AN AMERICAN WEEIA IN PARIS

A WEEIA MARSHALS NOVEL

ELLE BOCA

POYEEN PUBLISHING

Published by Poyeen Publishing
2901 Clint Moore Road #265
Boca Raton, FL 33496

ISBN: 978-1-932534-22-1

Sign up to receive news and updates about Elle Boca titles and special offers at

elleboca.poyeen.com/weeia-marshals/an-american-weeia-in-paris

Other titles by Elle Boca:

Unelmoija: The Dreamshifter
Unelmoija: The Mindshifter
Unelmoija: The Spiritshifter
Unelmoija: The Timeshifter
Unelmoija: Paradox
In the Garden of Weeia
Gypsies, Tramps and Weeia
Weeia on My Mind
Smells Like Weeia Spirit

Author's Note

This is an original work of fiction. Any relationship to real people is unintentional and a coincidence. At times I took literary liberties, creating fictional places, modifying existing locations, names, addresses, and so forth as necessary to adapt to the story. The setting is Earth. The geographic boundaries of the book encompass the city of Paris, France and its environs, real and imagined. I relied on personal experiences, online and print sources (some of which are listed below). Any errors are my own.

How Paris Became Paris The Invention of the Modern City by Joan DeJean
The Other Paris by Luc Sante
The Seven Ages of Paris

Acknowledgments

I am deeply grateful to my beta readers who made time from their busy lives and commitments to read my unfinished manuscript and share honest and kind feedback: Melissa Manes, and fellow author Nicholas Rossis. Thank you to beta readers Melissa Manes, Mary van Ede and Katja van der Heijde.

Table of Contents

To my mother, words are never enough

Chapter 1

Despite my relatively short stature, when it comes to mealtimes, I'm no dainty diner. My French friends call me a gourmand, a polite way of saying I eat a lot. I prefer to think I enjoy the heck out of food. But, seven courses with wine pairings in one of the finest restaurants in Paris, France will dampen the appetite of even the best of us. So my hunger level was dropping.

My meal partners did nothing to stimulate my appetite. If anything, their haughty attitude dimmed the fine restaurant luster. We were six courses and as many wineglasses into the meal when the maître d'hôtel, manager of the public area of the restaurant, returned to our table. He had greeted us with much fanfare when we arrived and escorted us personally to our window side table, with the best views of the city, he had explained. Even with the sky cloudy and a light rain falling, the view was stunning. Plus, we were dining at one of the most famous restaurants in the world halfway up the iconic Eiffel Tower.

At seven hundred euros per person for the customized chef's tasting menu with truffles, we had already spent far more than my monthly food budget in a single meal. I didn't know the price of the wine pairing, selected personally by the sommelier, because it wasn't on the menu, but I guessed it would be north of one thousand euros. That didn't include the price of the aperitif drinks we had when we arrived. The menu included coffee and dessert and a service fee, but a tip was still customary at such a restaurant, my friend Sébastien explained when I asked what to expect.

"Monsieur Walker, I trust everything is to your taste," the

maître d'hôtel said, his concerned expression attracting my attention.

Ted Walker was the stereotypical Texas man. He even wore cowboy boots and a hat and smoked cigars. His ego was big, and I mean big with capital letters. In my job as a marshal, I dealt with large and extra-large egos on a regular basis. This guy could compete with them. He let the maître d'hôtel sweat, allowing the silence to stretch, not glancing at him or responding right away. I was tempted to jump in, but the man had not addressed me, so I waited.

"Yes, Mr. Benjamin," he said, pronouncing the name with a twang, after what felt like a long while.

I bit my tongue instead of telling my guest the maître hôtel's name was Benjamin Pavot so he should call him Mr. Pavot. For all I cared, he could call him Mr. Sweet Potato. I wanted the night to end so I could go home, away from those people, and remove the high heels and uncomfortable clothes I was wearing.

"I noticed your children leaving," the man said without any sign the error in his name bothered him.

"Young people are impatient," Ted replied, his manner dismissive.

Despite his nonchalant attitude in front of the employee, the wrinkles on his face deepened when his children announced they were stepping away from the table. It bothered him that his adult children preferred to run around the tourist attraction than finish dinner with their parents even though the view was fantastic and the chef prepared our meal himself. I empathized with them and wished I could leave as well.

"They won't be a minute. They went to take some photos at the top of the tower," Amanda Walker, Ted's wife, said in a sugary voice.

"Should we hold dessert until they return?" the maître d'hôtel asked.

Amanda looked like she was going to say yes. Before she had a chance her husband spoke, "Absolutely not."

The maître d'hôtel opened his mouth to speak, but before he had a chance to say anything a thin uniformed man with a worried expression rushed to his side. Staff should always be discreet and unobtrusive, my mentor's voice intruded into my thoughts unbidden. The man's fast walk drew our eyes toward him before he reached our table. The tightness around his lips and furrowed brows communicated alarm. Perhaps there had been a run on caviar or foie gras in the kitchen, I mused.

I was on duty, watching over Ted Walker, a visiting United States Elder, and his family while they were in town. The man was intolerable, and his wife was a doormat. As if that wasn't bad enough they had their two offspring tagging along on the trip. It seemed a ginormous waste of my time to have to escort them just in case. In case what? If the man's body language was anything to go by, my small compensation our gourmet dinner, was about to be spoiled. Some people could hide their feelings behind a neutral face, but most failed to mask their body language.

As he leaned into the older man's ear, I watched him. His uniform was wrinkle free like all the others. Where the servers wore dark red ties, the maître d'hôtel's was white. The younger man wore a light pink tie and a pin on his lapel. I thought it was the restaurant logo on his pin, but as he reached us, I saw the shape of a bunch of grapes, identifying him as a sommelier. I remembered seeing him when we ordered our meal, but there had been so many staff at our table it was hard to keep track.

It wasn't that I cared about their clothes or fashion, I didn't. As a marshal among Weeia superhumans, it was my job to gather clues and stay informed so I could gauge a situation accurately and anticipate danger. That humans were clueless about the existence of Weeia made my job much less complicated than it might have been.

Although we were in a private room, I had noticed the sounds within the restaurant had become louder in the past few minutes. I assumed it was the mixed drinks and wine that were causing people to be rowdy. I strained to hear the sommelier's whispered conversation. I caught the word hostages. Despite the rich food and wine, I was alert. In two movements, I rose from my seat and reached the men.

"What hostages?" I barked at the man in the pink tie.

He shrunk back as if I had punched his midsection, eyeing me with a mix of surprise, concern, and confusion. I could almost read his mind. As a guest at the most important table that night, he didn't dare challenge me. Something in his gaze, fear perhaps, told me whatever had brought him over took precedence. He straightened before finding his voice.

"Mademoiselle," he said in a pleading tone. "Please keep your voice down. You will frighten our guests unnecessarily."

I wanted to slap him, but I clenched my fists instead. My main job was to protect Ted and Amanda while they enjoyed the sights of the City of Light for several days following a Weeia gathering. There was no threat and no particular concern. It was a courtesy Ted received as a superhuman of high rank, my friend Sébastien who knew way more than I did about protocol, had explained.

As the acting marshal in charge of the Paris office, I had to pay my respects and escort them personally. Delegating the job to my staff would have been bad form. Not that I cared overmuch about form, but I was keen for my position to become permanent. Nor did I have much staff to delegate unwanted tasks.

"I am one of your guests, and I want to know what's going on," I said, stressing am, so only he and his boss could hear me. "One more time. What hostages?"

"Some madmen have—" he blurted.

Before he could finish, Ted was by our side. "What the

hell is going on?" Ted, standing with his legs spread wide like a gunslinger, asked the maître d'hôtel and sommelier.

His voice boomed way louder than mine, but the men said nothing to him. They exchanged glances. What a surprise, if my experience in Paris was anything to go by, France was nothing if not male oriented. I was learning how to deal with gender bias, but the anger prickling my gut told me I had a long way to go.

Their faces reflected misgiving. Judging by their reaction and newly furrowed brows they appeared much more concerned about the Texas man's opinion than mine.

It was my job to find out if the situation merited concern, and Ted was getting in my way. On the other hand, results took priority over asserting my authority. He let the maître d'hôtel sweat, allowing the silence to stretch. I almost jumped in, but the man looked ready to break. I waited.

Chapter 2

"I came to invite our guests to exit," the sommelier said after glancing at his boss for approval.

"Exit?" Ted and I asked almost in unison.

"Yes, sir," the restaurant manager said. "We think it would be safer if you leave as soon as possible."

Ted spread his legs further apart as if centering himself in readiness to toss the two men out the nearest window for suggesting we leave before we finished dinner. I was none too pleased myself. I figured it was all a misunderstanding.

Taking two small steps forward, I stood close to the men and asked in a low voice so only they and Ted could hear me, "Safer from what exactly? What was it you said about madmen and hostages?"

They hesitated. The maître d'hôtel shifted feet. I placed my hands on my waist, holding my position to let them know I demanded an answer.

"It seems several armed men have taken control of the tower," the sommelier explained. The tension in his face softened as he spoke. His voice trembled slightly. "They have hostages."

Ted and I must have looked unconvinced because the sommelier pulled out his smartphone and showed us a video of the chaos that was the ground floor of the famous monument. From where we stood, I saw the tens of thousands of twinkling lights of the city. The restaurant's expansive views were breathtaking. Nothing seemed amiss. The view was as fantastic as when we arrived. Of course, I couldn't see the base of the tower itself. As the four of us crowded around the small screen, I wondered how to get Mr. and Mrs. Walker to safety.

A dozen thoughts and as many questions flooded my mind

at the same instant. Was that why the voices had become louder in the past few minutes? I opened my mouth to speak, closing it seconds later as I realized I had little to say. We had to leave immediately. Later I would want to know what had happened. At that moment, my priority was escorting my charges to safety and ensuring their children were out of harm's way. One reason I had agreed to dinner at the Eiffel Tower restaurant had been its protected status. After the Elysée Palace, the official residence of the president of France, the national monument was the most guarded place in the city.

I thought Ted was upset, but as I watched him, excitement blossomed on his face. His eyes widened and tiny lines formed on the edges of his lips. He pressed the play button on the sommelier's smartphone, and we watched the video once again.

As it was nearing the end, I interrupted him, "Ted, we need to go."

I steered him back to our table while the maître d'hôtel and sommelier spoke in hushed tones. I felt a pang of annoyance at myself. I should never have agreed to dinner at such a place. While well-guarded, it was on the target list of every terrorist with a grudge against the Gallic nation. It wasn't as if I had much choice. The Walkers had demanded we dine there. When we arrived earlier that evening, I had felt reassured at the sight of dozens of well-armed men wearing bulletproof vests standing around the base of the structure.

A chain-link fence surrounded the entire Eiffel Tower. Only paying visitors, after standing in long lines, could make their way to the upper levels of the monument by climbing an open-air staircase or paying extra to take elevators. In addition, to reach L'Etoile, where we were, two armed guards stood near the ground floor entrance of the prestigious venue. After confirming we were on their list of guests for the evening, they invited us up several steps to a narrow entrance. Once past the metal detector, two more armed guards had escorted us to a private elevator and up to the restaurant's arrival hall.

As soon as we were back at our table, his wife asked, "Ted, Danni, what is it?"

"A bunch of hee-haws attacked the tower," Ted answered louder than I would have liked. Motioning to the sommelier, he added, "That young fellow has a video. They want us to leave the restaurant before the attackers make their way here. We have priority over the other diners."

In an effort to assert my authority, I added, "I agree. We should go."

When Amanda turned to me, there was fire in her eyes. It was impossible to mistake it for fear, so I assumed it was anger.

"I'm not going anywhere without my kids," she said in a voice of solid steel.

Gone was the Texas drawl and polite indifference that had marked her attitude since our meeting. In their place was a stranger.

Several staff tried to escort us out. We declined. After a few minutes, servers and other uniformed personnel I didn't recognize joined the senior staff. They were rounding up guests from the dinner tables and pointing them toward the back of the restaurant. I had taken a tour of L'Etoile when we arrived and memorized the layout. They were taking guests out through the staff entrance. That meant the main entrance was blocked or unsafe.

"Where are they?" Ted asked.

"I don't know," she said, faltering. "I haven't heard from them since they left." She glanced down at her smartphone before announcing, "It's been forty-five minutes."

"Call them," he ordered.

"They're not answering," she replied, urgency ringing her voice.

"Once you and your husband are safe I'll look for them," I said.

"I'm not going anywhere until we find them," she said in the same steel voice from moments earlier.

I turned to her husband, hoping he would sway her. The tense lines of his bravado had waned. Now there was confusion, his slack jaw and slightly open mouth told me.

"Ted, the staff will be back once they evacuate all the guests," I said. "While your safety is my priority you know the prime directive takes over. We may not reveal ourselves and our abilities in the presence of humans."

He turned to his wife, who was punching the screen on her smartphone with nothing to show for it, and back at me. He looked like a deer in the headlights.

"As acting marshal of Paris," I began, hoping to assert my authority and convince them to leave.

Before I could finish, Amanda Walker raised her head from her smartphone and announced, "I'm going to look for them upstairs."

"We're not splitting up," I blurted.

She didn't bother to reply or even turn around. Ted and I watched for an instant helpless to stop her. She walked with alacrity, arriving at the door that led to the restaurant exit to the next level up in seconds. She spoke with the man at the door before Ted and I arrived there. At first, he blocked her way and argued with her. She continued speaking without raising her voice until moments later, he stepped aside, and opened the door for her to pass.

"Yes, Ma'am," the guard at the door said to her as we arrived. There was a resigned expression on his face. "I'll be here."

"That's my wife," Ted said in a commanding tone.

As he spoke, I had time to notice the man. He was clean-shaven and less young than I had thought at first glance. He wore a military uniform with a helmet, a bulletproof vest, and an automatic rifle like the men we had seen at the base of the tower. Dressed in black, he had a wire running out of his ear.

A stiff material covered his knees. His belt held spare clips and tactical pouches. He looked like a professional soldier, despite the posh venue.

"What is the situation on the ground?" I asked, assuming he was in radio contact with his colleagues.

"Bad," he said. Lines appeared across his forehead and lips. "Once you leave the safety of the restaurant, I won't be able to protect you. As I said to the lady, it's best if you flee. Follow the public. If you can't get out, come back, and I'll let you in."

I nodded, stepping across the threshold of the door he held open. Ted followed me. As soon as we were through, the soldier closed the door behind us, standing at the ready once more. I turned to the Elder. I stiffened against the chill wind blowing, wishing I had my coat. It was in the coatroom. Ted didn't notice the cold.

"Stay behind me," I ordered, inching next to him so he could hear me above the noise, a blend of wind and people. "If you see your wife let me know by tapping my shoulder and I'll stop. Whatever happens, we have to stay together."

His only reply was silence. Like me, he was scanning the crowded area for Amanda. People were moving in all directions, like panicked caribou hunted by a wolf pack, searching for an exit.

"There," he pointed.

As soon as I saw her, I made a beeline toward her figure, searching for their children along my path. Ted followed me.

"Any luck?" She asked when we joined her in an alert yet casual voice as if we had been hunting for a favorite ice cream flavor.

"Nothing," Ted said in a hollow tone.

We spent precious minutes searching without success. Nervous men, women, and children bunched up by the entrance to the staircases. Others rushed toward the elevators, where frustrated staff yelled at people in various languages to stand in line. The mass of bodies paid little attention to their commands. Some circled aimlessly as if they might find a way out that none of us knew about. The icy wind whipped at my face, making my eyes tear and muffling the voices around us.

After half an hour circling the same area several times I asked them to stop. We stood against the railing to avoid being jostled by the fast-moving crowd. At the foot of the tower, the familiar lines of people queuing for tickets and admission were gone. In their place stood a few dark and indistinct figures armed with what looked like automatic weapons. From one hundred and fifty meters away I couldn't see their faces. Their legs spread apart and their rapid uneven, movements told me they were jittery and menacing. A pang of fear shot through me. I forced myself to look away. There was nothing I could do about the men at ground level, and much I could do about the couple by my side.

"They're not here," I said. "If they were, we would've found them by now."

"Or they would've returned to L'Etoile," Amanda conceded.

The woman held herself with a confidence she had not shown before. Her eyes were alert and watchful, like a trained professional, I thought. Ted's focus was glued on her. The roles had reversed from only a few minutes earlier. Between them, she was in charge. That might have been the case, but it was my job to protect them.

"The exit on this level is blocked," I said, drawing their attention by raising my voice above the surrounding sounds. "The restaurant is safer than being out here in the open."

"I agree," Amanda said. "I doubt that guard can hold them for long, but it's better than nothing. The attackers have control of the stairs." She spoke in a calm voice like a commander assessing a military scenario. "If Tina and Sammy got on the elevators they may be safe. Let's return to the restaurant in case they go there."

I thought of arguing, but there was no point. It didn't matter who said it. We agreed the restaurant was the best alternative.

Chapter 3

As soon as the guard by the restaurant entrance saw us, he opened the door and stood aside to let us through. The warmth inside was pleasant after the searing cold of the tower deck. Written on the small lines around her lips and wide eyes, Amanda's hope made me feel sorry for her. It made me want to help her find her children.

"Did they come this way?" she asked the guard.

"Sorry, ma'am," he said, shaking his head from side to side. "No one has been here since you went out. Everyone is leaving. You should too."

As soon as we entered, he locked the door behind us and resumed his position. He was alert and anxious, his eyes searching as if he could see something beyond the cramped and shadowy space where we stood.

"When will reinforcements arrive?" Amanda asked as if she was his boss.

"I don't know," he said in a kinder tone than I might have used had I been in his place.

There was a bleak determination in his face. He held his head high, his hands grasping his weapon as if it was a lifeline.

"Surely, the city has prepared for such an attack, and there's a plan in place," she said to the guard.

He said nothing, staring toward the outer stairs and the floor above. Ted tugged gently at his wife's arm to move further into the hallway. She stood her ground.

"Are there other guards in the restaurant?" She asked.

The man was in his twenties, clean-shaven, and thin. His hands were red, either from exposure to the cold or from a skin condition. The latter made more sense as there was ample heating inside the restaurant. He looked uncomfortable, shifting from one foot to the other and avoiding her gaze. I guessed that either what he knew was bad news or he didn't know anything more than we did, and that too was bad news.

Ted intervened, "I bet he's not allowed to discuss that. We know there were four other guards, two at the entrance and two in the elevator."

Amanda relented. The guard shot Ted a grateful glance.

"I saw two guards when we walked by the kitchen," I added more to fill the awkward silence than anything.

The guard glanced at me as if noticing me for the first time. That happened more often than I liked to admit. It was because I was, as my direct report said one day when she thought I wasn't in the office, short, plump and had no sense of fashion.

"You can't hold your position against men armed with explosives. Is no one coming to back you up?" she asked, her face reddening with emotion.

The guard sighed as if resigned to answer her in the hope we would leave him be. Amanda stared at him. It was all I could do not to smack some reason into her. If it hadn't been because they were in my care and she appeared not afraid in the slightest, I might have given in to temptation. At least that would make me feel better. I pressed my anger down and waited.

"For the moment, I'm the only guard in this position," he said, his stiff exterior cracking for the first time. I saw a flash of fear in his eyes. I couldn't blame him. If the attackers made it to the restaurant, unless something changed in our circumstances soon, he stood little chance of surviving. "If superior forces approach before back up arrives, as we expect they will, I won't be able to hold my post for long. I advise you to leave while you still can."

"Thank you," she said, walking into the restaurant to my relief. "They should be ashamed."

"Who?" Ted asked.

"The city, the tower authorities, whoever is in charge of

this," she said spreading her hands. "Their security set up is a shambles, and that boy is too green to do much on his own." I disagreed. I thought he had combat experience, but there was nothing to be gained by pointing that out to her. "He's Tina's age, only a little younger than Sammy. He's going to get killed."

"We don't know that," Ted snapped.

"People," I said in the calmest and most authoritarian voice I could muster. "There's nothing we can do about him. At the moment my hands are full keeping the two of you from danger and finding your errant children to boot. We have to get out of here."

Amanda stopped in her tracks, making me turn to look at her after a few steps on my own. Ted was by her side.

"In case I didn't make myself abundantly clear before let me do it now," she said in a commanding, yet, unemotional voice. "I'm not going anywhere until I know my kids are safe. If they're somewhere on the upper floors, they'll return to the restaurant. I plan to be here to protect them if they do." Looking at Ted and me she added, "You're free to do whatever you please."

Anger rose through me like a cobra. Breathing deeply, I pushed it down with much effort. It was my job to protect them even if they behaved like asses. I wasn't going to leave without them.

"If you stay, I'm staying too," I said. "How do you propose we do that without being found out?"

She shrugged as if she couldn't care less. Ted's eyes widened and his mouth opened in a helpless expression that reminded me of the dead fish on display at the fish seller's stall at the street market.

Chapter 4

The restaurant manager and wine steward were busy herding the remaining diners and dining room staff toward the kitchen and hadn't seen us. If we were going to wait for Tina and Sammy, we had to hide somewhere, and fast. The problem was the restaurant's open circular design, while ideal for visitors to soak in the panoramic views of the city, offered no good places to hide.

As if reading my thoughts Amanda said in an authoritarian tone, "We have to find a hiding place before they see us."

"I took a look around when we arrived and when I went to the bathroom," I replied. "The only possibilities are behind the bar, inside the bathrooms. and the kitchen. The bathroom stalls are tiny. The bar is almost the same size; don't know much about the kitchen." Another possibility popped into my head. "The coatroom might work, but it's kinda small." Ted's blank expression prompted me to explain. "Remember that when we arrived someone took our coats and umbrellas?" He nodded. "He handed them to the woman in the coatroom who gave us a ticket."

I pulled the crumpled gray stub out of my pants pocket, showing it to Ted. He nodded once in acknowledgment. Amanda had walked back toward the guard. The more I thought about it, the better it seemed. It was a matter of seconds to reach it. I hoped Amanda would follow us there.

"Empty," I said after inspecting the interior. It had a door and a glassless window where an employee had stood earlier that night. Ted glanced at me with disinterest, like a politician considering someone who doesn't vote. "It's small, but we should be able to squeeze in, and it has a door we could lock." I inspected the doorknob. "Fortunately for us, they left the key in the lock in their hurry to leave. Our coats are still here, our umbrellas too."

Somehow that was reassuring. The cloying smell of expensive perfumes and colognes from the many items of clothing stored there in the past assaulted my nose. I rubbed it with my hand to clear it if only temporarily. Ted stood in the hallway, his head turned sideways toward where we had last seen Amanda. His eyebrows were knit together, and his lips pressed tight in worry. There was no trace of his bravado.

The sound of voices approaching drew my attention. I yanked Ted into the coatroom with a single motion, causing him to stumble. His narrowed eyes and open mouth revealed his annoyance. Before he could say anything, I placed my index finger over my lips, whispering, "Shush." At that moment, I noticed Amanda had slipped in behind her husband.

Our coats and umbrellas and a few old neglected items were all that remained in the coatroom. We could crouch down, but there was only enough space for one. If anyone looked through the window, they would see us. The voices were much closer to us than moments earlier. There was nowhere to hide. Once again I pulled on Ted's arm until he stood behind me. I did the same with his wife. After an initial moment of resistance, she complied with my silent request and stood next to her husband.

Whispering, "Whatever you see or hear be quiet." I encircled us in an illusion.

Illusions are my superhuman ability. I'm pretty good at using them, too. I can make people see whatever I want, within reason. I made us invisible to the humans as they passed. Ted's loud breathing behind me was unnerving. His pungent citrus scent, perhaps from soap, tickled my nose, making me wish there was more distance between us. He shifted feet every couple of seconds like a nervous child. Time slowed to a crawl as we waited for the sommelier and another man whose voice I didn't recognize to appear. When they glanced at the closet, I extended my illusion to include our coats.

Ted exhaled with relief as they passed us. I couldn't blame him. I was so nervous that for a split second I had doubted whether my illusion would work. Projecting an illusion required energy. We didn't know how long we would have to remain in the restaurant or what confrontation we might have with the terrorists so I better conserve my energy. I released my illusion, allowing Ted and Amanda to step back.

"There are no coats left. I think that's everybody," the man said from a short distance.

"Yes," the sommelier replied. "Let's get out of here."

I had just enough time to step closer to Amanda and Ted while lifting the illusion back up before they passed us. They didn't even look inside. I waited until their voices faded before dropping the illusion and moving away from the power couple.

"I think we're alone," Amanda said.

No sooner had the words left her lips than we heard loud thuds and voices. Ted tensed, taking a step back and away from the noise. Amanda and I turned toward the ruckus. Her eyes glowed with excitement.

The intensity of the sounds doubled. They came from the elevator doors where we had first arrived. Men's voices reached us, but I couldn't understand them.

"They're foreigners. Use the translation feature on your badge," she commanded.

I did as she suggested. Because I kept the volume low, I had to place my badge next to my ear to hear the translation. Amanda leaned in to listen. Ted's eyes were wide with fear. I thought he was going to run. Amanda followed my gaze. She placed a calming hand on his arm, which soothed his nerves a smidgen.

"Where do we put them?" the translator's disembodied voice asked.

The men were approaching the coatroom. I placed my

index finger over my lips, staring at Ted first and then Amanda. I saw two scruffy bearded men in dark fatigues carrying small machine guns. They moved with quiet competence, each looking in a different direction. I held my breath as one of them paused at the coatroom door, staring right at us. For a moment, I thought he could see us, but he just saw my illusion of an empty coatroom. I exhaled softly, not daring to move. Although they were only there for milliseconds, it felt like time halted. Fearing the translator might give us away I pressed the mute and record buttons on my badge just as they moved past us.

My senses were on high alert, or I might not have noticed Amanda as she tried to step out into the hallway. Wait, I mouthed with urgency. Where Ted's panicked eyes gave away his fright, the small lines around Amanda's eyes and the tension in her body told me she was in the opposite state of mind from her husband. In the hallway, the men continued their conversation.

"Let's hear what they're saying," I whispered, trying to keep Amanda's attention on me so she wouldn't follow them.

"He did not say," the device translated a second man's words. "Does not matter. As long as all the explosives go off at the same time on the restaurant level, the whole tower should topple. I will take care of the armed guard."

"Sounds like gunfire," Amanda said, springing to action. Ted's eyes widened in alarm. "Honey, wait in there," she ordered. She turned to me, her face softening as if she was talking to her daughter. "You too. I'll be back in a jiffy."

"Hell no!" I choked back my frustration, unwilling to draw attention to us. "You're not the boss of me. Besides, I'm supposed to protect you." I emphasized the last word for effect. "Stand behind—"

She covered my mouth with her hand before I could finish speaking. In two long strides, she was around the corner and beyond my sight. I heard crackling ahead like a live wire. I thought of running to find her but decided against it. If there was danger, I would walk into it without knowing what it was or being able to protect us.

"Do it," a man's voice was followed by silence.

When I reached Amanda a moment later, I saw streaks of white light that reminded me of lightning strikes. Four figures stood around the room, one of them raising a boxy machine gun to point at her. Surprise replaced the confidence in the men's faces and a second later, pain. The black-clad men writhed in agony as unintelligible grunts left their bodies. Smoke spewed from them, hanging in the air around them like a horrible gray specter. I held my breath, feeling a little queasy. Their bodies twisted and wrenched at impossible angles. I heard bones and joints snapping until their legs buckled under their weight. After what seemed like a long while, they fell where they stood as she watched impassive.

"What happened?" I asked as I reached Amanda's side. An unfamiliar nauseating odor that reminded me of cooked meat threatened to make me double over and wretch. I gagged, dry heaving. Before it happened again, I covered my mouth and my nose with my sleeve. "What's that smell?"

"Seared human flesh," she said in a calm, patient tone. "It can be quite revolting even if you're used to it. You might want to step away before you lose your lovely dinner."

"How?" I asked feebly.

She raised an eyebrow as if I had asked the silliest of questions. Of course, she must have used her ability on them, duh. I had no idea she was so gifted. I had been so consumed with the drudgery of the task of providing them a VIP escort while they were in town that I had never bothered to read their files. As an Elder, Ted had to be a Maximus, the highest ability level among the Weeia, but it hadn't occurred to me that Amanda might have such a powerful ability of her own. She acted like such a wallflower it never crossed my mind. I kicked myself. What kind of a marshal was I? That was sloppy.

"You-"

"Yep," she replied in a calm voice as if we were discussing the weather. "I'm a bit out of practice. I've been retired since I became pregnant with Tina you know. I'm afraid they suffered. Back in the day, they would've been dead before they knew what hit them. And, before I could stop them, they were unnecessarily cruel to that nice guard."

She motioned toward a bloody figure behind the bodies. He moved. I ran to his side. I had seen fights and even killed people as part of my job, but what I saw forced me to turn away until I regained my composure. He was alive, hanging to life by I thread. Although I wanted to ease his suffering, my basic medical training was useless. He needed a massive painkiller. Salty tears reached my lips. I was equal parts angry, frustrated, and sad. Get it together, Danni, I told myself. I hated crying. It made me feel weak and useless.

Amanda crouched beside the guard on the other side of where I was. His breathing was ragged and fast. She placed two fingers on his neck as if taking his pulse.

"He's alive," I croaked.

"I know, sweetie," she replied in a soft voice. "How's your energy level, marshal?" as she held both hands toward me and looked down at the injured man.

"Holding steady, take what you need if you can help him," I said as I realized what she intended and grasped both her hands. I felt a pull of energy as she drew some of my reserves to recharge herself. Although I had heard the theory I had never known anyone who could manipulate energy like that.

She broke our connection and reached with two fingers to touch the worst wound in his neck. When she held her fingers against his skin, his breathing eased as he trembled. "I can't guarantee he'll survive, but at least he'll sleep for a while. It's the best I can do under the circumstances. I can't spare more resources until we find the kids."

I couldn't argue. Until we were out of harm's way, we had

to conserve our energy. In time, I could recover lost organic fuel I had spent on my abilities. Food helped speed up the recovery. Replenishing energy was one of my favorite excuses for snacking.

Her kickass electric ability was impressive and uncommon. Most Weeia had only mundane low-level abilities. Few had more than one ability. That she had a second one made her even more exceptional.

"You're a healer too?"

"Only for my family," she said, dropping her fingers and rising. "But, you looked so sad I decided to help him."

Many Weeia grew up in communities composed of only our own kind and thought of humans as harmless yet inferior beings. My aunt and uncle had raised me in rural Canada among regular humans and taught me to value and respect all life alike.

The marshals rules protected humans from Weeia exploitation, but if a human threatened a Weeia's life, he or she was justified in taking that human's life without penalty from Weeia authorities.

Part of the job of a marshal was to keep the involvement of Weeia and our abilities from coming to the attention of human authorities. Considering what the attackers intended to do and their cruelty to that poor guard, I had no trouble concealing Weeia involvement in their deaths.

Chapter 5

"We need to go," I said, regretting leaving the injured guard before help arrived.

In response, Amanda walked back to the hallway to find Ted. I followed her until the three of us were together. Ted glanced behind us at the bodies and scrunched his face in distaste.

"The guard?" he asked.

"He's still alive," his wife's gentle tone surprised me.

"We have to go now before more terrorists come up the find out what happened to their friends," I said.

I knew my clipped words showed my impatience, but I didn't care. My priority was to keep Amanda and Ted out of harm's way. I would worry about ruffled feathers later. I didn't trust them to do as I said, so I inched into their private space.

"Now," I said as loud as I dared. "Our best way out is toward the back of the restaurant."

"Why don't we take the elevator?" Ted asked in a little boy voice as we passed the elevator.

I squelched the sharp reply that was at my throat. Taking a deep breath, I explained, "Two heavily armed terrorists came up that way less than ten minutes ago. Do you really think that is a safe exit?"

He glanced at the closed doors of the mechanical device we had taken from the ground floor up to the restaurant foyer earlier that evening. Everything had been serene and normal or as normal as a well-guarded national monument appeared in Paris these days. It was hard to believe we were under attack.

"With any luck, we'll be able to leave through the staff entrance," I said, hoping I was right.

"Monsieur and Madame Walker, mademoiselle," the sommelier's familiar voice said as we reached the kitchen. I thought he was going to scold us. Instead, he escorted us to a dark and narrow doorway. "Please, this way."

Moments later, we reached the street level of the Eiffel Tower, where black-clad policemen directed us away from the structure. I had braced myself for questions about our late arrival, but none came. Amanda hesitated until I placed the palms of my hands against her back, pushing her less than gently forward. One of the policemen stared at us until one of his colleagues called him on the radio strapped to his shoulder.

"We're not going to find them here," I said between clenched teeth. She moved a few feet, looking back at the door as if to return. "The minute the police go up there they're going to find the bodies. We need to be gone before that happens or we could face some awkward questions."

"Don't you have a police contact?" she asked.

Feeling inadequate as the interim head of the office without the connections, money or social standing that my predecessor had I sighed. I didn't have time to justify my actions to her, but that was exactly what I would have to do.

"No," I stated. "This is a small office, and I'm new at this job." I left out how inadequate I felt at not being Parisian, let alone French. Madame Marmotte, my direct report at the office, never let me forget that I was French Canadian. "If they take us in for questioning it may be a while before we're released." Although I was confident the marshals influence would secure our release, I didn't know how long it would take. They were much more influential stateside and in North America than in Europe. "The country is in high alert, and after the attack on the tower, security will be extra tight. At the first sign of the body of one of their own it's likely they would throw us in jail first and ask questions later. We're better off out here looking for them on our own. The police will not make your children a priority, but I will."

At my last words, she seemed to take notice. She glanced at the uniformed men and followed my lead away from the tower. Although I wasn't sure which way to go, I knew it had to be away from the chaos of the tourist attraction that was under siege. We traversed the Champs de Mars, a large grassy park where I had always seen people take photos of the tower in the past. Usually, dozens of camera-clad onlookers and couples in romantic poses hung about even late in the evening. That night there was only a hand full of people. The grass was wet, and puddles of varying sizes peppered the dirt paths that crossed the park. I walked around them to avoid getting my prissy shoes soaked. When was I going to learn to wear my comfortable boots no matter the occasion? The rain had dissipated the smell of urine I remembered from previous visits, yay.

The green lawn continued, but I preferred to avoid the telltale lights of a police car by the Wall of Peace monument steps from Place Joffre and across the street from the Ecole Militaire.

"This way," I said turning left on Avenue Joseph Bouvard toward a pizza place I knew was open late.

"Slow down," Ted ordered in a ragged voice.

That was when I realized how fast I was going. Amanda had been on my heels. We turned toward him at the same time. In my hurry to get them to safety, I had been moving so fast we were almost running. She kept up, but he was battling to follow. The arrogance he had worn since he had arrived into my care was gone, and he wasn't lippy anymore either. It was a small comfort given the downturn the evening had taken.

"The children," Amanda began. Before she could finish her sentence, the electronic sound of her phone interrupted her. As she glanced down at the device, her lips widened, and her expression softened. "It's Sammy."

Ted's heavy breathing was returning to normal. We both waited for Amanda to tell us more.

"They're okay. They went for ice cream," she said.

The lines of tension around her eyes eased, her brows unknitted, and she sighed. It seemed everything would work out after all. I had had my doubts a few minutes earlier.

"Ask them where they are, and we'll find them," I said.

She did as I asked, and within ten minutes we arrived at a tiny ice cream shop on rue des Champs de Mars, a narrow street two blocks away from the pizza shop I knew. Amanda's composure melted as soon as she saw Tina and Sammy through the window. Ted opened the door, and she rushed in. I glanced around the quiet sidewalk before following them inside.

It was shoulder to shoulder in the shop. The rowdy crowd overwhelmed the handful of tables and chairs. While Amanda chatted with her offspring, I took the opportunity to observe Tina and Sammy. Tina was more still than I remembered her being the entire night at the restaurant while Sammy had an almost imperceptible twitch of his left eyebrow. For once, they weren't looking at their smartphones. Sweat poured down Ted's face as he stood next to his wife.

After a few minutes, Amanda approached me and started talking. I snatched a word here and there such as video, attackers, and hotel. The noise level inside made it impossible to hear her.

"Can't hear you," I yelled.

Amanda cupped her hand around my ear and said, "Thank goodness they're fine. When they tried to return to the restaurant the police were blocking access. They told them to get as far as possible from the tower. They've been trying to reach us since then, but their texts weren't getting through, and the calls bounced."

"I see," I said, wondering why they had to go out for ice cream in the middle of dinner. "We should go."

"Yes," she replied. "We want to return to the hotel."

"I'll try to get in touch with our driver," I replied. On the sixth ring, the driver picked up. "We're ready."

"The police forced me to move. Where are you?" she said. I provided her the address. "Most of the streets near the tower are closed off or blocked. I will be there as soon as I can."

"She's on her way," I said to them all, but the background noise was too loud. I took two steps and cupped my hand around Amanda's ear, repeating my words and adding, "I'm sure we'll see the car when she arrives."

Tina swapped places with Amanda so her mother could sit down. Sammy offered the same to his father, but Ted preferred to go to the bathroom.

Handing me her smartphone, Tina said, "Mom wants you to see this."

A still image with a play symbol in the middle occupied the entire screen on her Korean phone. I placed my index finger over the symbol and watched the events of the evening unfold in an unexpected way. It looked like a newscast stitched together from amateur video clips. At the end of one clip, several of the masked men lay unmasked and trussed to one side of the ground floor of the tower, near the entrance to the restaurant.

"Did the police do that?" I asked Tina.

She shrugged. The nearness exposed me to her over sweet perfume. It made me think of the unholy blending of sugary candy and night jasmine. Since I had worked on the perfume case, I took note of scents.

"That's odd," I said to no one in particular since Tina's back was to me and her mother couldn't hear me.

After Ted sat down on his return from the men's room, I watched the movie multiple times, found other versions of the same clip elsewhere online and watched them with media reports and updates. One reporter said the police were looking for the good Samaritan who had captured the terrorists. There was no mention of the bodies in the restaurant. I felt relief when one station mentioned a guard was in critical but stable condition. I was looking for more information when Tina tapped my arm, pointing to the street.

"She's here," I yelled so Tina could hear me. "I'm going out to make sure it's safe. When I signal you with my hand come out."

The street remained quiet. I wondered how the driver had managed to wedge the stretch limo into the street. At least there were no other cars. She jumped out as soon as she parked, opening the rear door of the limo when she saw me. Moments after I signaled to Tina that they should come out, we were on our way to the Walkers' ritzy hotel in the eighth arrondissement.

"At this hour, there should be no traffic," the driver said when I asked how long the drive would be to the hotel. "Five minutes, tops."

True to her word in what seemed a surprisingly short drive, which could have been five minutes, we arrived. After I made sure the Walkers were settled in for the night I went back to the limo for my return home.

"Were you at the tower when it happened?" the driver blurted as soon as we were on our way.

"We were at the restaurant," I replied. "We were having dinner, and then all hell broke loose. What did you hear?"

"At first nothing," she said, turning south toward the Left Bank where I lived. The dirty blonde woman in her fifties looked at me via her rearview mirror. I returned her gaze. "I couldn't figure out what was wrong with my phone. It wouldn't get online."

"Oh?"

"It was dead. No texts, no calls, apps, Internet," she said. "I was fiddling with it when a military officer rapped on my window, ordering me to move away. I tried to explain the spots were designated for limos, and that I was waiting for VIP clients. He said he didn't care, that the area was closed off effective immediately. He did the same with the other cars.

I tried to circle back around, but when I reached the end of the second street, a long line of police vans blocked the road. I figured you would need a ride when you came out, so I drove until I found a place to park. They must've have been blocking cell phone and Internet signals because as soon as I was a few streets away, my phone started to work again."

That would explain why Amanda couldn't get ahold of her kids, and I couldn't get online. It was standard procedure in cases of terrorism to prevent team members from communicating with each other. I wasn't sure how the police themselves stayed in contact. It also explained why once we broke free of the perimeter of the tower Amanda's phone, and moments later mine returned to normal.

"We're here," the driver said, shaking me from my contemplation. "Please sign."

She handed me a tablet. I approved the total for the night and added a hefty tip. She had earned it.

Chapter 6

I lived in an old building in the heart of the city, in a vibrant pedestrian-friendly neighborhood full of restaurants and museums and the people they attracted. I loved its location, convenient to most places I visited, except the marshals office, and spectacular views of the River Seine.

As soon as I walked in, I took off my wet and muddy shoes, feeling a twinge of guilt for the mess we must have left in the limo. I set aside the heartache I felt every time I returned home and the memories of Iaen flooded my brain. I missed him so much. I promised myself I would grieve later. I would spend time on his boat, and celebrate the months we were together before he died in a traffic accident.

For most of the night, there had been a light drizzle. Walking a few steps was no problem, but we had done more than that with no umbrella or raincoat. Without looking in the mirror, I knew my hair was wet and untidy not to mention my clothes. After emptying my bladder, I prepared to call my boss at marshals headquarters using my badge. It allowed audio and visual communication on an encrypted line safe from human eavesdropping. I glanced at the twinkling lights of the city across the river on the Right Bank and took a deep breath to arm myself with courage before selecting the audio mode.

"Yes?" my boss answered almost right away.

That single word put me on edge. Since Francois, my Paris boss, had moved to the marshals headquarters in Moosehead Lake, Maine to "grow personally and professionally" I had been acting head of the Paris office. Francois had recommended me for the position, high praise from him as he had gone out of his way to distance himself from me from the day of my arrival in the City of Light. The final decision was up to the powers that be in Maine, and they had said nothing one way or another about what I might expect. For the moment, I had a temporary and significant boost in salary and benefits, the only issue, reporting to a pompous and indifferent career man.

"I'm sorry to bother you, sir," I said feeling self-conscious.

I was unsure how to begin. Dealing with superiors at Moosehead Lake had been my former boss's duty. He was good at it. I dreaded reports and interactions up the chain of command. It didn't help that many, if not most, in the marshals ranks disapproved of me on principle due to the tarnish my parents had left on our family name after they disappeared when I was a child. I suspected my boss was among them. An awkward silence filled the air, making me feel worse than when I began.

I raced onward, "There was a suspicious incident at the Eiffel Tower tonight I thought you should know about. Terrorists attacked while Elder Ted Walker and his family were there. They're unharmed."

"Very well then," he said, sounding disinterested and ready to hang up.

"There's more," I added before he could end the conversation. "Mrs. Walker took down four of the attackers, sir."

"Mrs. Walker?" he asked.

"Yes, sir, Amanda Walker," I said. "She seems rather capable."

"I see," he said. "Why were they there again?"

"Having dinner, sir," I replied. At the last minute, I left out that it had been my idea. "After they attended the regional European gathering near here they decided to spend a few days in town."

I guessed that meant he hadn't read the detailed report I had sent him a week earlier. It was the same way Francois had behaved when he was living in Paris, never reading my messages or returning my calls. "There's a famous restaurant there." Silence engulfed us.

"After we made it to safety and located their children I saw a video of the events at the base of the tower. It's hard to know for sure, but I suspect Weeia might've been involved."

His voice doubled in volume as he asked, "What?"

"A Weeia may have been involved, sir," I said. Finally, I had his attention. "While Mrs. Walker confronted the terrorists one level up someone subdued the suspects at the base of the tower."

"Why was she involved in the first place?" he asked.

"We were in the restaurant when the terrorists arrived, sir," I said, hoping that satisfied him. "I asked her to wait, but she—"

He interrupted me, "It's of no consequence. If she felt threatened she was well within her rights. Regarding the other attackers that doesn't sound exceptional. The French police have a solid reputation."

"But sir, I didn't see anyone in the videos," I said. "In a matter of minutes, an invisible person or persons took down a handful of heavily armed men. Before the police knew what was going on, he, she, or they tied them up and left."

"What do you mean an invisible person?" he asked.

"I don't know," I replied. I was uncertain how the attack involved the marshals if at all, but my gut told me it did so I plowed on. "One minute the attackers are standing alert, holding their machine guns, the next they're tied up and lying flat."

"How is that possible?" he asked, speaking slowly as if I needed extra time to reply.

"I don't know," I repeated. "I will try to find out."

"Don't do anything until you hear from me," he ordered.

I slipped out of my wet clothes and showered. I hadn't realized how cold I was until I felt the steaming hot water on my skin. I kept looping through the events of the night, trying to make sense of the evening. I fell asleep, waiting for my boss to call with instructions. I was tired when my alarm woke me. I double-checked my badge. No one had called.

I was cleaning the gunk out of my eyes and working on my second black coffee when I received a text from Susanna: *Sorry to bother you. Need to talk ASAP. Can you make breakfast today?*

When she and her two children first arrived in Paris as refugees, I had taken responsibility for them. Now they were settled in Paris and doing great.

I thought about last night's events and considered begging off, but nobody was calling me with instructions.

I texted back: *Okay. At the Club in an hour.*

Oh well, I had been trying to work up the energy to go running. It would have to keep. On the other hand, I could warm to the idea of breakfast at the Club, the Weeia Club that is. It was the unofficial gathering place for Weeia in Paris, where we could speak about Weeia matters without fear of human eavesdropping. Membership dues were outrageous. As the provisional leader in the marshals office, the Club had extended a courtesy membership.

The Club had the added advantage that it was on my way to work and a two-minute walk for Susanna from the perfume shop where she worked. If I had to meet someone for breakfast, my least favorite meal, it couldn't be more convenient.

Ten minutes later, dressed in my usual black on black outfit and uber comfortable custom-made leather boots, I went to the door. As soon as I picked up the keys from the glass bowl, a gift from my friend Mara, Ceri appeared. Her look reminded me of two tasks I had to take care of before I could head to the Club.

The first task was to clean up her toilet corner, the designated newspaper covered space where she could do her business on days I didn't make it back home in time to walk her. I had walked her before dinner the night before, so there wasn't anything to pick up. She was a fastidious creature who would only drink bottled water and fresh food, nothing canned for her royal highness. If her newspaper was less than pristine, she wouldn't deign to stand on it. How did I end up in charge of the city's most stuck up dog, I mumbled to myself. I spread clean newspaper on the floor, folded the thick stack of old paper and shoved it into a garbage bag. Then I refreshed her water and food bowls.

Ceri, short for Cerise, was Francois's pure breed red poodle. I had nearly fainted when he had asked me to take care of her after he announced his departure. He and Ceri were almost inseparable. They went to lunch together, to the Club, and just about everywhere. I had assumed she would move with him to Maine. It never crossed my mind she would stay behind, let alone with me.

He explained dogs were not allowed where he was going, but what did that have to do with me? I pointed out that I had a hectic schedule with unpredictable hours. Patrick, his best friend and my unofficial mentor, was a better choice, I said. When I mentioned that she didn't like me, he dismissed my objections saying it was all in my mind. I begged off the request for as long as I could. In the end, he wore me down with surprising insistence. For a man who seemed not to care about me at all, he managed to persuade me to feel guilty if I did not take in his pet.

Ceri used to bark every time she saw me before Francois decided to leave her with me. After he announced his decision her barking increased. She would bark before I reached the front door of his house and continue throughout my visit. Weeks after his heartbreaking departure, it had stopped altogether. After he left, she became quiet and droopy. She ate little, and nothing interested her. To my surprise, I missed her perky personality. I had convinced myself that she annoyed me. Now that we lived together her sadness touched my heart.

She didn't bark or scratch at my legs as many dogs due

their morning walk might do. She was too dignified for that. After all, she was a refined society dog. While looking after her was not my choice, it wasn't her fault. Francois had more or less made recommending me to the marshals for the interim position conditional on my agreement to look after Ceri. Poor thing, she ended up in the care of one of the least refined people she had crossed paths with in her short life.

With Iaen gone, my life was ruled by the demands of my job. Where Francois was a gourmet, like Ceri, my palate wasn't as educated or refined as his. Worse yet, these days I paid little attention to what I ate at home. I seldom cooked, not that I was much of a cook. I bought foods that were quick and easy to prepare, filling and affordable.

I received a huge salary bump thanks to my new job, but it was provisional until the committee in Moosehead Lake confirmed me as the permanent head of the Paris marshals office. I didn't want to expand expenses to match my earnings only to have my income drop if I lost the temporary position. I sent my aunt and uncle in Canada, who had raised me like parents, a share of my salary to help with their expenses. I had learned to be frugal from a young age and clung to it out of habit.

Ceri would only eat fresh food, low-fat meat from a nearby butcher and organic produce. I thought Francois would send money for her upkeep, but he didn't. He had left a week's worth of supplies and one month's budget. After that, I hadn't heard a word from him. I spent more on Ceri than I did on myself. When I wasn't working, I was home. Fashion, make-up, perfume, décor, or the superficial social trappings that occupied the attention of most Parisians just held no interest for me.

"I forgot you were here," I said.

She lowered her head as if she understood my words. At first, I thought it was my imagination, but she did that too often to be a coincidence. I could take her with me to breakfast the way Francois used to do. Well-behaved dogs were welcome at many places in Paris, including the Weeia Club. Ceri and I tolerated each other, but I wasn't sure how taking her to breakfast would go, and given everything that was happening at work, I decided to err on the side of caution. If I had to investigate last night's case or follow up on something Susanna brought up, it would be inconvenient to have a prissy headstrong dog on a leash in tow.

I grabbed my keys and put my shoes on by the door. She watched me. As soon as I lifted her leash, she walked to where I was so I could attach the strap to the diamond-studded collar around her neck. I pulled a plastic doggie bag and tucked it in my pocket before closing the door behind us. She walked down the stairs of the old building at a fast clip. I sped up my pace to match hers.

Outside the sky was clear. We crossed the street to the Quai des Grands Augustins, where a few pedestrians rushed by on their way to start their day, and down the stairs to the riverside. There were far fewer people by the river. Ceri liked it best, and I couldn't fault her for that. It was quieter than usual. I thought perhaps we were late. When I lifted her to clean something that had gotten stuck on her paw, I noticed she was gamey.

"The time has come and gone for a bath, young lady," I said in a soothing voice. I talked to her sometimes. As long as I didn't mention Francois's name, she didn't react. She turned her head in the opposite direction, sniffing at the ground as if it held a secret I knew nothing about. "We'll have to figure out what to do. I know your dad left the name of a groomer, but I'm sure that's expensive. It will save a ton of money if I bathe you at home."

It was half an hour before we returned. I refreshed her water. She had only eaten a bite or two from her dish, but she wouldn't touch day old food. After cleaning her plate, I set a handful of fresh morsels on it, hoping she would eat more than the previous day. She drank some of the water without so much as smelling the food before walking to her daybed and lying down.

Glancing at my watch, I realized I had less than twenty minutes to dress and make my way to the Club. I had to hurry. I selected the new pair of pants, top, and red scarf I had bought at a "gently used" shop steps from the rue de Rivoli on the Right Bank.

Although it was easy to find a match as most of my clothes were black I made a special effort to look presentable since I was going to the Club. Despite my new clothing allowance, except on special occasions like dinner at the Eiffel Tower, dressing up and fashion were seldom top of mind for me.

When I had arrived in town from Portland, Maine I had dressed in the clothes I had brought with me. I had bought them because they were cheap, practical, and sturdy. At the marshals office, Madame Marmotte had described me as a country mouse when she thought I wasn't around. Patrick, Francois's childhood friend, had impressed on me the importance of wearing the right clothes for the right occasion. I remembered his words, "Among Weeia in Paris, more than perhaps in any other city, people judge you by your appearance."

Chapter 7

I reached the rue des Deux Ponts on the Isle Saint Louis in two minutes. From there to the Club was another matter. Because the one-way streets on the small island were narrow, all it took was for a single vehicle to stop to load or unload for the entire section to become clogged. Patience, I reminded myself, thrumming my fingers on the steering wheel. Glancing at my watch, I chastised myself for cutting it so close.

I was about to text Susanna about my delay when the way cleared. I turned into the Club courtyard, leaving my keys in the car for the valet and dashed inside. While the exterior of the building appeared dilapidated on purpose, the interior was sumptuous. I still marveled that I was a bona fide member.

The maître d'hôtel was busy. I took advantage and waltzed in past his station. Susanna waved at me from a table for two at the back of the room.

"Nice," she said after we exchanged kisses a la French. As usual, she smelled wonderful like exotic flowers and spices I couldn't name. That wasn't surprising since she and her partner made perfumes for a living. "Did you get them at that new shop you told me about?"

"Yep," I said, pleased she had noticed the additions to my wardrobe.

While Susanna was not as svelte as Parisian women, and sometimes the busy patterns she chose accentuated her weight instead of minimizing it, she was, in general, a smart dresser. I appreciated her opinion. She was being polite, but I could tell from the tight lines around her eyes and tension in her shoulders that she was eager to dispense with the small talk. Instead of asking about her two children as I meant to do I waited for her to speak.

"Someone is watching the shop," she said in a soft voice. "Before you ask, yes, I'm sure."

In the months we had known each other since her arrival in Paris with her kids, Susanna had proved to be an intelligent, capable woman with much strength of character. She wasn't prone to hysterics. If she said someone was watching the shop, I believed her.

Before I could respond the maître d'hôtel arrived at the table. I was grateful to see he brought an elegant silver coffee pitcher with him.

"Bonjour Mademoiselle Metreaux," he said, refilling Susanna's coffee cup as he spoke. With a subtle gesture, he indicated my cup, adding, "May I?"

The coffee, like the food at the Club, was excellent. I nodded my assent.

"Would you like to see today's specials?" he asked us both.

Despite the previous night's elaborate meal, the mention of a menu made me notice the breakfast smells in the dining room for the first time since I had arrived. The odor of coffee, pastries, and sautéed butter was in the air. My stomach growled in response.

Turning to my friend I said, "I know what I want. Susanna?"

"Yes, I do too," she said, pouring hot milk into her coffee. "I'll have a continental."

"Mademoiselle?" he asked.

"Some fruit, an omelet, and viennoiserie," I replied, feeling a bit self-conscious about my much larger order.

"Plain?"

"With ham," I said. "And fresh vegetables, spinach, asparagus, tomatoes, whatever the chef has in the kitchen."

Marla, who had adopted a healthy California lifestyle and looked fantastic, had been after me to eat fruits and vegetables. On our next chat, I would be able to boast that I had ordered fruit and an omelet with veggies. The nine-hour time difference between France and the West Coast meant we didn't talk as often as we would like. I made a mental note to call her soon.

"What do you think they want?" I asked once we were alone. She raised an eyebrow and lifted her shoulders to indicate I knew the answer. "Mathis?"

"What else?"

"When did you notice it?" I asked.

"I'm not sure when it started, but I've had an odd feeling for a couple of days," she said. She ran her fingers through her bangs in a nervous gesture. "At least. Mathis has been on edge too. You know how he gets. He frets over every little thing, afraid he'll get in trouble again, you know, make a mistake."

Mathis, her partner, had been at the center of a complicated case I had worked on that had spiraled out of control. In my job, I had learned it was hard to know what people were like for sure. All I had to go by was the way they behaved. Where she was resourceful, clean, generous, and kind, he appeared to be an odd and selfish slob. He had a rare ability, and at one point he had, using a family instruction book, created scents with powerful effects, intended and unintended. Before we realized what was going on, the perfumes fell into the hands of a twisted young man, and the situation spiraled out of control.

Her shoulders relaxed as if sharing her thoughts with me was all it took to make her problems go away. I didn't have the heart to remind her there was only one of me and a new direct report to cover the entirety of Weeia issues in Paris. Or that he was a well-connected twerp on a mission to steal my job from under me.

"Has he made any mistakes?" I asked to give myself time to think.

"None that I know of," she said, plucking a piece of baguette from the napkin covered basket on the table and buttering it.

"Have you noticed a particular person or a car?" I asked, hoping for a clue.

"Not really," she said.

"Have you seen anyone that didn't belong?"

She smiled as she said, "Ninety percent of the people on the island, especially during the day."

Visitors often crowded the Isle Saint Louis, the smaller of two interconnected islands in the center of the Seine River on the eastern side of the city. Parisians and tourists alike pounded the pedestrian-friendly streets in search of ice cream, souvenirs or a bite.

"I've met everyone in our building and many of the neighbors," she said. "Visitors far outnumber residents, many of whom are retirees. Mathis told me two men followed him home from the tabac the other night."

"What did they look like?" I asked.

"He didn't say much, and I didn't see them, but he was pretty shaken up," she said.

"I'll look into it," I said, hoping my bland words would reassure her, knowing I couldn't very well patrol their building twenty-four hours a day.

Our breakfast arrived, making my stomach rumble in anticipation. I hoped Susanna hadn't heard it. She showed little interest in the food. I pounced on mine with gusto.

"How are you holding up?" she asked.

"You know, some days are better than others," I said. "Nights are the worst. That's when I remember our quiet time. On some evenings, I can almost sense his breath. You?"

Susanna's husband had been missing for months. We never used the "d" word, but I felt certain he had either abandoned them or been killed.

"The sadness and pain are always with me," she replied, placing the flat of her hand over her chest. "For the sake of the children, I hide my feelings. They deserve a normal life."

She lowered her eyes. I didn't want to cry either, so I

changed the topic.

"How do you like being in business with Mathis?"

"It's not so bad," she replied. "I've been incredibly lucky since I arrived here. If it wasn't for you, I don't know where I would be. And, after some initial disagreements, Mathis warmed up to me. He needs me, and he knows it. I need the work. It's not just the money. A challenging job like this one fills my mind, leaving little space to think about anything else. Taking care of the children uses up any time that remains, so I have few opportunities to fret."

"I know the feeling," I said. "With my new duties, my days are overfull with no end in sight."

"Speaking of your new duties, how do you like being in charge?" she asked.

"That part hasn't changed much since the only staff are Madame Marmotte and the new guy," I said. "She was devoted to Francois and never my fan, to put it mildly."

"I hear the new guy is good-looking," she said, fishing for the latest.

"Don't even think what I know you're thinking," I replied. "Never mind that I wouldn't ever date a direct report."

She raised her eyebrows and opened her eyes in a surprised expression as she asked, "Oh?"

"It's not only that he's trying to take my place and that he's seriously well-connected," I said, mulling over in my mind what exactly bothered me about him. "He's arrogant and entitled. Other than he made it clear that he wants my job, I can't put my finger on anything he's done, but I don't trust him."

"I thought he was young," she said.

"He is, my age," I replied. "If you see a photo of him he might pass for a catch. He's tall enough, fit, his features are angular, and he has good manners when he chooses to use them for his benefit."

"Nothing like Sébastien," she said.

Sébastien, my previous direct report, had become a close friend and ally. To my disappointment, he had stepped down from the marshals service to work in his family's business. I was sure he had waited until I had recovered from the grief of losing Iaen before taking an indefinite leave of absence. He was an excellent young marshal and had saved my tail more than once. He finally relented to his family's constant pressure to return to the fold and dedicate himself to "something worthwhile". He was a decent man determined to do what was right even if it made him less than happy.

His parents and sister supported him without reservation, mostly. They thought joining the marshals had been a rite of passage for him, a way to prove himself before he accepted his rightful place in the powerful and influential company. They believed it was just a fad. When we first met, I thought he was a spoiled rich kid like so many other Weeia youth. It didn't take long for his true mettle to shine through the privileged trappings of his life.

Working side by side, sometimes in dangerous conditions, we had gotten to know each other well. Being a marshal wasn't a whim for Sébastien. It was his true calling, and he was good, better than good. In time, he might have been excellent. Replacing his father as the head of the company was his duty and his destiny. In the end, he did what his family expected and demanded of him and gave up his dream of being a marshal.

"Not in a million years," I said.

"Have you heard from him since he left?" she asked.

"We keep in touch," I replied in a sharper tone than necessary, defensive because it had been days since I had reached out to him and he had yet to respond.

"Don't worry, I bet he'll be in touch soon," she said, recognizing my distress for what it was.

"What makes you say that?" I asked.

She drew in her breath as if remembering something before

replying, "I've seen you two work together, remember? The bond you have is strong and—" She paused as if searching for a word. "long-lasting. It doesn't disappear overnight."

When we met, I had not appreciated Sébastien. I had to overcome my own prejudices first. So, it had taken me some time to look past his obvious qualities, his drop-dead gorgeous face, Greek god body, and wealthy status, to discover the intelligent, caring, and thoughtful man beneath. By the day he had resigned, he had become more than a coworker I relied on. He was a close friend, and I missed working with him every day.

"You're right," I said, eager to talk about something more cheerful. "How are the kids?"

"Wonderful," she said. A sad expression crossed her face so fast I would have missed it if I hadn't been looking at her at that moment. I imagined she was thinking about raising her daughter and son in a strange city without her husband. I felt pity and wished I could have done more to help them. As it was, I had stretched my authority to gain asylum for them in France and among the Weeia. "Their French is getting better every day, and they are adapting to life in Paris like fish to water."

When I glanced down at my watch, I was surprised at the time. I gulped down some coffee and shifted in my seat.

"There's a situation I have to deal with today," I said. "I have to go to the office. I'll check in on you as soon as I can."

"Thank you," she said.

Chapter 8

Perhaps because I drove out of the island frustrated there was little I could do to protect Mathis and Susanna, I forgot about the massive yellow vest (for the bright yellow emergency vest many participants wore) strike scheduled for that day. I never ceased to be amazed by the many benefits the French took for granted. One of the rights they most exercised was the one to strike. It seemed everyone went on strike at some point during the year. In the short time I had lived in Paris, garbage workers, street cleaners, teachers, oil refinery workers, air traffic controllers, pilots, flight attendants, and all other transport system employees except taxis had gone on strike. It was helpful that the unions scheduled the strike days and times weeks in advance to minimize disruption.

As I drove northeast and away from the island, traffic stopped again. Looking ahead at the gnarled mess of cars unlikely to go anywhere fast I realized what was happening. With some effort, I maneuvered my way around to the Boulevard Périphérique, a highway that circles the city. Two hours later, I reached my destination, pleased to have gotten myself free from the congestion yet annoyed at the delay. My boss in Portland wouldn't give a fig about little issues like massive citywide protests. There were never strikes in Maine. He didn't have any interest in Paris strikes. Besides, while he had never told me he disliked me to my face, I had the impression any excuse to discredit me would do for him.

The marshals office was in a gated compound that took up an entire city block in the twentieth arrondissement, one of the neighborhoods furthest from the city center. With some much-needed renovations, it could house dozens of people, maybe more, although the only occupants were our office, Susanna and her children, and two Lithuanian workers I had hired and their families. It was in a mixed neighborhood. Some streets were upscale with clean sidewalks, well-maintained short buildings, and even houses, while others, strewn with garbage and dog poo, had graffiti-covered walls and tall government housing buildings bursting beyond capacity.

The central district I called home was touristy and popular with pedestrians at all hours. Tourists seldom visited this neighborhood on the edge of the city, except to explore the well-known Pere-Lachaise Cemetery, the only tourist attraction in the area. Despite its flaws, I had grown to like it. I appreciated the authenticity of the family owned shops, even the ones with grumpy staff. It was nice that the owner of the produce shop around the corner from my office recognized me and remembered I liked apples. They treated Susanna and her kids like extended family. In contrast, it was so busy when I went to the produce shop near my apartment, there was little time for small talk. Besides, the owners were never there and the employees couldn't care less.

Madame Marmotte was a bit more alert when I arrived than usual, which wasn't saying much as she moved at a glacial pace. The woman had made an art form of doing as little work as humanly possible even if she wasn't human. Instead of ignoring me when I arrived or more often arriving after I did, she looked up at me from the continuous manicure position she took up at her desk. You would think her nails were perfect judging by how she was always filing, touching up and fussing with them. They were nothing of the kind.

She watched me enter and set the croissants I had picked up by the coffeepot without replying to my greeting. As soon as I sat down with a cup of coffee and a pastry she raised her hand, waiving small pieces of paper at me and saying, "For you."

Pressing down the annoyance I felt I took a bite of my croissant before replying, "Okay, thanks."

I never saw her address Francois that way when he was in charge of the office. Around him, she behaved like an adoring fan rather than a direct report. Even when he wasn't around, which was most of the time, as he hardly ever went to the office during my tenure in Paris, she referred to him with reverence and respect. She treated me with disdain and contempt.

Attempts to reason with her had no effect. On the other hand, she was elderly and worthy of my pity. I used to try to intimidate her, but it felt wrong, my aunt and uncle had raised me better. Treating her in a less than kind way was like kicking a mangy puppy. She waved the papers again, signaling me to get them by drawing her hand in her direction.

"What is it?" I asked, unable to hide the frustration.

"You'll want to see these right away," she replied.

It wasn't that I minded getting up and retrieving the messages as much as allowing her the win of making me do what she wanted. Why did she have to be so petty?

"Just tell me," I replied. "What?"

"I took the trouble to write down the details. The least you can do is read them," she said.

In seconds, I walked to her desk, snatched the messages from her hand, and without uttering a word returned to my seat. Her musky perfume made me want to sneeze and cry at once. I rubbed my nose in an unconscious effort to make it disappear. She wore her usual heavy make-up like a faded movie star. Bits of her foundation powder covered the bright scarf around her neck and excess lipstick stuck to her front teeth. It tore at my heart, deflating the anger she provoked.

It was no surprise the message notes were almost illegible. The same arthritis that slowed down her gait made the joints on her fingers knobby. She never said anything, but I suspected writing was difficult and painful. She could have texted or called me if there was something that needed immediate attention. I drew in a breath to help me keep my composure.

"The first one I get," I said, referring to the message from my boss. "What does the other one say?"

"If you're not too busy Elders Ted and Amanda Walker would like a word with you," she said in a tone that suggested how busy I was made no difference at all. "They were expecting you at their hotel first thing this morning."

I made the mistake of replying, "I never said I would be there."

"I told them I'm not your keeper," she said. "They were upset that you didn't give them your number." I had, but there was no point in telling her. "They expected you to report your findings as any self-respecting marshal would do with her superiors."

The Walkers were not my superiors. Well, in a sense they were as they ranked higher than I did, but I didn't report to them. I was head of the Paris office. It wasn't my job to keep them updated. As a courtesy I would whenever I had any news to share.

"I…" I began, thinking better than to argue with her, I stopped speaking. "Where is Rupert?" I asked more to change the subject than because I cared.

"In the workout room," she said, avoiding the use of his name as usual.

The only positive following Rupert's arrival had been that I had gone from least liked person on her list to second least liked person. Since I had joined the office she had made it clear she was not my fan, and I had accepted it. Knowing someone well-connected, better dressed and with more social graces than me had earned her scorn amused me for some reason.

As a new marshal, he had no field or supervisory experience. For all intents and purposes, I had been running the Paris office since my posting nearly two years before. I had years of field and supervisory experience and a higher level of training than he did. The potency level of Weeia abilities is self-defined, divided into Lowes, Medius and Maximus in order of strength. I considered my skill Medius while I estimated his to be Lowes, which meant I had superior abilities. Despite that, he was on a mission to undermine my authority and steal my job with the support of influential Weeia back home.

The big black mark on my family name made me unpopular among the conservative ranks of my fellow superhumans. It made no difference to them that the tarnish was from the actions of my parents and not my own. They had died when I was a little girl. Despite unfavorable odds, I had chosen to become a marshal, following in their original footsteps. In the Marshal's Academy, I had passed every written, oral, and practical test on my merits. Once assigned to a post I had to overcome deep distrust and open hostility from my colleagues, many of whom resented my superior grades and abilities. Because they went out of their way to thwart me, every victory had been hard won.

Madame Marmotte's dislike for Rupert was due to his open contempt for her. He made fun of her to her face, calling her a relic and encouraging her to resign. He mocked her clothes, her limp and slow movements, and described her make-up as garish and inappropriate for the office. While I made a point of chiding him when I heard him, I suspected he had curbed his behavior to ensure I didn't hear him, yet continued to harass her behind my back. She was too proud to complain, but I was certain it hurt her feelings to receive a dose of the same medicine she had given me for so long. I couldn't help a touch of glee.

I postponed my desire to train in favor of calling my boss. He picked up on the second ring.

"Did you just arrive at the office?" he asked.

"I had a meeting at the Club early this morning," I replied. I held back the further explanation that I had little sleep the previous night. He wouldn't care. He might even hold it against me. "Any news?"

"As a matter of fact, yes," he said in a neutral tone I had come to dread. "Detailed analysis of the video we found online indicates the person involved is likely a speedwalker."

I waited while he gave orders to someone in his office before speaking. I could hear many voices and phones ringing in the background.

"We don't have any speedwalkers in Paris, sir," I replied. "It must be someone from out of town."

"I thought as much," he said.

"I was in touch with the Walkers this morning," he said. "I agree with them that this is a high profile case because of the setting and that it could involve one of our own."

I remembered Sébastien's words when we were sparring one day before he quit: high profile cases, while risky are the path to promotions. At the time, I had teased him that he was his father's son, always with his eye on making a buck. He was right. This could be my opportunity to be confirmed as permanent head of the Paris office. My spirits lifted.

"I'll start looking into it right away," I began.

As if I hadn't spoken he went on in the same tone, "All eyes are on this, human and Weeia."

"Yes, sir. I will do my best," I said.

"That won't be necessary," he said.

"But, sir, I'm the acting head of the office," I said, sounding whinier by far than I wanted to.

"I'm afraid there is too much at stake, Officer Metreaux," he said. "You have two days to resolve the case or we will send an urgent response investigative task force."

I felt the energy drain from my body. It was the first serious opportunity to prove myself and he was ready to pass it to someone else. To avoid screaming at him and saying something regrettable, I mumbled that I would send updates ASAP, and hung up at as soon as I could.

I paced around my office, feeling like a caged lion in a space too small to hold my frustration and anger. I had to do something. I wondered what the video analysis revealed and what the Walkers had said. They were influential enough to get the case reassigned. There was little I could do either way. On the subject of the video, I needed to learn what they had found.

I texted Ernie, a friend based in Portland, Maine. He was a technical expert and the second in command in his department behind only the weapons master at the marshals headquarters. The lack of an immediate reply made me realize it was still too early in Portland and he wouldn't be up. I wanted to work out in a bad way to let some of the excess energy escape, but if I ran into Rupert I might not be able to hold back. A black eye would set his attitude to a proper setting, but I was his boss and had to behave myself.

So I did the next best thing. I closed my office door and called my friend Marla despite the nine-hour difference with California.

Her sleepy voice answered on the fifth ring, "Danni?"

"Yes," I half yelled. "Sorry to call you so late. I'm so mad I could scream."

"You sorta are screaming," she said.

"Sorry," I said. "Would you believe that man? He plans to bench me on what could be the highest profile case in my career." I spoke almost without pause. "Solving that case could guarantee my post in Paris would become permanent. But, no! He's going to micromanage the case from Portland. He's giving me two days. What am I, Merlin? I can't do magic. If by the deadline I have no answers, he's sending an urgent response investigative task force, people who may never have set foot in Paris, who may know nothing about French culture and sensitivities."

"The last time we spoke you were ambivalent about staying in Paris," she said in a tone that was way too reasonable for my taste. "Why do you care so much now?"

"I don't know," I said in a louder tone than she deserved. "I just do."

An awkward silence filled the air between us. I thought about her question.

"If I leave I want it to be on my terms, the way Sébastien left the service," I said in a calmer voice than the one from a moment before. I took a deep breath and let it out before continuing to make sure I kept my composure. "Almost without realizing it Paris has become my home. It's not just a job. I care what happens here. You were right. It's an amazing city and it's gotten under my skin."

She waited for me to speak, but hearing the truth in my words had been like a soothing tonic for me. My frustration had lessened. I was ready for her response.

"I thought I heard some ambition there, too," she said.

"Maybe," I conceded. "And what if I want the case? There's nothing wrong with that. It happened on my watch, in my city."

"True," she said. "You've always focused on doing the right thing rather than moving up the ranks is all. What changed your mind?"

"I, uh," I stuttered.

"Never mind," she said. "How can I help?"

I thought I heard a voice in the background. Remembering her boyfriend, I felt a pang of guilt.

"Oh no, are you sleeping over at—" I began.

"No, he's out of town, don't worry," she replied. "That's just the TV."

"Okay, if you're sure," I said.

"Yep. Talk to me. What do you want to do?"

The answer came without effort. "Solve the case," I said. "Not because I want to keep my job or for any personal advantage, but because it's the right thing to do."

"That's the Danni I know and love," she said. "So what's

stopping you?"

"Well my boss said I only have two days to solve the case," I said. "I don't think I can do that."

"Can anybody?"

"I don't think so," I said. "Even if he sends a team there's no way they'll be able to either."

"So?" she asked.

"So nothing," I said, still frustrated.

"So what's holding you back from doing what you want?" she asked.

"My boss," I replied.

"Did he say you couldn't work on the case?"

"Not in so many words," I said, thinking before answering further. "I see what you mean. I can work on it for the next two days officially and continue working unofficially after that." A smile spread over my lips. "You're the best. Thank you. You can go back to sleep now. Sorry I woke you."

"Just like that?" she asked in an amused tone.

"Yes, unless you want to talk some more," I said with a smidgen of regret at having to hang up. "I would love your thoughts on the case if you want to discuss it, but I figured you want your beauty sleep."

"I'm here if you need me, but if not I have a big day tomorrow and I need to get some rest," she said.

"I understand completely," I said. "Call me when you have a minute and I'll catch you up."

"Deal," she said and we hung up.

I was sure when I told her later what it was about she would be interested. If she ended the conversation now it was because she really had to. She had been a great help, and I was grateful.

Rupert was gone when I arrived in the workout room. I banged around for an hour. When I left, sweat pouring down my red face, I was excited with the possibility that I might solve the case even if I had to do it single handed. There was a reply text from Ernie saying he had a meeting and would be available at the end of his workday.

I reached out to a police contact for clues on the attack, but she knew little. I was too restless to focus on paperwork. Figuring it would take me a long while to get back home I left early. I stopped at the Walkers' hotel to discover they were out and hadn't bothered to let me know where they were going as they were supposed to. I left a voice mail for Ted and waited half an hour before leaving.

Chapter 9

If traffic had been a mess that morning it was ten times worse in the afternoon. The Périphérique was all but a parking lot. The rain didn't help. A sea of cars inched forward in an awkward soppy dance. I was grouchy when I entered the sixth arrondissement in search of a parking spot.

Ceri's greetings for me when I returned home were a shadow of those I had witnessed for Francois. My consolation was that at least now she greeted me. When he left, she pined for him and sulked in the new bed I bought her without so much as a bark. Some days when I returned home after a long day at work, I would find she had bitten one of my shoes or a pillow. She wasn't any happier about the arrangement than I was. We were stuck with each other.

I hadn't eaten much since breakfast, but I wasn't hungry so for dinner I had a quick sandwich. Ceri watched me in silence. I was starting to miss her habit of barking at me whenever she saw me in the days when she lived with Francois. For a change I hadn't found any shoes with tooth marks or any other signs of mischief. As a reward for her good behavior I took her on an extra-long walk. We strolled toward the Isle Saint Louis to check on Mathis and Susanna.

On our way we passed by Francois's favorite café, where he used to go with Ceri and Patrick. I was lost in my thoughts letting Ceri have the lead when I heard the headwaiter's greeting. For an instant, I thought he was talking to me and was about to reply until I saw him crouch down to speak to Ceri. She let him pet her without growling or barking.

It shouldn't have surprised me that he all but ignored me. He always treated me with contempt. I suspected that because I wasn't from Paris and refused to obsess about outward appearances, he judged me undesirable. Perhaps because I was in Ceri's company, at the last moment he acknowledged me with a casual good evening. I nodded and mumbled a reply before continuing toward the bridge that connected the two islands.

A construction project marred the busy road next to Notre Dame. From there, a pedestrian bridge connected the two islands. As usual it was filled with street performers, tourists, residents walking their dogs and all manner of curious people. That night a trio of musicians was playing a haunting song nobody seemed to like. Their tip hat had only five or six coins. It was also a favorite haunt of pickpockets and gypsy tricksters said to travel from East Europe to Paris to make their living conning fools in the city.

As soon as we reached the Ile Saint Louis, I relaxed a smidgen. The narrow cobblestoned streets, especially the side ones, were quiet. They had sidewalks so narrow it was difficult to walk along them. We sometimes had to step off the sidewalk when a motorcycle blocked our way or a group of people spilled out of a building. Short old-looking and uneven buildings lined both sides of the one-way streets. The shadows and distinctive facades made me wonder what the island might have been like a century or two before my time.

While the neighboring islands shared some common history and a part of the Ile de la Cité was in the same arrondissement as the Ile Saint Louis they had distinct characteristics and vibes. The Ile de la Cité was perhaps twice the size of the Ile Saint Louis and home to the famous Notre Dame Cathedral. Although the Ile Saint Louis was popular with locals and tourists it was modest in attractions. It was the intimate setting of the smaller island that I liked most. As the day drew to a close the crowds disappeared, leaving those out for dinner and island residents.

Sometimes when I arrived home past dinner, I went to the deli shop that stayed open late on the Ile Saint Louis. The limited selection often included at least one baguette.

Prepared foods, cheeses, chocolates, jams, and deli meats satisfied late night cravings. Except for the prepared foods, which were pricey, most of the prices were the same as at my neighborhood supermarket, and the attendant was always helpful.

Despite the many tourists that flocked to the island, it retained a certain dignity that other neighborhoods had lost. The popular streets were a double-edged sword of sorts. They made it difficult to identify threats to Mathis and Susanna. At the same time, they allowed me to pass by unnoticed. Having Ceri allowed me to fit in with the locals. People's eyes were drawn to the beautiful poodle with her fancy hairstyle while ignoring me.

Mathis's shop was on the basement and ground floors of a venerable old building owned by his family for generations. He lived in the upper floors. At that hour, the shop, which had limited hours to begin with, was closed. There was nothing peculiar about the exterior and no one stood out as a potential threat. Ceri and I circled the block twice. To be sure, I turned on the Weeia detection feature on my badge, which to the casual observer appeared to be a mobile phone. There were no Weeia anywhere along our path.

I knocked on the door of the well-lit shop, expecting no reply. To my surprise Susanna answered the door. After the compulsory exchange of kisses, French style, and greetings, she invited me in.

"I thought you would be gone by now. I was hoping to speak with Mathis," I said, feeling guilty that it was the first time I checked on them since we had spoken.

"I came in late to be with the kids at school all morning," she said. "You know, they're off Wednesdays and have class Saturday morning." I nodded even though I hadn't known until that moment. I found shop and business hours in Paris erratic and baffling. Why should schools be any different?

"I'm in the middle of a project I want to finish so I may be a while longer. He just stepped out. If he stays true to his routine he's probably at the tobacco shop on the main avenue. Want me to show you?"

"Naw, I know it," I said.

They special ordered the brand of snus I liked. Whenever I popped by to pick it up the owner and his nephew looked like they had swallowed a porcupine quills and all. I didn't get the impression it was personal. They treated almost everyone as if by entering they were interrupting something more urgent or important than they were. It was an attitude I had witnessed many times around the city.

Instead of following Mathis to the shop, we kept our distance. Ceri had already done her business, and I had picked up after her so we were in no rush. I watched the shop entrance from the corner of my eye, allowing Ceri to linger on favorite smells. Fifteen minutes later, Mathis exited with a bundle under his arm. An average-looking man, not too tall and not too short, followed the perfume maker until he reached his home. As the man turned toward us, I snapped a selfie of Ceri and me with him in the background. I didn't recognize him, and the Weeia function on my badge didn't light up, meaning he was human rather than superhuman. In the morning, I would check our database, small as it was, for any matches. It was better than nothing.

Chapter 10

Since I had set my system to notify me if any big events such as the recent terrorist attack took place, there had been no news. It was past midnight, and I was about to head to bed when the alerts on my badge began to ding. Judging by the number of media alerts something was newsworthy in the city. A French media outlet said a good Samaritan, nicknamed MGV, had foiled a robbery on the famed Champs Elysees. Activity on the main social media sites showed it was a big deal, although I couldn't get details of what had happened. There was no evidence that it was Weeia related, so I convinced myself to get some sleep after an hour of reading and watching videos with little progress.

The following morning, I went for a short run before walking Ceri and heading to work. I was stunned to discover the office full of marshals. Approaching the nearest one, a tall man with dandruff on his shoulders, I cleared my throat to draw his attention.

"This is my office. Who might you be?" I asked in the calmest tone I could muster when he turned to face me.

"Marshal Metcalf, ma'am," he said. He was young, a newbie. It reminded me of my days as a newly minted marshal. "I'm part of the investigative team reporting to—"

I stopped listening after investigative team and interrupted him with a hand gesture. To his credit he didn't react.

"Why are you here?" I asked in an angry voice despite my best efforts at staying calm.

"We are assigned to the Eiffel Tower terrorist attack incident, Ma'am," he replied.

"I see," I said, not seeing at all. There was no point in

venting at him. He didn't make decisions. He followed orders and I doubted he knew much about the case. "What happened to two days?"

"Ma'am?"

"Never mind," I said, stepping around him to find Madame Marmotte and Rupert.

"They were here when I arrived," she said as soon as she saw me. The anger must have shown on my face because she went on before I could ask any questions. "I have no idea who let them in." The truth was marshals could come and go without being let in, but it was common courtesy to at least notify the marshal in charge before arriving. "It must've been Rupert. I heard something about an emergency assignment. One of them mentioned your boss's name."

Before I had a chance to ask where he was, I heard Rupert's voice, "Gentlemen, this way. There is a private room where we can meet. We can assign nonconfidential tasks to staff members later."

Susanna and her kids were in the residential wing living in my old apartment. The other occupants of that section, our Lithuanian handymen and their families, had returned home on leave. Madame Marmotte and I were the only people in the office part of the complex, making it obvious that he meant private from us.

Madame Marmotte's face fell when she realized they were leaving both of us out of the investigation. If they had included her, she wouldn't have hesitated to exclude me. After all the times she had treated me like an outsider, I should have been glad that she was getting a taste of her own medicine. Instead, I felt pity for the tragic old woman.

"Better to keep Francois's office locked," she said after the men were well out of earshot. "Unless you have told Rupert, only you and I know how to open it. I'd rather those young fellows not go in there."

My old boss's office was the best space in the building. At

some point in his career when he cared about his job he had furnished it with mementos and high end furniture. Rather than an ego wall, he had an entire ego office. While it was too masculine for my taste, I had to admit I had felt grown up when I took it over. More than that, moving into his office had been a huge triumph for me, in particular because he had gone out of his way at every turn to discourage me from staying in Paris.

I was tempted to remind her that Francois's old office was my office. And I wanted to scream that she had been the one to try to win Rupert over since his arrival. Instead, I took a deep breath and counted to ten before replying.

"He's so full of himself and so confident he will get his way that as soon as he arrived, he told me of his intent to dethrone me, as he put it," I said. "I haven't told him how to open it."

I couldn't make out what she replied. She didn't enunciate well, and I was distracted.

Realizing directing my anger at her wouldn't accomplish anything I nodded. Her shoulders relaxed and the smallest tension lines around her deeply wrinkled lips softened.

"I'll need to use your computer if I can't get into my office," I said, expecting her to object.

Instead, she moved away from her desk, motioning with her hand she drew a wide arc in the air in invitation. Half an hour later I had nothing to show for my efforts. I was anxious and annoyed. I didn't want to be there.

A workout was what I needed to help me calm down. To my irritation, the private meeting place Rupert was referring to was our workout room, the one I had spent so much effort modernizing. Granted, it was the only temperature controlled, refurbished room large enough for the group to meet.

Did I mention it was a huge sausage fest without a single woman among them? The marshals were founded by a woman and in my experience, women were well represented among our ranks. Judging by what I had seen of the team, the selection criteria consisted of lack of experience and willingness to work under Rupert.

I was so distracted when my phone rang I answered without looking at the caller ID on the screen, "What?"

"And a good day to you too, Sunshine," a familiar, cultured voice replied.

If anyone else had said that at that moment I might have thrown a foul word their way. His good humor stole some of the angry wind from my sails.

"I thought you had disappeared off the face of the earth," I said, but I couldn't throw any of my fury toward Sébastien. "To what do I owe the supreme honor of a call, from you high and mighty CEO?"

"Sorry, I've been out of touch," he said in a soothing tone. "I was at a retreat and the instructor confiscated all electronics for the duration. You're among the first people I'm calling. I take it you heard about MGV?"

"Last night," I said, the anger and humiliation of being excluded from the investigation in my own office threatening to swallow me whole. I breathed deep and counted to ten before continuing. "I was supposed to have two days to investigate whether Weeia were involved in the attack on the Eiffel Tower. Did you hear about that during your electronic isolation?" I didn't give him a chance to reply. "That was an impossible deadline and we both knew it."

"By we, do you mean you and your boss who issued the deadline?" he asked.

"That's the one," I said. "When I got to the office this morning a team, with Rupert's help, had assumed responsibility. They're in the gym as we speak."

"I heard," he said.

I knew who had told him, but for once I didn't mind. Madame Marmotte had a direct line to Sébastien and worshiped the ground he walked on. It was no surprise. He stood for everything she believed in, a wealthy, powerful old

Weeia family with social standing. And, he was a man. No matter how hard I worked to overcome my social flaws, I would never be able to make up for being a woman in her eyes.

"Why are they calling the rescuer MGV, any idea?" I asked.

"It stands for *Mec a Grand Vitesse*, a play on the speed train, which is *Train a Grande Vitesse*," he said. "Think he or she is Weeia?"

I loved that Sébastien didn't automatically assume it was a man. It was impossible to know for sure from the videos I had seen.

"It's starting to look that way," I said. "The thing is that speedwalkers don't live around every block. We don't have any here." I paused to emphasize the point. "Whoever it is must be from out of town or out of the country."

"Have to go," he said, and we hung up.

As I glanced around Madame Marmotte's messy desk I saw the time and remembered I had somewhere to be. I needed to make some progress. Better yet I needed to crack the case before the team did. That was what it would take to reestablish my credibility and keep my job. If the team solved it, there was every possibility that Rupert would replace me. Not only that, but he had made it clear there would be no room for me in Paris if he became the head of the office.

I forwarded Ernie the photo I had snapped of the man watching Mathis. Then I sent him a text asking for his help, in confidence, and to send the results to me and nobody else. It was an imposition, but under the circumstances I had no choice. My own MGV investigation would continue, but meanwhile, I would make myself scarce. There was no way I was going to be the errand girl for Rupert and the task force working to oust me.

Chapter 11

It was five after one when I arrived at the Quai de Montebello restaurant. As the name hinted, it was on the Quai de Montebello facing north toward the River Seine. Central Paris was among my favorite areas of the city. The old streets oozed character and history. Each one was unique and each building was distinct from its neighbor.

Where the famous grand boulevards made clear paths across the cityscape, these streets were almost whimsical. The boulevards Saint Germain and Saint Michel set a grand tone, but there were also many narrow streets that veered at unexpected angles. Some streets were short as if a giant boulder had blocked the builders while others, like the quais de Montebello, followed the river without hindrance.

Although I preferred to self-park, finding a convenient spot at that hour would steal too much time, so I took advantage of the complimentary valet service. At a cursory glance, the old building was like all the others on the street, except it had floor to ceiling glass walls. Inside the small restaurant was half full. The staff were busy, and no one said anything as I made my way to the back, where I climbed the spiral staircase one floor. I saw Kate Marlow, the bottle redhead in her fifties who was my lunch date, waving from a table for two next to the window.

"Great table," I complimented her.

I liked the restaurant's clean lines, neutral colors and minimalist décor. The manager had explained one day that the designers had selected the colors and style to emphasize the view. And what a view it was. From the second floor of the three-story building, where the best tables were located, we could see Notre Dame Cathedral on the Ile de la Cité and the sidewalk that fronted the river.

"I got here early and had my pick," she replied, giving me a smile without teeth. After making sure none of the staff where within earshot she continued, "The food is okay and the service is uneven. What I love is the view of the bouquinistes and the riverfront. They remind me of Jonathan." The smile faded as she mentioned his name. "Even though nowadays most of them only sell tourist junk made in China, he was convinced you could find rare books and memorabilia if you knew where to look. We were childhood sweethearts you know."

The bouquinistes sold souvenirs, books and collectibles on the banks of the Seine. They peddled their goods from wooden boxes perched on the walls along the Seine. I felt a pang in my heart too, but I didn't mention that Iaen had run one for a while. Her second husband, Jonathan Bitter, died of injuries inflicted during a mugging gone wrong while in Paris on their honeymoon. Marshals investigate Weeia deaths within their jurisdiction, and prevent exposure of our kind. I met Kate during the investigation.

Despite the age difference and perhaps because we had both lost a loved one to tragedy in Paris we connected right away. I had been a basket case following Iaen's death before Kate and I met. I understood her grief because my own pain was just below the surface. All it took was a familiar scent, walking by a favorite place or something as simple as the background sounds of the city on a given night and tears would bubble up in my eyes unbidden and impossible to contain. After his death, I had found solace in my family and friends who had come to my side. She had lost her son years earlier and her parents were gone. If there was anyone else she had never said. I had offered companionship and understanding, expecting she would leave after the funeral, but she had stayed.

"Oh?"

"We dreamed of traveling to Paris together," she said, her

eyes focusing to one side as if in some faraway place in her mind. "After so many years apart, we finally got together. When we arrived here for our honeymoon we explored the city like high schoolers. It was wonderful." She averted her gaze and rubbed away a teardrop from her cheek. After a moment, she turned to me. "Enough of my mushy stories. How are you?"

"Annoyed as all get out," I said.

Leaning in she asked, "How come?"

"It's a long story," I said. She let the silence fill the space between us until I spoke again. "To make a long story short, I was supposed to be in charge of a big investigation, but this morning a team from the home office arrived. A new guy, who is trying to take my place as head of the office, is using this opportunity to jump past me."

"By big investigation do you mean the Eiffel Tower case?" she asked, still leaning in with interest.

"That's the one," I said glad not to have to explain.

I don't have a habit of discussing work with people outside the office so I didn't elaborate. She had guessed about the case on her own. I hadn't revealed anything that hadn't been on the news.

"I thought you were the head of the office?" she asked.

"I'm acting head of the office," I replied stressing the second word. "It's up to my bosses in Maine to decide if I get to keep my job in the long-term."

She leaned back in her seat and was quiet for a moment. The morning's events had unsettled me and the silence stretched on.

"I bet you're good at your job. Solving this case could secure your position," she said in a matter-of-fact voice.

"Yes, it most certainly could," I said. "But, it's difficult to crack a case when they leave you out of the team investigating it."

"Wow, so they're excluding you from your own case?" she

asked.

I nodded to avoid screaming with frustration. I could feel her eyes on me. Before I could say anything, the server arrived to take my drink order and bring us menus. He was in his mid-twenties or so with the sides of his head shaved and a tiny ponytail of bleached hair piled on top.

He poked the screen of his digital tablet and turned to go.

"I'm hungry. If we let him go now it may be a while before he comes back," she said, calling him. "Can you pick something quickly while I give him my order?"

In response I grunted, "'Kay," and zeroed in on the two-page lunch menu.

"I'll have the chef's menu," she said. "What fish is that?"

When he didn't reply, I looked up. The server's lips were pursed to one side to indicate he had no idea.

"Never mind," she said. "Bring us more bread and butter, please. Danni you ready?"

"I'm between the lunch menu and the chef's menu. I'm concerned the chef's menu might be too much," I replied.

"Since when?" she asked.

"It's not that I can't finish it, just that I shouldn't," I said. "Ever since I joined the Club officially, I've been eating there regularly." To her wide smile, I replied, "I'm not complaining. The food is great and it's my job to go there, so the company pays for most of my meals." Company was the term we used in public when referring to the marshals. "I've been trying to watch what I eat."

"You exercise like a demon," she said. "You must lose a ton of calories with those killer sessions not to mention that you run. You're in enviable shape."

The server shifted his feet and looked back toward the top of the stairs as if to leave.

"It's easier for the kitchen if we order the same dish," she said. "Eat whatever you want and leave the rest. I might take it off your hands."

"Okay," I said unconvinced about my ability to resist temptation. "I'll have the chef's menu."

The server poked his device one more time, took the menus from the table where we had set them and walked away. Before either of us had said anything, he had returned with my glass of house Burgundy.

"Speaking of being in shape, what's up with you?" I asked.

"What do you mean?" she asked.

"You look fantastic," I said. She did. When we had first met she had been on the plump side. Now she was thin. "When we met, you had a few extra pounds and now you are in shape and trim." I left out that she had been unkempt, sometimes smelled like she hadn't showered for days and appeared like a bus had run her over. There had been a time when that description would have fit me. "More importantly there's a gleam in your eyes I've never seen before. What's your secret?"

Her smile showed her even and bleached teeth that time. She shrugged just as the server returned with a basket of bread and a dish of butter stamped with the restaurant's logo.

"No secret," she said. "I still miss Jonathan like a son of a gun. I can't bear to leave Paris because this is where we were happiest. This is where he's buried. I'm making peace with that and finding a way forward. He had done well for himself, better than he had ever told me. I was surprised at the fortune he left me. I guess he wanted to be sure I married him for him and not for his money. I had a nest egg of my own. I can afford to stay here for a while."

Work was what had gotten me out of my rut following Iaen's passing. Whatever she meant by finding a way forward it was making a visible difference.

"Whatever it is, keep doing it," I said.

"How did you manage, you know, after?" she asked.

"There was a big case," I said, looking down as if to shake the sad memory.

"Work is a good distraction," she said.

Wanting to talk about anything else I asked, "Are you still at the hotel?"

"I'm moving to an apartment tomorrow," she replied. "Finding a decent rental was much harder than I expected. Apparently most of the owners prefer to rent on a weekly or nightly basis because they make much more money that way. And central Paris, oh la la, pricey." Her eyes widened. "You live around here. How do you manage?"

"I had company housing in Maine and when I arrived," I said as if that answered her question. I wasn't sure if or how to answer it so I asked her a question instead. "How did you find your place?"

"It took no small amount of effort," she said. "There are a ton of agencies online, but many of them wouldn't or couldn't answer basic questions about the properties they claimed to have in their inventory. One agency wanted advance payment for the rental before they would show me the apartment or even disclose the address. None of them would tell me the name of the owner. Can you believe it?" She continued before I could reply. "Others were only available online or by email. That is a definite red flag. Sure enough, I would ask to see an apartment only to discover that what they described as a two room was not a two bedroom, but something else entirely. I learned to insist on getting the size in square meters and to make sure they had all the appliances. You wouldn't believe how many apartments are the size of a closet or how many owners throw a curtain up and call the space a bedroom. Many old buildings have no elevators." Like mine, but I didn't want to talk about my apartment so I kept quiet. "To say quality standards enforcement is poor is an understatement. Nobody seems to inspect the listings for accuracy. It's a free for all."

"So what did you do?" I asked, curious.

"I was getting seriously frustrated when I found an agency that handles corporate rentals," she said. "They charge a hefty commission of one third of the rental fees, but at least their apartments are clean and they call me back."

I was about to ask where it was when the first course arrived, erasing all non-food related thoughts from my mind. Judging by Kate's expression, she too was hungry.

"It's sushi," she said.

"I wouldn't have guessed that's what it was from the description on the menu," I said, piercing a tiny morsel with my fork.

"Me neither," she said, scooping a piece of her own onto her fork and putting it in her mouth. "Not much flavor."

I ate mine, hoping she was wrong. There were two maybe three more small bites on my plate. When I looked back up to agree with her, her plate was empty. When I reached for a slice of baguette the basket was empty. I had been so distracted talking I hadn't noticed Kate had eaten all the bread and butter.

"You'll have to come by sometime for a drink once I move in," she said while we waited for the server to clear our empty dishes.

"Sure," I said, hoping she wasn't expecting a reciprocal invite to my place. "I'm not much of a homemaker so I won't ask you to my place. It's messy, especially now that I'm looking after my former boss's dog."

"That guy Francois? I thought he had blocked your way at every turn," she said.

I guess I talked about work more than I thought I did, at least to her. Despite the thirty-year age difference, we got along well. In the days after her husband's death she had bared her soul to me. To a lesser extent I had done some of my own baring.

"Yes, he did," I said. "He was also the one who recommended me highly for the job when he left. Since he had opposed my posting from the beginning, his vote of confidence held a lot of weight. Besides that, he's an influential guy."

"You mean here?" she asked.

"Here and at the headquarters," I replied.

"I thought his dog was a prissy spoiled b—"

The server plunked down our next course before she could complete her sentence. It smelled of mushrooms and something else I couldn't identify. We tucked in, finishing it almost at the same time.

"She is," I said after I set down my sauce spoon. "Plus, I'm pretty sure she's never liked me."

"Truffles," she said.

"What?" I asked.

Scrunching her nose, she said, "The other ingredient in the soup was truffles. I had identified the mushroom flavor, but the other one was eluding me. It's black truffles."

"I was wondering, too," I said. "The flavor combination was good because neither one overpowered the other."

"Exactly. That's the fun with chef's menus, you don't know what they'll bring," she said. "I like guessing. Don't you?"

"Yeah, I guess I do," I replied.

"You feel obligated," she said. "You're looking after the dog because you feel you owe your old boss."

"More than that," I said. "Francois made his recommendation conditional on my agreement to look after her. He's not allowed dogs during his training for at least the first year."

"I like dogs. Maybe I can help," she said. "What kind of dog is she?"

"A toy poodle," I replied.

"They're very intelligent," she said.

"I can believe it," I said, remembering how she had hidden where I couldn't find her when it was time for her doggy bath or stashed items away for some inexplicable reason.

"I'm not sure when my place will be ready for guests, but why don't you bring her next time we get together?" she asked.

"Could do," I said. "She's well behaved in restaurants. Francois used to always take her with him to lunch and dinner, and, except when she barked at me, she was quiet as a mouse."

"Is she home alone all day?" she asked.

"Uh, yes, unlike Francois who used to stay at home or whatever it was he did with his time rather than going to work, I have a full-time job," I said. "I take her out for a walk in the mornings before I leave and in the afternoons when I return home."

"If she was used to being with him all day and now she's alone she may be lonely or bored," she said.

"She seems depressed to me," I blurted. "She hardly eats and doesn't want to do anything."

"Poor thing," Kate said.

"How about poor me?" I said. "I'm stuck with her."

"She's a dog," she said, grinning.

"A high maintenance dog," I added.

"She's small. How much maintenance can she need?" she asked.

"If I followed Francois's instructions, a lot, but I don't," I said.

"Why didn't he leave her with someone else?" she asked.

"That's what I asked him," I said. "I suggested his close friend Patrick, for example. Francois said Patrick has pets at home that wouldn't get along with her. I was the only one available apparently."

"Give her time to get used to you," she suggested. "Who knows, one day you might enjoy her company."

"She'll have to improve her attitude," I said.

Lunch sped by as we chatted about anything and nothing in particular. We commented on the dishes. Kate shared her impressions of the city, many of which mirrored my own.

"It's funny, I've always dreamed of living here, but I never imagined it would be the result of such a huge loss," she said.

She brushed her hair in a nervous gesture I had seen before

as if to push unpleasant thoughts aside. There was nothing I could say to make her pain disappear so I said nothing.

After a while, she spoke again, "It's hard to put my finger on why I like it some much. There are many things I don't like, especially the never ending strikes, but all in all it's an amazing place."

"I know what you mean," I said. "It has a little of everything and it's relatively easy to get around."

"It's small enough to be intimate yet so diverse," she said, her eyes gleaming.

I took advantage of the server's arrival with coffee to look at my watch. Kate followed my eyes.

"You don't miss a beat," I said, amused. "Unlike the idle wealthy like you I have a job."

"I don't feel wealthy," she said. "And, I don't think I'll ever be idle."

"What do you plan to do with your time?" I asked.

"Don't know yet," she said. "I'll figure something out. I'm not going to retire to sit at home eating bonbons, that's for sure."

I chugged down the espresso. She sipped at hers lost in her thoughts.

Plucking some money out of my wallet and setting it on the table I asked, "Do you mind if I leave you to sort out the check?"

"Not at all," she said. As I was heading out she added, "Good luck with your case."

Chapter 12

A message from Ernie arrived as I was exiting the building. He had identified the man in the photo. He was a local private investigator, no one I had ever heard of. In reply, I called him.

"I'm heading to a meeting," he said. "Did you get my message?"

"I'll keep it short," I replied. "Yes, I called to tell you thank you." He was silent so I added, "And that I owe you."

We hung up after he mumbled something like yeah you do, and we agreed to catch up later. I couldn't tell if he was sleepy, distracted in preparation for his meeting, or annoyed at me for the favor I had asked. I planned to find out when we spoke.

From the restaurant, it was a two-minute walk across the bridge to Mathis's shop on the Ile Saint Louis. I strolled around his block and the ones on either side, scouting for a place to observe the entrance without being obvious. The two nearby cafes had no view of his street. The sidewalks in front of his building and across the street from it were so narrow it was difficult for two pedestrians to pass side by side.

On a whim I called Madame Marmotte. I was hoping to find out what was going on at the office, but doubtful that she would be much use. She had a history of brushing me off and disregarding my role as her boss.

She answered the call with a question, "Find out anything?"

"It's slow going," I said. "What's going on over there?"

"They asked about you, you know," she said.

"Oh?"

"I told them I'm not your keeper," she said in an angry tone. "They asked me to make coffee and order lunch, like I work for them. They wanted your computer password so they could copy the case files."

"What did you—"

She interrupted me before I could finish, "What do you think? I don't work for them." She barely worked for me, I thought. "Where do they get off giving me orders? That young boy called me old woman to my face."

"I'm sorry, Madame Marmotte," I said, meaning it. There was no excuse for them to be hurtful to her. While she wasn't the most pleasant person she was harmless. "I wish there was—"

She cut me off again with a question, "Have you found out who's watching the perfume shop?"

I couldn't find it in me to be angry at her given how they were treating her. I should have been there to protect her. As her boss it was my job, but there was little I could do.

"I'm working on it," I said, annoyed at my lack of progress. "How is their investigation?"

"What a laugh," she snorted. "They couldn't find their hindquarters with a map, never mind that none of them speaks any French." I was tempted to point out that although he had a thick American accent, Rupert spoke French and decided not to. "What were they thinking sending a bunch of nincompoops to solve a complicated case? And pushing you out of the case is plain silly."

You could have knocked me over with a feather. That was the closest to a compliment I had ever received from her.

"Have they found out the identity of MGV?" I asked.

"Don't think so," she said. "They waste time like nobody's business, and they're starting to snap at each other."

If it wasn't because I wanted her to keep me updated about their progress, I would have told her to take some vacation days. I offered the best I could.

"You can go home early today," I heard myself say.

"I will," she replied.

Although I knew the Ile Saint Louis island well, I walked its streets searching for a solution. Walking often helped me think. After more than two hours, I headed home. It wasn't until I was in front of my building that an idea came to me.

Once inside my apartment, I called Ceri's name. The lack of response wasn't surprising. She was in her usual place, the basket Francois had brought with him the day she moved into my home. On seeing her leash in my hand she got up and took two steps in my direction, allowing me to clip the end of the leash to her collar. That was something.

"We're going to play a waiting game," I said to her as a way to figure out my plan by speaking it out loud. "We're going for a walk around your old neighborhood because I need to check on someone while we're there to make sure he's safe. His name? Mathis. Although he makes perfumes for a living he's a smelly guy, but don't you worry because we won't be talking to him tonight. Your delicate doggie nose won't be offended. We're only going to observe without any interaction. To do that I'm going to make us look like someone else by using my Weeia ability. You'll appear like a white poodle." She looked up at me as if she had understood.

"Red poodles are rare. You and I were there recently and people might remember. It's unlikely for there to be two red poodles on the island in the same week. So in my illusion you will be you with white hair. I will look like Sébastien's sister. She fits in the neighborhood much better than I do thanks to her fashion sense and poise." Her ears perked up. "Yes, I know. That will be very different from my usual appearance. I will use the photo I have of the two of them for inspiration. I'm that good. I could probably fool her family if they saw me from a distance. The clothes are the trickiest part. That's not a problem because I'll use the ones from the photo. She never spends time around the island, so the chances are tiny that someone might recognize her. The single modification I will make to her outfit will be that I will wear my comfy boots instead of her three inch heels. It would be downright hazardous to walk around the island's uneven streets in shoes like hers."

She stared at the door as if to say what are we waiting for? I took that as my cue to get going. Before we left, I enveloped us in the illusion. It took a few minutes of concentration to create the illusion after I refreshed my memory by looking at the photo of Sébastien's sister. I didn't think she would mind, especially if I didn't tell her. It required more effort to maintain the illusion of an imaginary being than a real one. Every time I used my ability, it drained me. I recouped lost energy by eating, which wasn't so bad. On the way home, I would pop into the grocery store to make sure I had something for dinner. The illusion would have no effect on Ceri, except I was hoping the walk and fresh air might brighten her mood.

Anyone who saw us would see me looking like Sébastien's sister and Ceri as a white poodle. Knowing we might have a long wait later, I allowed her extra freedom to explore the sidewalks at the beginning of our excursion. I was eager to be done with the Mathis investigation so I could turn my attention to the Eiffel Tower case. My future in Paris, and perhaps my career prospects, depended on it. She seemed to smell every scrawny tree and corner or it might have been that my impatience made it seem that way.

Knowing what to look for made my surveillance easier than the previous night. Moments after we arrived, I spotted the P.I. I took notes about everything I could think of, including his clothes, what he did, the direction he came from, the direction he went and the brand of cigarettes he smoked. It occurred to me there might be more than one person tailing Mathis so I watched and waited.

We had been there more than an hour when I thought I saw someone. I turned but there was no one there. I dismissed it, thinking I was oversensitive because I had had several cups of coffee that afternoon. As we were leaving, I had the sensation there was someone just outside seeing range. I pulled out my badge. Our badges were our ID, weapon, shield, and telephone rolled into a single device. Made of obsidian stone, marshal badges were designed to look like a mobile phone at a casual glance. I had no idea how they were made. It was impressive that each badge responded to its owner and no one else.

My badge had a Weeia sensor, which could pinpoint the presence of nearby Weeia. I switched the sensor on and it revealed a Weeia, but when I searched the old fashioned way with my eyes there was nobody there. That I had imagined someone was one possibility, but that I had imagined someone and there was a glitch in my badge was not likely.

Two hours later, the effects of the coffee had worn off. I was chilled and Ceri was shivering.

"Time to head home," I said to Ceri, who looked up at me and wagged her tail a couple of times before sagging. "I didn't realize you were so cold. I'm sorry. It should be nice and toasty there."

Ceri went straight to her basket as soon as we entered the apartment and got under her supple cashmere blanket. It was the nicest blanket in the apartment, a gift from her daddy of course. I wouldn't dream of spending that kind of money on myself. As soon as I set food on her plate and refreshed her water bowl I called her. She didn't even look up from her slumber.

I was famished. I ate everything I had picked up on our way home, two large slices of vegetarian lasagna, a tuna sandwich, a spinach salad and a spring roll, washing it down with a glass of red wine and a glass of water. If Iaen had been alive he would have greeted me with a foot rub and a hot dinner. I sighed, missing him for many reasons, the least of which were his amateur cooking abilities.

That night, I had been concerned about the pooch. Poodles are prone to pneumonia, Francois had warned me before leaving. He left a long list with instructions. I was always to dry her hair if she got wet, using a blow dryer if necessary. I checked on her several times that night, finding her fast asleep.

I was relieved to find Ceri was back to her normal self the next morning.

The following two days were similar. I got up early and went for a long run, taking Ceri for her walk on my return. I had a light breakfast before researching the P.I., his firm and anything that could lead to the identity of the client who order the surveillance on Mathis and his business. I kept an eye on Mathis's shop and watched for signs of the P.I. and anyone else. Both nights I had the same sensation that someone was there. Although my badge confirmed there was another Weeia, I never saw a soul.

"I'm seriously peeved," I said to Ceri on the third night. "I'm sure something wonky is going on, but I can't figure out what exactly. Today I'm going to try those pebbles that Ernie gave me when I first arrived in town to amplify signals in the area. I'll spread them around during the walk. They should expand the reach of my badge and magnify the signals it picks up. With the pebbles, I should be able to find the mystery person."

I had taken Ceri for a walk and was getting ready to go to the island. She was in her basket. There was something subtle about the elegant way she sat, looked around her and held her head that reminded me of a queen on her throne.

"Sweetie, these past few days have been heavy work," I said, watching her. I hadn't meant to say sweetie. I hoped it wasn't a sign that I was growing attached to the grouchy canine. It was too late to take it back. "My cover is more credible with you by my side, but I understand if you would rather stay here."

She barked once, lowered her head onto her paws, and closed her eyes. I took a deep calming breath and then closed my eyes in preparation for the illusion, adjusting details here and there, and wondering what I would do for my cover without Ceri. On the Ile Saint Louis there were a handful of boutiques and several art galleries of the kind a young and wealthy society woman might visit. I decided to stroll as if I was window shopping.

Ceri followed me to the door although I hadn't pulled out her leash. I lost sight of her while I put my boots on so I assumed she had gone to sit in her basket. Moments later, she was back.

"I already took you for your walk," I said, hoping she would join me. "I'm going to work now. You sure you want—"

Before I could finish speaking, she barked. Her leash was on the floor. I took that as a sign that she wanted to go with me, and hooked the clip of her leash to her collar.

"We'll take the bridge to the Ile de la Cité and circle the entire circuit so I can check on the pebbles I placed there this afternoon," I told her as we left our street. "It won't take a moment. If it's very crowded around Notre Dame I'll pick you up."

She looked up at me. Despite her size she kept up with me without difficulty. She knew her way around the island, her neighborhood, better than I did. And she was headstrong. Sometimes I had to rein her back when she wanted to follow a path and I preferred another.

When we reached the plaza in front of Notre Dame, marked as the Place Jean Paul II in the signs, she slowed down. Looking over the hedge at the corner I saw it was bursting with people. The first time I saw the plaza like that, I assumed there was a special event. Since then I had seen it overflowing with crowds so often I stopped wondering why. As usual, there were police cars and uniformed police on foot. Before she could resist, I scooped her up, tucking her under my left arm. From there, she had a clear view of the path ahead of us.

I crossed the plaza diagonally to rue du cloitre Notre-Dame, the narrow street that ran parallel to the river behind the cathedral. It was a favorite of pickpockets searching for distracted tourists in line to climb to the top of the attraction, so I avoided it whenever possible. But I had dropped pebbles in the cathedral garden and wanted to check on them. Besides the area was so congested I doubted it made much difference which street I took. The rue du cloitre Notre-Dame led to the Pont Saint Louis, the bridge which connected the Ile de la Cité and its smaller neighbor the Ile Saint Louis. As soon as we reached the bridge, I set Ceri down. She shook with vigor as if to shake the memory of me carrying her away.

"Sorry, I know you prefer to walk. It wasn't safe for you through there," I said in a soothing voice.

In response, she took the lead. I followed her into the island, slowing down to look for the pebbles every so often. To the naked eye, they looked like tiny stones of no particular interest. I had seen enough of them to reassure me that they would serve my purpose of amplifying the badge's signal so I could locate the mystery Weeia.

We returned to our usual area of interest near Mathis's store. Fifteen minutes into our watch, I had the sensation we were not alone. My badge confirmed there was a Weeia half a block away. Nobody was visible on the block. Looking in the same direction Ceri barked, a lot. She pulled on the leash and almost got away.

"Ceri," I admonished her. "Stop."

While the barking ended her eyes remained on the empty sidewalk and she stood at attention. It was rare for her to bark that way in public. She was a well socialized dog, accustomed to being surrounded by people in crowded streets and restaurants.

I couldn't pursue my lead and risk placing her in harm's way. I needed help, but the only other staff person in our office with field experience was Rupert. Asking him to assist me was out of the question. He would either block my progress or blab our findings to the out of town team. I pulled my phone out of my pocket, dialing while I prepared my plea.

"Hey you, what a surprise," the familiar voice said on the third ring. "Miss me, do you?"

"Yes," I blurted. "I need help. Can you come to the Ile Saint Louis now?"

"I wish I could," my former colleague said. His words were slow and deliberate. He spoke with a subtle upper crust enunciation the result of attending the best schools and universities. "I'm in the middle of something. Unless it's an emergency it will have to keep. How about tomorrow?"

"That'll do," I said, annoyed at the delay yet grateful.

"Is it the same situation we discussed before?" he asked.

I wasn't keeping information from him. I had to be vague because we weren't supposed to discuss Weeia issues on open lines.

"No, another one," I said.

"Okay," he said. "Did you hear MGV made an appearance tonight?"

"Uh, no, I switched off the news alerts on my phone," I replied. "They were distracting me. What happened?"

"Dunno," he said. "I've been in and out of meetings all day. My brain and my body are numb. I saw the headline scroll through in a news update five minutes ago. I'm looking forward to tomorrow."

"Meet me at my apartment at, what time can you make it?"

"Sevenish," he said. "Gotta go. See you tomorrow."

He hung up. Feeling better than I had in three days, I said "Thanks" to the dial tone.

Chapter 13

The following day I rose before sunrise to go running. I returned sopping wet after getting caught midway by heavy showers. After changing into dry clothes and shoes, I took Ceri for her walk, detouring to the Ile Saint Louis on our return to catch a glimpse of Mathis's storefront. Everything was quiet. I doubted Susanna had arrived. Behaving like a tourist, I took a ton of photos of everything I could think of, including the street and shop signs, entire streets, and the sidewalks.

I was tempted to pop in to the Club for breakfast, but I was wearing a pair of torn pants, stained t-shirt and weather-beaten shoes sure to raise the manager's blood pressure. It was just as well that I stay out of sight in case the out of town investigators went there. Rupert didn't have a membership like the one that came with my position, but Madame Marmotte had told me he had a courtesy membership thanks to his family's membership stateside.

Instead, I picked up a dozen chouquettes, sugar topped light as air pastry puffs, at a new bakery on the way home to enjoy with my coffee. It was the first time I entered the bakery, which had a high end minimalistic design. Until a couple of months back, the space had been vacant and in a bad state.

The owners must have spent gobs of money and greased many palms because it went from an eyesore to a glitzy shop in record time. Although the interior was well lit, I saw no baked products. The name of the bakery and bakery items were written in large block letters on the walls along with phrases like bread is good for the soul. There were elaborate displays of fake cakes, breads, croissants as well as boxes of chocolates and teas on faux wood shelves. The young saleswoman wore foundation so thick I wasn't sure what her skin color was, black eyeliner, so much mascara, I wondered how she was able to open and close her eyes without using her fingers, and at least three shades of eyeshadow. She accentuated her sensuous lips with dark liner and a shade of pink I was certain couldn't be found anywhere in nature. Her fragrance was so intense, I rubbed my nose in an unconscious effort to rid myself of it. I doubted I would be back.

For Ceri, we headed to the island butcher shop to buy fresh meat as a treat. Francois had always shopped there so they took special care of him. He had introduced me to the owner before he left, instructing me to buy his dog's food there. Thanks to the introduction and because the staff recognized Ceri, I too was welcome. As soon as we walked in, I saw the owner, a man in his late fifties with a generous belly covered by a blood stained apron, standing in the back of the small space speaking to an assistant. The flesh below his chin wobbled a bit as he spoke, lending him a comedic air like a comic strip character.

"Good day, Madame Metreaux," he boomed. "How are you?" Without waiting for my reply he went on. With two long strides, he crossed the shop and appeared at my side. Glancing down at Ceri he asked, "And the little princess?"

If it wasn't because I knew dogs couldn't smile I would have sworn Ceri was smiling. She looked up at the man, holding her gaze steady on his. Without asking for permission or even glancing at me, he bent down to her level with surprising speed. He fed tiny red morsels to the pooch, who with dainty motions worthy of a real life princess, took them one by one and chewed them slowly before swallowing. When she was finished he used his clean hand to pet her. She didn't allow strangers to pet her, but she had known him since she was a puppy, so she showed no sign of displeasure. He returned to an upright position with greater agility than I expected.

Looking at Ceri as if she was his long lost child he said,

"We've missed you."

She followed him with her eyes and barked once. It was a friendly bark rather than an alarm bark. I was becoming familiar with the different barks and moods.

Where he regaled Ceri with a warm expression I received a reproachful one as if I was mistreating Ceri by not feeding her his gourmet products daily the way Francois used to. Jerk, where did he get off judging me without knowing anything about me? I was tempted to explain to him that I worked for a living. I summoned my patience, drawing a breath and let it out before speaking.

"I was hoping for some meat for Ceri and a steak for me," I said in a small voice, adding the steak on an impulse.

"The usual for Ceri?" he asked.

"Yes, and a flavorful cut of meat for me like the one I bought a while back," I replied.

If I made such a request at the average butcher shop they wouldn't know who I was, let alone what I had ordered in the past. That man was the favorite purveyor of top meats of the city's elite for a reason. Francois had told me that the owner appeared aloof, but that he was far from it. He explained to me that the butcher had inherited the family business and knowhow from his father. They both cared a great deal about every item in the store. Unlike the growing number of shops who sold merchandise of unknown or suspicious origin, he could trace the animals in his shop to their source.

In contrast to the ample space at the bakery, the butcher shop was cluttered. The refrigerators were bursting with all manner of cuts of meat. I wondered how they found anything the case was so crowded. Birds I couldn't begin to name hung upside down with most of their feathers plucked and there were deli meats ready for slicing. Knives in multiple sizes and shapes hung from a place on the wall and were strewn about on the counters. Every inch of the display cases was taken up with packaged goods such as condiments, pasta, pickled vegetables and crackers. While there was a slight odor of death with a hint of metallic aftertaste, the store was clean.

"Madame, everything we sell is of the highest quality," he said. "We only offer our customers fresh, natural French products handled expertly by us." They charged a premium for that. It was fair, just way more than I was willing to spend. He stood with his arms relaxed and his eyes challenging me to disagree. He made no secret of the pride he felt in what he did for a living. "There is no doubt you'll love your steak."

That was the problem. I would love my steak and want to buy more. My former boss swore the butcher knew every customer's habits and preferences and average spend. Despite the dirty looks he gave me on Ceri's behalf, he was never pushy. On the contrary, more than once I had seen him chase away prospective customers by delaying responding to them and answering their questions in single words until exasperated they left. Remembering those scenes, I felt glad to be among the lucky few he counted as regulars. Ceri seemed to walk lighter and be more cooperative after we left the butcher shop than she had in days.

Although it started raining again, we stopped at my favorite island cheese shop. There were three cheese shops on the Ile Saint Louis. I usually stopped for butter and a slice of Roquefort. The strong odors of the shop always took me aback. It was like that in all the cheese shops, the better the cheese, the stronger the smell, as one owner once explained to me. Inside the Fromagerie de l'Ile there was no one to greet customers. That was not surprising. Often the gregarious owner was nearby chatting with neighbors. I wondered sometimes if he would rather be outside than in his shop. I knew to wait and he would appear, greeting me with kisses and asking about my health like an old friend. If I let him, he would fill me in on the neighborhood gossip too.

Refrigerated cases filled the rectangular shaped store. Tourists and locals stopped to look and snap photos of the display of dozens of cheeses behind a floor to ceiling glass wall that was half the width of the shop. In the shelves, which reached the ceiling, there were imported specialty products as well as French honey, chocolates, and fresh bread. Should I need deli meats the refrigerator in the back of the shop was my best bet. His was a cheese shop and more. I liked it because of the friendly and knowledgeable service. I also appreciated that his products tasted good and were free of preservatives. I was lost in my thoughts when the shopkeeper greeted me.

"I should have the Roquefort by tomorrow if you want to pass by," he said in reply to my unspoken request. Like the butcher he knew his regular customers. I glanced behind him at the dozens of cheeses on the shelf as he leaned forward on his wood cutting table. "How about some of this?"

He was middle-aged, of average height and weight in Paris. His dark blond hair, balding at the top, was short. He always wore a white shirt, black pants and a white apron. He had added a moustache since my last visit.

He handed me a generous slice of hard cheese. I felt Ceri's eyes on me as I accepted it. Placing the lion's share of the cheese in my mouth I offered her a tiny bit. She smelled the yellow item and ever so slowly took it from my hand. It had a rich nutty flavor with a smoky finish.

"Comté?" I asked.

"Aged five years," he replied. "I have an older one if you prefer. It's a bit saltier."

That would be pricier, I thought. There was no point in worrying too much about prices in that shop. There were no cheap cheeses. Besides, if I wanted that I could go to any supermarket.

"This one is fine," I replied.

He placed his knife across a narrow section of the round Comté, looking up at me for instructions. I nodded to indicate the slice he proposed would be fine. In one smooth motion he cut the hard cheese, then wrapped it in wax paper before sliding it inside a thin plastic bag and handing it to me.

We also went to the neighborhood street market for walnuts, fruit and salad greens. Perhaps because of the rain and the early hour there was no line at my favorite produce vendor. There were days when the line was eight or ten customers thick even with several sellers behind the colorful fruit and vegetable laden tables.

Located in the center of the thrice weekly street market on the Boulevard Saint Germain, east of the Boulevard Saint Michel, the produce stand I preferred was organic, bio in French. It took up several long tables worth of prime market space in an "L" shape. Two men and one woman sold a variety of produce, including root vegetables, leafy greens, onions, squashes, and all manner of French and European fruits. I liked that the vendors were service oriented and knowledgeable. If I was unsure how to prepare a particular vegetable, they always had suggestions that panned out when I tried them at home.

I busied myself researching every scrap of information I could find about the Eiffel Tower and its surroundings. I studied the maps of the neighborhood. When I was finished, I did the same with the entire Ile Saint Louis, learning the names of the few streets I didn't already know. I studied the photos I had taken. When I was done I memorized the layout of the perfume shop's street as well as any landmarks and features that seemed noteworthy, including a nearby elementary school. I noted entryways and courtyards where an assailant might hide.

When I became peckish, I ran out for a sandwich to the bakery near my apartment. If Ceri was surprised that I remained home instead of going to work, she showed no interest in me, except when I was munching, she raised her head and watched me from her basket. She was a polite dog, I had to give her that. Any other dog I had ever met would have been drooling at my feet. She had a drink of water and circled back to her spot.

I called Madame Marmotte for an update, but she had nothing new to report. I was relieved. Before I knew it darkness had fallen. As soon as I lifted her leash from the hook where I kept it Ceri was by my side.

"We better get you walked before Sébastien arrives," I said to the dog as I attached the clip to her collar. We had an hour, which was enough to walk Ceri, make a couple of calls and get ready. "After that I'll have to work. We're trying to catch some bad guys." She raised her gaze toward me and barked once. "It's better if you stay home. We don't know what we might find. It could get dangerous."

I took advantage of my workday at home to do laundry. I would have done more, but even the shortest cycle in the washer ran shy of two hours. The dryer required the same duration. Often I had to run the clothes for another cycle, or hang them to dry. For the first time in weeks, I was caught up. All my laundry was clean. It gave me a small feeling of accomplishment. Even if I was making little progress in either of my cases, at least I had done something productive that day.

I was pulling a pair of black pants on, when Sébastien Poyager arrived. As soon as I opened the door Ceri ran to greet him. He lifted her into his arms with ease. She didn't bark or object in any way.

"Hey you," I said as he bent down from his six-foot two-inch frame and we exchanged cheek kisses.

He had tucked Ceri under his arm, where she remained like a queen surveying her kingdom from up high. He had lost weight since we had last seen each other. His hair and light brown bangs, a journalist described them in an article as chestnut, were so short they made him look younger than usual. It was hard to imagine that he was the chief executive officer in training at one of the most powerful and influential companies in France. There he was in my living room. I had him all to myself.

"Hi," he said. "How are you?"

With him there to lend a hand, I was excited at the prospect that we might crack the case, annoyed at what was happening at the office, and anxious about losing my job. Instead of telling him all that I shrugged. He waited, giving me a further chance to update him.

"That was a warmer greeting than I ever get from that ungrateful dog," I said, pointing at the bundle under his arm, changing the topic and killing the awkward silence. "You should adopt her."

"I wish I could. She's such a sweetie," he said, petting her with a gentleness that belied his tough guy self-image. "She can't be that bad to live with, can she?"

"Not really," I replied. "It's an odd fit, you know? She's a prissy elegant dog and I'm, let's say the opposite of prissy and elegant, less than ideal for her needs. I can barely spare the time to look after myself let alone someone else's high maintenance pet."

"Has she given you any trouble?" he asked.

His brows furrowed with concern. That dog managed to win everyone over. People, including strangers, fawned over her.

"Well no," I said. "It's not anything she does." He let the silence hang until I continued. "If you must know it bothers me that I try so hard and she doesn't like me."

"What makes you think that?" he asked.

His eyes widened and a smile began to spread across his Greek god face. I knew that expression. It meant that he thought I was too serious. Sébastien had a way of calming me. It was one of the many qualities I admired in him. Where I felt like a volcano ready to blow more often than I cared to admit to myself he was the portrait of calm, cool and collected no matter the circumstances.

"She always barked at me like nobody's business whenever

I saw her with Francois," I replied, searching for examples.

"That doesn't seem so strange," he said.

"She didn't bark at anyone else," I said in a louder tone than was necessary. "Not the server, Patrick, people at nearby tables, only me."

"She probably knew the server since she was a puppy," he said. "The same with Patrick. She wouldn't notice people at nearby tables unless they approached or spoke to her. You were a stranger at her table. I bet that was all it was."

"Why does she tear my clothes and shoes?" I asked.

"Dunno," he said. "Maybe she misses Francois. It must be difficult for her. I find petting our dog Monsieur always calms him down when he's stressed. Have you tried petting her?"

"Uh, no," I said, feeling silly. "I'm afraid it would upset her or that she would bite me."

"Such a tough kickass boss and you're afraid of a toy poodle?" he said, handing her to me. Before I could object he had positioned her under my arm and was showing me how to hold her. "Try tucking her legs like that and petting her."

At first her legs scrambled in separate directions in the air. After a moment, she settled down. She relaxed and her eyes began to close as I stroked her head.

"Color me surprised," I said, surrendering to the satisfaction of seeing Ceri relax in my arms.

"That's a first," he said.

His smile spread showing his even teeth. I was powerless to object.

"What?"

"Nothing," he said. "Nothing at all."

Feeling self-conscious I asked, "You going out like that?" to take the attention away from me.

"I wasn't going to," he said, lifting a bag I hadn't noticed until then. "I brought a change of clothes. As soon as I get out of the monkey suit, you can bring me up to date. May I borrow your bathroom?"

I nodded my agreement. As he stepped away in the direction of the bathroom I yelled, "It's a bit messy."

Housekeeping was not a priority for me. As much as I liked having a clean and organized home spending the effort and hours required to keep it that way was another matter. Sébastien was willing to go the extra mile for a clean desk and his car was pristine. It helped that he had no housekeeping responsibilities at all. He had staff at work and at home tasked with ensuring everything was just as he liked it. He never mentioned his staff or his money. It was only after we had become friends that I learned how obscenely wealthy he was, and not because he brought it up. Unlike Rupert, who tried to influence me by using his family name as soon as we met, Sébastien had been a model of discretion. Marla, who was up on gossip more than I was, told me the Poyagers owned the company outright, and that their fortune far outranked Rupert's family many times over.

From his first day as a newbie marshal, under my supervision Sébastien had taken his job to heart. Even when I had been grouchy and less than welcoming, he had my back, and a good thing he had. I had been foolish enough to place myself in harm's way and Sébastien had arrived at the perfect moment to rescue my bacon. Over time, we became close colleagues and fast friends.

While he was in the bathroom I busied myself, pouring Ceri's home cooked seasoned beef into her doggie bowl, hoping the human style seasoning would entice her. Sébastien came out as I was refreshing her water bowl.

"I was getting ready to call fire rescue," I said when he came out. He gifted me with an unguarded smile. "We're going to do surveillance on Mathis's house, not to a photo shoot for a fashion magazine."

"We're going to the Island, and you said we should fit in," he said. "This fits in with that crowd."

He wore designer jeans and a brown cashmere sweater with

shoes that matched the color of the sweater. He could have been on the cover of a men's magazine. In fact, since he had stepped down, he had been on the cover of several magazines.

I acknowledged his efforts by saying, "You take longer to get ready than I do."

"Perhaps, but I look the part," he said, leaving out the obvious conclusion that I didn't, which was true.

"Fair 'nough," I replied.

If most anyone had said it I might have taken offense. I knew Sébastien wasn't alluding to expensive clothes, but rather my unwillingness to dedicate the effort to my appearance that many people, women in particular, dedicated to theirs.

"Is this about Mathis and Susanna?" he asked. I nodded. "What's the problem?"

While to a casual observer he might appear relaxed I saw the tension in his chest as he took a shallow breath. During the dozens of hours we had spent working together on stakeouts, at the office and in a variety of situations in between, I had come to recognize his body language. There was the way he stood with his legs spread out to the width of his shoulders as if ready to sprint, and most of all, his eyes gleaming with excitement.

"Seems someone is stalking Mathis," I said, gathering my thoughts to explain the situation. "I have been watching the shop and Mathis for several days. I saw one P.I. following him." I showed him the photo. "So far there hasn't been any contact."

"Why would a P.I. follow Mathis?" he asked.

"Exactly," I said. "There is no evidence that he's on the radar of any police investigation or the French government. The best explanation I have is that whoever hired the P.I. is Weeia. It's a discreet way to discover how easy he is to approach, assuming that's what they want."

"They?" he asked.

"I assume it's more than one person, but it doesn't matter right now," I said, impatient to explain. "If Weeia are behind it, and they know what he is capable of, they might try to hire him or offer him money."

Mathis Tartan's ability was rare. Sébastien and I had worked on a case in which a man had twisted the effects of Mathis's custom made fragrances for his own nefarious purposes. For a while, the situation had gotten out of control and people had died. Mathis was forbidden by the marshals from ever producing the same fragrances. With Susanna's help, he had reinvented his business and everything had been copacetic until she contacted me.

"I thought he owned the entire building. That has to be worth a mint," he said.

His partway open mouth told me he was curious. The slightly narrowed eyes revealed his mind was racing.

I couldn't help myself and blurted, "Says the man worth several mints." He lowered his eyes to concede my point. "Since when has being wealthy kept any millionaire from wanting to grow his fortune?"

"His fortune?" he asked, emphasizing the first word.

"Oh, don't try to change the subject by playing the gender card," I replied. "You know very well the list of millionaire men is much longer than the list of millionaire women."

We laughed. It was nice to have someone I trusted to laugh with sometimes.

"He could have cash flow problems," he said. "There are a number of reasons someone who appears rich could take risks to acquire more money. Let's assume for the moment that Mathis might be vulnerable to a high offer, why is it our affair?"

"Because Susanna asked for my help," I said. I paused to highlight the importance of her request. "She's worried for his safety. He's worried too. And if he ever uses his ability the same way as before it would violate the terms of his freedom.

It would be my duty to arrest him and remand him to the marshals immediately. More importantly it could wreak havoc again."

"Understood," he said. "It could be something entirely benign, you know."

"Or it could be the opposite," I said. "We don't know anything until we know something."

"Okay, we know nothing, well very little," he said. "Where do I come in?"

"I was hoping you would ask me," I said. "A couple of days ago when I was watching over Mathis I thought I saw someone. When I looked there was nobody there although my badge indicated a Weeia presence."

"Could you be mistaken?" he asked.

"I wondered too," I said. "There are two reasons I'm convinced I was right. I used amplification pods, you know the ones that look like pebbles to humans. They boost the badge signal. When I returned to the island the Weeia indicator lit up again, the same each time."

"And the second?"

"Ceri barked," I said.

"Ceri could have barked at anything," he said in a tone that told me he wasn't convinced. "Could your badge have a glitch?"

"It's possible," I said. "You can try your badge. If our efforts bear no fruit, I'll consider the badge issue. It's also possible that whoever has been watching Mathis might not be there tonight."

"Only one way to find out," he said.

"I agree," I said. "Once we are in position there is only one way in and out. When we get to the street, I will stand in the same place while you block the exit. I'll use my Weeia finding function. If there is anyone there it should be pretty straight forward as he or she will have to get through me or you to pass."

As soon as we headed toward the door Ceri, who on a regular day sat in her basket when I went out, followed us. She looked at Sébastien and me, wagging her tail.

"Sorry, Ceri." She wagged her tail more. "You can't come," I said, closing the door before she could scurry between our legs. We dropped his bag off in his car and headed along the Seine to the nearest bridge to the island.

Chapter 14

Rainy weather had emptied the streets. When Sébastien arrived the downpour had waned, although it was still coming down in chubby drops. The cafes and restaurants were open, and the shops closed. Only diehard tourists and locals running errands on their way home were out. The sound of heels echoed in the distance. Further away the drone of an emergency vehicle filled the night.

Half an hour later, we were in place. We had separated several blocks earlier, arriving five minutes apart. Given our disparate appearances no one had any reason to guess we were together.

I was buzzing with excitement. We were the only ones on that street. That was what we needed. I checked my badge. Two Weeia signals appeared. Taking a deep breath, I counted to ten, then ten more. When I estimated several minutes had passed, I glanced at my badge. The device revealed three Weeia on the street, Sébastien, me, and one more.

When I approached the place where the dot for the third Weeia appeared on my badge, the signal blinked and reappeared behind me, moving at a fast clip. I followed it until it disappeared. I walked back to where I had first seen it, hoping it would show up on my screen once again. At that moment, I saw Sébastien walking fast toward me, wearing a fine line of worry between his eyebrows. When he saw me his lips parted in surprise.

"What are you doing here?" I asked.

"What do you mean?" he asked. "You told me, not a minute ago, to run to the shop, that someone was hurt."

"That's not possible," I replied. "I haven't talked to you since I got here." Lowering my voice, I continued, "My app showed three of us, I don't see anyone else. I walked toward where the third signal should have been. It disappeared only to reappear behind me. This is so weird."

I knew I hadn't spoken to Sébastien, but I didn't doubt him. He thought he had seen and spoken to me yet he hadn't. He must have met someone like me capable of creating illusions.

"The third signal on the screen was a mindshifter," I blurted in a hoarse whisper. "It's the best explanation."

Although there was no one else on the street we had to be careful in how we discussed Weeia matters in public. We had to assume there could be eyes and ears even if we couldn't see a soul. Sébastien's eyes widened in surprise. To his credit, he expressed no doubt.

"It makes me wish I had brought Ceri," I went on. "She wouldn't have been fooled as easily as we were. She would have known my scent."

"I didn't think there was anyone else like you in Paris," he said, confirming that he understood what I meant.

"Nope," I said. "It must be a visitor or someone with newly developed abilities."

"That didn't seem like the work of a newbie," he said.

I looked in both directions. There was nobody around.

I checked my badge as I replied, "My thoughts exactly."

After a long moment, he said in a voice so soft only I could hear him, "I thought it was odd that I caught a glimpse of your thoughts, well the duplicate you. Your mind is usually locked tight, but I saw an image of the place you or she was headed next."

"Ever since the encounter with that woman," I let the words trail off. When he showed no sign of knowing what I was talking about I continued. "Ursell Morland."

He nodded as soon as I said her name. He knew the case I was referring to.

She was a powerful Weeia who had invaded my mind and made me do things against my will. It was a horrible feeling, having someone in my mind controlling my actions against my will. "Where did she go?"

"I'm not sure," he said. "It was so fast. Let me see if I can figure out the location."

"Of course," I said. "We might as well call it a night. I doubt she will return."

I walked Sébastien to where his car was parked, and after the usual exchange of kisses, we each went our separate ways, agreeing to stay in touch.

When I arrived home, Ceri was curled up in her basket. She lifted her head in greeting. By the time I locked the door and removed my boots, she was asleep. What surprised me was that her dish was empty. It was the first time since Francois had left and she had been living with me that she had eaten all the food in her dish. Maybe she didn't dislike me so much after all.

Chapter 15

I was looking forward to lunch with Patrick, Francois's childhood friend, at the Club. Patrick was wealthy and powerful, not just among the Weeia, but among the French elite. We had met when I first introduced myself to my old boss while they were at lunch with Ceri.

Where Francois had been dismissive and unfriendly, Patrick had been patient and encouraging. Francois had been a snob, acting as though my assignment to his office was a personal affront. Patrick had offered kind suggestions and help, and he had made a huge difference in the quality of my life in Paris. I suspected that I provided amusement for him. One day, out of the blue after his best buddy left town, Patrick invited me to join him for breakfast. I accepted with a lingering concern that he may have saved up his favors for something objectionable, illegal or both.

Many other less important Weeia behaved as if they deserved special treatment, calling on the marshals to take care of their difficult problems as if we were their private fixers. I should have known better. Patrick had an army of staff at home and at work. There was nothing I could do that they couldn't. As my fears abated I relaxed and enjoyed his company. He was handsome with a hint of naughty for good measure. He was stylish and fashionable in an understated manner. He seemed to know everyone and be up to date on everything that mattered. For some mysterious reason, he had taken a liking to me.

Marla had asked if he was flirting, but that couldn't be further from the truth. It wasn't that Patrick was a faithful husband. I knew he had a longtime mistress. But I had never caught him looking at me with any kind of carnal desire nor had he ever said anything inappropriate. I wasn't objective, at least not one hundred percent. As far as I could tell his attitude toward me was a mix of amusement and benevolence with no strings attached. I admired him, although I wasn't attracted to him. For me, he represented a sort of father figure.

As usual, I arrived early. The maître d'hôtel offered me a glass of bubbly while I waited. I was about to reply with an order of sparkling water when I spotted the Elder and his family. I made a beeline to their table.

"Hello," I said as I arrived at their table.

Amanda returned my greeting with a warm smile. Tiny lines formed on Ted's forehead as if he was displeased to see me, like finding something sticky on his shoe. He glanced at me, nodded and turned away. Their children looked up from their smartphones one after the other in my direction. Neither replied. Instead, they went back to their screens with the urgency of rush hour drivers on their way home at the end of a day in the city.

Small talk wasn't my thing, so I went straight to the point, "I've been trying to reach you. Did you get my messages?"

Ted made an o with his lips. I let the silence hang in the air. He owed me a reply.

"Uh, yes I think so," he said. "We've been very busy. Is there something you need?"

The ton of questions I had all disappeared in that instant. He and his family might know something that could move the investigation forward, they might have seen something. I couldn't know until I asked them. No one at the table was looking at me. Amanda, who had called a server, faced the dining room entrance as if I wasn't even there. Ted held my gaze for a millisecond before returning to the wine menu he had been reading when I arrived at their table. Their offspring remained glued to their gadgets. I wasn't going to let him know I was annoyed that he had been ignoring my messages or that he was treating me like an unpopular kid in the schoolyard. I tried to gather my thoughts, but his dismissive attitude got the better of me.

Before I lost his attention I managed to ask, "When will you be heading home?"

"As soon as possible," he said, glancing at his wife for confirmation. "Amanda has been shopping, and the kids want to explore the city a bit longer. I understand the team is making good progress on the case."

He emphasized the word team, implying he knew I had been sidelined. I wanted to tell him he was an ass for pulling rank and getting me shoved aside on my own case. Instead, I was fishing in my mind for something that would get a rise out of him. Maybe in his smart remark I would find out something useful. I saw movement in the background. I looked up to see Patrick arriving at the entrance, where he was chatting with the staff member.

"Is there something you need?" he asked.

"Nothing at the moment," I said, walking across the dining room toward Patrick, who in turn was heading to his regular table.

I reached the table seconds after him. Following the usual greetings, we sat down. The server placed Patrick's drink in front of him, handed us the handwritten lunch menu, and took my beverage order.

"How is it going with the Walkers?" he asked as soon as the server was out of hearing range.

"Meh," I said, shrugging. "I got booted off the case by a team they sent from headquarters courtesy of Ted and Amanda."

"You're still pursuing it on your own, aren't you?" he asked.

As I conceded, saying, "A little" a warm grin spread across his movie star white teeth. "How did you know?"

"It wasn't difficult. You're one of the most pigheaded people I know, and I know lots of stubborn people," he said. His eyes shone with amusement. "In your case, I mean it as a compliment."

He was one of the most polite and refined men I knew. While he never patronized me, I had the impression he favored me with his kindness in a way he did with few others. Not for the first time I was glad for the good fortune that made him supportive of me since we had met. I wasn't sure what I had said or done to have deserved it. The gentle sound of an electronic buzzer drew my attention.

"Forgive the interruption," he ordered in a soft voice. "It's something that can't wait."

I lifted my lips together in quick expression to let him know it was not a problem. In response, he pulled out his smartphone and focused his attention on the screen. I turned my attention away to give him privacy. I glanced around the room and back, lingering on the Walker table.

While the parents remained silent, as if they had had an argument, the siblings were horsing around. As I watched, Sammy bumped one of the crystal wine glasses by mistake. In a movement faster than my eyes could follow, he caught it before it hit the ground. The only trace of what had happened was a splash of red wine on the elegant off-white tablecloth. Without thinking, I opened my mouth in astonishment. I couldn't hear what Amanda said to Tina and Sammy, but it wiped the smile off their faces, and they stopped their antics.

"Do you know the Walkers well?" I asked Patrick when he had put away his smartphone.

"Only to say hello," he replied with disinterest. "They're loud, they put tomato ketchup on everything, they're from Texas, what more can I tell you? Why do you ask?"

"Nothing in particular, just curious," I said.

Until I knew more about Sammy and had a chance to explore my suspicions, I wasn't going to tell him what I had seen. On another occasion Patrick might have pressed me, but he seemed distracted. Although I usually enjoyed his company from that moment on I was eager to reread the Walker's file and dig into Tina and Sammy's abilities so our lunch dragged on until I thought I would burst with frustration. Putting on a patient face when I wished I was somewhere else was not my idea of a good time.

"Danni, I have a situation at work I need to take care of rather in a hurry," he said. "I'm afraid I'm going to have to skip the coffee. Please stay and order anything you like."

Patrick was never in a hurry. He had staff that took care of every eventuality so he never had to hurry. I wondered in passing what might qualify as serious enough for him to skip coffee. I was too preoccupied with my own case to push, and even if I did there wasn't a chance I would find out unless he wanted me to.

My thoughts raced while I waited for my espresso. Foremost among them was that if Sammy was a Timeshifter, he could be MGV. He had moved faster than normal speed, but that was not decisive. I called Ernie, but got his voice mail. I left a quick message asking him for anything he could find on Sammy. The server was setting down my coffee when Sébastien called.

"I figured it out," he announced with more excitement than I had heard from his lips in weeks.

"Oh?"

"It's on the rue Deux Cayrol in the eighteenth arrondissement," he said. "That's where she was headed. I'm ninety percent sure."

"I'll go check it out," I said. "Want to join me? If you do I'll tell you about my discovery that might blow open the MGV case."

"I wish," he said. "I have an emergency meeting with an important client, and tonight I have a function. There's no way I can get free today."

"Your loss," I said in a light tone I hoped hid my disappointment.

"Who will watch your six o'clock?" he asked.

"Wouldn't you like to know?" I said in the same tone.

"Seriously, be careful," he said. "Whoever that was had some power behind her. If you wait I'll clear my calendar to go with you."

I could tell from the strain in his voice that such an action would be difficult. It wasn't that he didn't want to go with me, on the contrary, I was confident he would rather be by my side than do almost anything that was on his calendar.

"I bet you have no openings for days," I said, testing my theory.

"I don't," he said, sounding defeated. "I'll figure something out."

There was no way I was going to put that kind of pressure on him. I had my job, and he had his.

"Don't you worry your pretty CEO head," I said, goading him. I knew it wasn't his fault, but I couldn't help being a little mad at him for leaving. If he hadn't, that jerk Rupert wouldn't have taken his place. "I can take care of myself."

"I know you can, but you shouldn't go alone," he said without taking my bait.

On another day, he would have responded to the poke about his pretty CEO head. That he didn't, told me he was distracted, concerned or both.

"You left. It's not your problem," I said in a sharper voice than he deserved. "It's not like I have a direct report I can call anymore."

I was glad the dining room had emptied and there wasn't anyone nearby to hear me. Sébastien didn't reply for so long I thought he might have hung up. He was too polite to do that.

When he spoke, it was in a concerned tone, "Promise me you'll be careful."

The anger I felt evaporated. Instead, I was grateful to have a friend who despite his important standing and many responsibilities cared about me.

"Yeah, all right," I said.

"Call me when you get back no matter the time," he said.

"You can tell me about the MGV case then."

"I thought you were going to be in a meeting," I began.

"Don't you worry about that, call me," he said, stressing the last two words. "I have to go. I will wait to hear from you."

Talking with Sébastien left me elated. Even if he couldn't go with me he had my back. And, for the first time in days, I had a solid clue about the Mathis case. I grinned as I remembered I also had one about MGV, lucky me.

Chapter 16

It took me longer to find rue Deux Cayrol than I had expected. It was on a quiet, dead-end street west of the Basilique du Sacré Coeur, a catholic church, and popular tourist attraction. While the area near the church was boiling with people, the narrow cobblestoned street I was searching for had an almost otherworldly calm. The only business was an art gallery, which might have been closed, attached to a two-story building. Across the street there was an open area with the same cobblestones, leading to a steep staircase.

My eyes were drawn to the ivy that covered the walls of a three-story building next to the staircase. I was searching for the address when I saw a middle-aged man exit the building and walk onto the street at a brisk pace. There was something familiar about his face. My gut told me he was Weeia. My badge confirmed it. I followed him. I was about to tap his shoulder as he neared the intersection of the rue Deux Cayrol and Calvaire Plaza when I realized what I was seeing.

Without thinking I blurted, "Dad?"

The man turned around so fast, I automatically began to take a defensive position. In a nanosecond, his gaze fixed on mine. The tension in his shoulders dropped and the lines on his face softened as he spoke, "Danni?"

I let my arms drop. My mouth felt so dry, I wasn't sure I would be able to swallow. Tears formed in my eyes. Time stood still as I watched my father. How was it possible that he was alive and in Paris? Why hadn't he gotten in touch with me? I had so many questions. His image became blurry as tears rolled down my cheeks. I nodded, unable to speak, move or stop crying.

He walked toward me, taking slow deliberate steps like someone approaching an injured animal that might become frightened and sprint at the slightest provocation. When he was within arm's length, he spoke again.

"It's not safe on the street. We need to go inside."

I heeded the urgency in his voice, following him as he turned back the way we had come. He was taller than me by a foot, and better looking than I remembered. His voice was deep and commanding yet gentle. He moved with wide, efficient strides. I noted with detachment colorful graffiti and what was left of posters on the side and back walls of a small apartment building we passed. In a minute, we reached the entrance of the ivy-covered building I had seen earlier. A twelve-foot roof extended from the façade, providing a sheltered entrance. Like the building, it was weather-beaten and covered in thick ivy.

A buzzer sounded, indicating the door had unlocked after my father punched in a code into the panel. He held the huge wood door ajar, following me once I was inside. I might have asked where we were headed, but I didn't. I wasn't afraid. My heart beat fast with emotions I was struggling to contain. I walked with steady strides to match his quick pace, half noticing we were inside a house.

He motioned to a leather living room chair. I glanced at it, but decided against it. I had too much nervous energy to sit down. He stood and watched me, waiting for me to speak. My thoughts were conflicted. I was thrilled to be with my father, but also angry, no furious. My breathing was shallow. Where had he been all my life?

I directed my eyes away from him to give myself a few more seconds. I forced the anger down as far as it would go. Taking a deep breath, I released it slowly, counting to ten in my mind before looking at the handsome man whose face I had memorized so well from the photos I had that I could recognize it out of a crowd.

Frustrated to be clogged with so many conflicting emotions and not knowing where to begin, I asked the first question that popped into my head, "How long have you been in Paris?"

When he failed to respond right away I looked at him to see what he was doing. I hadn't trusted myself to look at him too much for fear that I might not be able to contain my feelings. He stood relaxed, his features soft as he gazed at me with what appeared like tenderness and smiled. His smile lit up the room. Like an adoring fan, I wanted him to always look at me that way. I shook my head as if the physical movement would rid me of the nervousness. I leaned against a table to hide the weakness in my legs.

"Is that what you really want to know?" he asked in a soft voice.

"For starters," I said, unable to keep my voice from trembling.

My heart beat so fast it rang in my ears. I was sure he could hear it.

"We arrived yesterday," he said.

"We? Who is we?"

I didn't dare speak the words I was thinking. Was my mother alive too? Time stopped while I waited for his reply.

"A colleague and I," he said.

"What colleague?" I asked. When he didn't answer right away, I filled the silence by rapid firing more questions, all except the one I really wanted the answer to. "Why did you say we weren't safe on the street? Why are you here? Where were you all my life?"

His intense gaze made me want to squirm like an unruly student in class. I thought of pacing and decided against it.

"I'll start with the easy questions," he began. Something about the way he moved reminded me of a panther. "It's dangerous because Argus has eyes everywhere and especially now, when their agents are in Paris. If they find out we're in town they'll come after us. If they see you with me, it would put you in harm's way."

Without thinking I blurted, "I can take care of myself."

"Yes, I know, you're a well-trained and highly capable marshal," he said, the hint of a smile blossoming on his face. "I'm so proud of you." He hesitated as if there was more he wanted to tell me. "But that's not what this is about. Argus is beyond the abilities of any single individual or even a group, and they're ruthless. They stop at nothing in their pursuit of their mission."

I wanted answers to the personal questions. I wanted to know what had happened to my mother, why I had grown up without parents. I didn't care about work at that moment. Despite that, curiosity got the better of me.

"Who is Argus?" I asked.

Before he could reply the front door opened and a slender woman about five feet four inches tall walked in. She wore chocolate brown pants, a khaki top, and leather shoes a shade darker than the pants. Her short messy hair was the color of mine.

My father turned toward her, sighing at the same time he said her name, "Claire."

She zeroed in on me, taking three long strides to reach us. As she neared me, she halted.

My question "Mom?" made her nod.

Her eyes filled with tears, which spilled out like a burst damn, rolling down her cheeks. She stared at me like a thirsty man looking at water. At first, she remained still, making no effort to wipe the salty liquid. They must have blurred her vision because after what felt like an eternity, she rubbed her eyes with the back of her hand. She inched closer to me, watching my face before spreading her arms wide.

In that instant, the many things I wanted to say and questions I had became unimportant. All that mattered was that for the first time in my adult life, my parents were in the same room with me. I gave in to the overwhelming desire for a hug. As I did her arms closed around me in a firm yet gentle embrace. We cried until there were no more tears.

She pulled her face away from our embrace to call my father, "Thierry."

Raising her arm, she made space for him in a three-person hug. He sobbed. I breathed in the scents of my parents, remembering them from my childhood. My father had an earthy smell while my mom reminded me of home cooking and guns. I don't know how long we stood that way, only that I didn't want it to end.

My mother pulled back an arm's length, pushing a wet strand of hair away from my face. For an instant, it drew me back to the same gesture when I was a little girl.

"Dan—ni," she croaked. Clearing her throat, she tried again. "Danni, I can't explain how happy I am to see you."

Joy filled my heart as completely as sunshine spreads on a summer day. I couldn't remember ever feeling so well in my life. I wanted it to last forever.

After a while, we separated. I watched my parents, wondering what was on their minds. I didn't want to think, but questions and doubts threatened to overwhelm me.

As if reading my thoughts my mother said, "You must be curious."

She pointed to the furniture. I sat on the edge of an end chair. My parents shared a red leather sofa. We turned to face each other. A wood coffee table in the middle made it difficult to move so I pushed it back, adding space to our seating area.

"That's the understatement of the year," I said, sounding harsh to my ears.

Her expression softened. My father wrapped his arm around her and rested his hand on her shoulder in an intimate reassuring gesture. The proximity of their bodies and the way they responded wordlessly to each other's nonverbal cues told me they were close. I felt left out. A pang of longing reminded me of all the years of parenting they had taken away from me. I tensed.

"Yes, of course," she said in a soothing voice. "Please

believe me when I tell you that leaving you behind with your aunt and uncle was the hardest decision we have ever made." Her composure broke at that moment. In place of her kind and warm features there was a pained expression on her face. She took a deep breath before continuing. "Every day I ask myself if it was the right decision. Not a day goes by that I don't miss you, not a day goes by that I don't want to contact you to ask how you are, to hear your voice."

If I hadn't been paying close attention, I might have missed her flinching. With the corner of my eye, I saw my father tightened his squeeze on her as she did, making me wish I had someone in my life who was as aware of my moods as they were of each other's.

My throat was dry. I was anxious, afraid of what might follow, but I soldiered on. I had to find out what had happened.

"But, why did you?" I asked in a shaky voice I didn't know I was capable of producing.

"We had no choice," she said with force. "Ruthless hidden enemies pursued us. After a horrible betrayal during a dodgy case, we barely escaped with our lives. While we cared little that our reputations were ruined, we feared what might happen if we returned home and they followed us there. It would've been impossible to protect you every minute of every day. There was only two of us, and many of them. Their resources were vast. We couldn't risk anything happening to you." She leaned forward, running the back of her hand over my cheek ever so softly. "I would never have forgiven myself if it had. The path we chose has been difficult, but you're well and safe. That's all that matters."

"I had no idea you were alive," I said, anger bubbling inside me.

"I'm so, so sorry," she said. "I know it was difficult to grow up without us. I wish there had been a better way. Our top priority was keeping you safe and we accomplished it. I hope someday you can forgive us."

"Are you forgetting someone?" I asked.

"Not at all, your aunt and uncle have done a tremendous job of raising you," she replied. "With their love and guidance, you have grown into a capable, hardworking, and ethical young woman, and a marshal to boot. Living on the run is expensive. I wish we had been able to help financially." She glanced at my father at that point. "Unfortunately we haven't been able to stay in touch, but we have followed your career as closely as possible. We know you send money to them every month to help with the upkeep of the farm. We couldn't be prouder."

A mechanical bell interrupted her. It sounded like a smartphone alarm. She glanced at her watch, looking at my father and back at me. He straightened his back and leaned forward as if to rise to his feet.

"I can go," he said, looking at her. "That way you can be with Danni."

Her lips spread in a soft smile without revealing any teeth. After a moment, she replied, "You had a long shift. Now, it's my turn. Danni will understand." Turning to me, she explained. "We have been watching Mathis Tartan, the spiritshifter who owns the perfume shop. That's where we first saw you. We were very careful to hide from you, but it seems you knew we were there despite our efforts, well done. Is that how you found us?" Before I could reply she went on. "Nevermind. Tell me later." My heart skipped a beat when she said that. It meant I would be able to see my parents again. Despite the many questions I had and how angry I was that they had abandoned me when I was little, never making contact with me, I was over the moon to have found them. "I don't think they would attack in broad daylight, but I prefer not to take any chances."

"Why have you been watching him?" my father asked, drawing my attention to the reason I was there in the first place.

"Susanna, his partner, and Mathis asked for my help," I replied. "They thought someone was watching Mathis, even following him. I found evidence of that."

"Yes, they hired local thugs to tail him, but we don't think they will do anything else," my father said. "They usually hire humans for the grunt work. Anything important is done by Weeia."

"But we can't be sure," my mother said. "We have to err on the side of caution. As you know Mr. Tartan can cause a lot of problems even without meaning to, as he did in the past."

"How did you—" I began.

My mother interrupted me before I could finish my question, "We know what he did."

"And how you handled the case," my father added. "You did a great job."

A grin spread across his face and his eyes lit up. Had they been keeping tabs on me? Before I could ask my mother continued.

"He has a rare ability," she said. "He would be a valuable asset to anyone. In the wrong hands, and those are definitely the wrong hands, he could cause chaos. We can't let that happen. I'm sure you will understand that I have to get back to the Isle Saint Louis. It's why we are in Paris. It's been a wonderful surprise seeing you."

I was torn. While it was my duty as acting marshal of Paris to keep the citizens in my area as safe as I could, I didn't want her to go. I had only just found her and had so much I wanted to say. In the end, the responsibility I felt toward Mathis and Susanna won the tug of war I felt, leaving me deflated. It must have shown on my face because she gave me a hug.

"Don't worry, chérie, we'll have a chance to talk again," she said, pulling a rebel strand of hair behind my ear with a slow and deliberate movement that made me miss her before she was gone. My aunt and uncle had been caring and loving in my growing years, and I missed them. Nothing they had done could remove the biting ache I felt at the loss of my parents. "I'm sure Thierry will take good care of you." She smiled showing pretty even teeth and winked at me. "If he doesn't, you let me know."

She gave my father a peck on the lips and like a gust of wind she left. Tears threatened my composure. To hide them, I turned away from my father and rubbed the liquid from my eyes. If he noticed, he didn't say.

Chapter 17

When I turned back to face him, my father was sitting in the same place, looking relaxed. A torrent of questions flooded my brain: what enemies could have forced them to abandon their only child? What dodgy case was she referring to that I knew nothing about it even though I had read everything I could lay my hands on about their careers? What hidden enemies were after them that they still feared them after all the years that had passed? Why was it that they were guarding Mathis and hadn't contacted me as the acting head of the Paris office? Were they still marshals? When would I see them again?

The silence between us grew heavy. I wanted to know the answers to my questions, and at the same time, I was afraid of what I might discover. At that moment, the possibilities were open. Once I dug around there would be fewer of them. I wished I could hold on to the intense happiness I felt at finding both my parents. The dread of losing them again hung in my gut like a nefarious flu. I studied my father, who waited for me to take the initiative, with undisguised curiosity.

He was handsome with a chiseled face and masculine features that might have been harsh if it hadn't been for the warmth of his eyes and the softness of his lips when he smiled. His fingers were thin and long, and his fingernails were clean and shone as if they had nail polish on them.

"You take after your mother," he said, interrupting my thoughts. "You have her coloring, her fierce determination, her kindness and her beauty."

"And her height," I said, feeling self-conscious about my weight. She was taller and slenderer than I was, but I could see it was her genes I had inherited in that regard. Preferring to focus on the positive, I shifted the conversation more out of habit than with any particular goal. "Did I inherit my ability from her?"

"It would appear so," he said. "She's a capable illusionist, and from what we have heard so are you."

"Medius?"

He moved his head to one side in what seemed to be a negative response. I held his gaze. Among the Weeia discussing abilities was a touchy subject. Most superhumans who had abilities, some didn't, never talked about the nature of their ability or their level with others.

While there are many kinds of abilities, some common and others rare, all fit into four major categories or henkis: material, mental, spiritual, and temporal. The possessors of the abilities are known as mattershifters, mindshifters, spiritshifters, and timeshifters.

"She has a Maximus mental ability and a Medius emotional one," he said.

My mouth opened halfway in surprise. I had no idea one of my parents had two abilities. Having two abilities wasn't unheard of, but it wasn't common either. Being a Maximus was uncommon.

"Wow," I said. "Do you have two abilities too?"

He nodded as he replied, "I'm a Medius temporal and a Lowes Material."

"I heard you were a healer," I let the question hang.

"I am," he replied.

Before I became a marshal, I had always wanted to be a healer, but my ability wasn't a match for my wishes, so I decided to follow in my parents' footsteps. Knowing my father was a healer made me feel good. It was the next best thing to having the ability.

I wanted to pinch myself to make sure I wasn't dreaming. Instead, I stared at him, wondering what my life would have been like if I had grown up with him by my side. Perhaps my thoughts were reflected on my face because he reached out and offered me his hand. Sitting next to him, I took it, and we remained side by side for a few minutes.

"What's that like?" I asked, breaking the spell. "Is it easy? Is it wonderful?"

His lips spread in a smile that pushed his cheeks upward, narrowing his eyes and brightening his face. He thought for a second before answering.

"I suppose that like all abilities it's difficult to describe," he said. Unlike the five human senses, which we shared, superhuman abilities varied with each individual. Two healers could have different experiences and produce opposite results even if they both had the same degree of power. A Weeia's ability was affected by his or her personality and effort. "I'm sure you heard this at the academy, but I can't emphasize enough how true it is. Each person's ability is unique."

I nodded to confirm our instructors at the Marshals Academy in Portland, Maine had drilled that into our heads. It was one of the ways in which we were distinct from humans, they always said.

"Nature or nurture?" I asked.

"Now you've opened a hornet's nest," he said, his smile returning. "I'm sure you know there is much debate on that point."

"Yes, but I want to know your point of view," I said.

"While there are those who disagree, I'm convinced it's both," he said. "Your genetic inheritance plays a critical role, of course. If you're lazy, it may be that your ability hardly develops. If you apply yourself, even if you start with a modest ability, you may be surprised at what you can accomplish."

"Are you speaking from experience when you talk about being lazy?" I asked, astonished at how relaxed I felt around a man I didn't know existed a few hours earlier.

"Absolutely," he replied. "At first, it was frustrating, and I wasn't especially good at it. To become a decent healer, I had to study, practice, listen, and pay attention, none of which I had the patience for back then. I preferred to goof around and play with my other ability, which was more fun and easier to learn, or so I thought at the time."

Lowes Temporal could mean any of many abilities so I broke past good manners and asked, "What's your other ability?"

"I can see ahead in time," he said in a matter-of-fact tone.

"That sounds amazing," I said, wishing I had inherited that instead of my illusion ability, which for years I had thought was lame.

"It can be useful," he said without elaborating.

"If you see the future did you know I would be here?" I asked, thinking he had been surprised to see me.

"There are situations when I see the future as you put it. Today, I had no idea you were coming," he said. "Would you like something to eat or drink?"

The thought of food had not crossed my mind since I had arrived. I was too excited to eat. My throat was dry, so I asked for a glass of water. I followed my father to the kitchen.

"This is a big apartment," I said while he fished a glass out of the cupboard and poured water from the tap into it.

"It's a house actually," he said. Before it was full he asked, "Ice?"

I shook my head from side to side. After handing it to me, he took one for himself and filled it the same way.

"I didn't think there were any private houses in Paris," I said.

"I think only a few remain," he said. "Many of the old mansions have been converted into government offices, others were parceled into tiny apartments, some belong to foreign millionaires with the money to restore them even though they seldom come to Paris."

"How is it that you know so much about it?" I asked.

"I was stationed here many years ago, and before we

returned for this project we did some research," he said. "It's changed so much."

I couldn't help it. I wanted to know what he meant. "In what way?"

"For one thing, there are so many foreigners and many more immigrants," he said.

"Isn't it like that all over Europe?" I asked.

"Yes, and in some cities, it's much more so," he said. "Here they were forced out of the city into the less desirable arrondissements and banlieues, you've heard of them, the suburbs?" I nodded and he continued. "The most noticeable change I see is that the small businesses that gave the city its character are disappearing. Chain stores are taking their place."

"Why do you think it's happening?"

He wrinkled his nose as he said, "I don't know for sure. If it's like in other places I have been, where the price of real estate has increased a lot in a short amount of time, it's because the value of property and rentals skyrockets. Small businesses are hit the hardest because they rent and don't own their place of business."

"What do you mean by small businesses?" I asked.

"The mom and pop cheese shops, butchers, bakeries, and cafes," he said. "If their rent increases twenty percent or more they usually have to relocate or close. If you look around, you'll see many vacant buildings and underused space."

I had noticed the empty storefronts, closed cafes and cookie cutter stores popping up. Although it wasn't the conversation I would had planned to have with my father the neutral topic allowed me an emotional brake. I was impressed at how observant he was.

"I know what you mean. I prefer the family owned shops," I said. "What do you think will happen?"

"It's hard to say. Sometimes people push back and the market rights itself. I read in one of the dailies that the city is subsidizing small businesses in the central district to offset the effects of the rise in rents brought on by short-term rentals."

"And they're supposed to be cracking down on illegal rentals," I chimed in.

"That should help," he said, leading the way back to the living area.

"Tell me what happened," I said in an uncompromising tone when we sat down again. "I want to understand why you left."

Was there any explanation that would justify parents leaving their daughter behind? I couldn't imagine one, but I would give him, them the benefit of the doubt. If he was taken aback by my request he didn't show it, points for him.

"Your mom and I were called in at the last minute to assist a team in a remote part of Canada," he began. He straightened in his seat, taking a deep breath before continuing. "We had almost no prep time and no advance contact with the team. We were told it was a routine case involving a Medius, so we drove up to the front door."

"On arrival, the situation was much worse than we expected. Instead of the no big deal Medius we thought we were after, it turned out that the team was there to catch a wanted criminal known as The Wizard, said to be hiding there. Because he was so dangerous and had evaded previous capture attempts the team was made up of several high-level marshals. They were supposed to trap him in stasis, suppress his ability, and collar him by creating a time bubble around him."

He drank some water from his glass and looked into my eyes for a second. He had all my attention.

"Soon after we arrived, there was a huge explosion, in which, as far as we know, all the marshals died," he said. "The compound was used to store fuel for the province. It burned extremely hot and left no trace of the team. It took firefighters days to extinguish the blaze. Nobody knew we barely escaped with our lives. In the official reports, we were listed among the dead. We were blamed for the explosion and labeled as traitors. It's taken us years of chasing every bit of information we could find and piecing together clues to figure out what happened."

I had opened my mouth while I listened to him. When he paused, I closed it long enough to ask the most intelligent question I could think of, "What happened?"

His eyes had been focused on the wall in what I imagined was the long ago past. His expression was pained. After he heard my question, he turned his attention to me.

"We're convinced it was a setup to get rid of the team, which posed a threat, and blame us. It was orchestrated by Dante the Dealmaker, a less than reputable spiritshifter who uses his ability to his advantage."

"Why?"

"For power, money, the usual reasons," he said.

"To pull off something like that, they had to have been working with someone on the inside," I said.

"We drew the same conclusion," he said. "We didn't dare return until we knew more, so we let everyone believe we had perished in the fire. As we dug deeper, it became obvious that the marshals' leadership had been breached. We didn't know how high or how many were involved, but we were sure someone powerful had manipulated the case, tagging us as rogue agents in the process. Remaining dead provided an enormous advantage. The more we learned, the greater our concern."

He paused. I was eager to hear more, but I held my tongue, giving him time until he was ready to go on.

"Eventually, we discovered we were only two of many victims that had fallen in their web," he said. "Their resources and reach are tremendous."

"Dante and The Wizard?" I asked.

"They're fringe elements, for hire mostly," he said. "It's the zealot leaders we're most concerned about."

"I'm not sure I'm following. The leaders of the marshals?" I asked.

"They call themselves Argus, after a many-eyed giant in Greek mythology," he said.

"I've never heard of them," I said.

"That's a good thing, because they're bad news," he said, drawing out the last two words for effect.

"Who are they?"

"They're a highly secretive, incredibly well-funded group of Weeia, a throwback splinter cell who believe superhumans are superior to humans and should be in charge," he said. "We had heard rumors about their existence before they set us up."

"Why did they set you up?" I asked.

"We don't know for sure," he said, rubbing his chin with his thumb and index finger. "We think someone felt threatened by us, maybe we got too close to one of their pet projects."

"If you didn't cause the fire why not come forward now? Your name would be cleared, you would be reinstated and could fight them with the resources and the backing of the marshals," I said, hoping it was as easy as that.

I almost said I could help. It wasn't all selfless thinking. If their name was cleared mine would be too. I had lived my whole life under the shadow of their bad reputation. It would be nice to hold my head up high for once among other marshals.

His brow furrowed and his lips moved up without revealing any teeth in an odd expression, a mix of concern and smile.

"It's not as easy as that," he said.

"Do you have proof that you're innocent?" I asked.

"Yes, but guilty and innocent are simplistic ideals under the circumstances," he said, sighing. "If we come forward, we lose the most valuable asset we have. Argus doesn't know we're alive. Leaving the record as is helps us do our work behind the scenes and keeps us safe. More importantly, if they find out we survived they'll come after us in the most direct and hurtful manner, you." His eyes dug into mine. "They'll kill you."

"I can look out for myself," I blurted.

"Of course you can," he replied in a soothing voice. "I'm not saying otherwise. No individual can remain safe in the open if Argus sets its sights on him or her. I don't care how capable or powerful that person is. It's like trying to take cover under a desk after a nuclear explosion. The scale is out of proportion."

Without realizing, it I was hugging myself. My world was changing in a frightening way. I took a long swallow of water to give myself time to think and process what my father had revealed.

Words failed me. I mumbled, "I...uh."

"Coming out would undermine everything we have fought, our sacrifices would have been in vain if they succeed," he said. "Your mom would be devastated."

"Is that why you left?" I asked in a strangled voice.

"Yes, that's what we've been trying to explain," he said. "We've missed having you in our lives, but knowing you were alive and well made it possible. If anything were to happen to you–"

I struggled to keep the accumulated tears in my eyes from running down my cheeks. I swallowed. In that instant, he seemed to age a lifetime. Where he had looked almost my age earlier in that moment, he looked old enough to be my father.

I was tired and overwhelmed with too many emotions to process at once. Glancing at my watch, it dawned on me that I had been there for five hours without realizing it.

Getting up I announced, "I need some rest. I'm going home. I'll come back tomorrow."

My father got up as soon as I did. I watched his reaction, hoping he would accept my return the next day.

"Tomorrow is not a good day for us," he said. "How about

the next day?"

Before he could change his mind I said, "I'll be here first thing, say 9 a.m.?"

"I'll wait for you at the corner where we met," he said. "Don't tell anyone about us, Danni. I can't stress how important that is."

Chapter 18

Despite being more tired than usual, I didn't sleep well. Thoughts and feelings tumbled in my head like an out of control rollercoaster. I kept remembering the day, the conversation with my parents, their explanations, the sadness in their eyes behind a steely conviction that they had done right by me. Strong emotions rattled me on and off all night. No matter how mad I was at them for disappearing from my life, I was over the moon with delight to have found them. Then I wondered if I would lose them again.

I must have dozed off on the sofa because I woke feeling a cold nose on my hand. I jerked myself up in a sudden motion that startled Ceri back.

"Sorry," I mumbled, struggling to dislodge the sleep from my eyes by rubbing my knuckles against them. She stared at me from where she stood across the room. "I didn't realize it was you."

She walked to her doggie bed and sat down as if to let me know she had forgiven me. After stretching my neck down and from side to side in a semicircle, I rose to my feet. I padded over in my socks to where she lay, crouching down to her level.

"I really need a hug," I said half to myself and half to the pretty poodle. "Is it okay if I pet you?"

I took her silence as approval or at least not disapproval, and I began to lift my arm toward her. Before I could reach her she crossed the space between us gazing at me as if she understood. Taking great care, I touched her. Her hair was soft like fine human hair. She moved closer and I grew more confident. I surprised myself when I lifted her, settling her bottom on the crook of my left arm and wrapping my right arm around her small body. It felt good to share a tender moment with another living breathing being. She closed her eyes when I ran my hand over her head, opening them when my palm was past her face. I'm not sure how long we stood there.

"I have an idea," I said, caressing her one last time before I set her down in front of her basket. As soon as I did she shook her whole body. "I'm going to follow those kids to see what mischief they get into when they're away from their parents. I have no other leads. Who knows? Their abilities might be better than they seemed to be at the Club."

She walked to her doggie water bowl. I followed her into the kitchen, making myself an espresso and thinking that having something to do would distract me from focusing too much on my parents. I felt better than I had since I had gone to bed the previous night.

It was still dark outside. That didn't mean it was early. In the fall, the sun rose around 8 a.m. I looked at the time, 6 a.m., early enough to feed and walk Ceri before I made my way to the ritzy Walkers' hotel in the eighth arrondissement.

I wore the dressiest top I had. It was silk with tiny flowers in a soft blue background, a gift from Marla. Black pants, black jacket, and my usual leather boots completed the ensemble. I sat in the lobby café of the five-star Bay Hotel, where a snooty server took my order with much fanfare, setting logoed napkins and a paper coaster atop the glass table before he left.

The hotel had white uniformed doormen standing guard at revolving doors, gilded high ceilings, gold leaf detailing, and chandeliers. I had heard people say it was the best in the city, but I wasn't as impressed as they seemed to be. I had dined there several times, mostly for work as I wouldn't spend the fortune it cost to dine there out of my own pocket, and found the staff stuffy. Worse yet the food, while colorful and artfully presented, ranged from bland to over spicy. It was also undercooked or overcooked, somehow never well prepared or tasty.

I sat behind a courtesy copy of the newspaper, waiting for Tina and Sammy to head out so I could follow them. Splashed all over the front page was a story about the mysterious MGV, who had rescued a well-heeled tourist couple from Singapore celebrating their honeymoon in the City of Light from a gang of street urchins. The children tried to mug them while they were taking a romantic stroll near their luxury hotel. Coincidentally, it was the Bay Hotel.

Ten minutes passed before the server returned with my cappuccino and an almond croissant. A tall man with gray hair and I were the only ones there. I wondered in passing why it took so long, but I was in no hurry. An hour and another cappuccino and croissant order later, the siblings strolled by my seat without noticing me. I left enough money to cover my order and a tip, and bolted after them, keeping a block between us to avoid being seen.

They walked east, passing the quiet rue du Vernet to the metro station George V on the tree lined Champs Elysées. The world famous avenue was, as usual, bustling with cars and motorcycles on the street, and pedestrians and the occasional bicycle on its wide sidewalks. I followed them past bistros, gourmet pastry shops, tea salons, restaurants, and pizzerias that spilled onto the sidewalk.

At the corner of the Avenue George V and the Champs Elysées three convertibles, two red and one yellow, with their tops down caught people's attention. They were parked next to a covered bus stop as if they belonged there. A printed sign stuck out of the back seat of the Ferrari, inviting passersby to test drive the cars for ninety euros. Sammy dragged Tina's arm forward when she stopped and stared and the eye-catching cars.

When they descended into the subway, I followed. The stench of exhaust fumes and body odor assaulted me as I did. It was so crowded, I feared losing them so I stayed closer than

I would have liked. It didn't appear to matter. They both had wireless earbuds and their heads down staring into their smartphones, and didn't seem to notice anyone around them. After five minutes, a subway car so full I wasn't sure we would fit arrived. Many people got off, and with some effort, we all managed to squeeze aboard before I heard the distinctive departure bell followed by the swish of the doors closing.

I was in the back of the same car as Tina and Sammy. When they exited the train three stops later at Place de la Concorde, I had to push my way past the wall of people standing between me and the doors to get off. When two beefy men with scruffy beards and caps that were in my way refused to move at my slight nudging I thought I would be stuck on the train. I took a deep breath before booming, "Coming through." The passengers standing parted allowing me to wedge through. I sighed with relief once I was out of the train.

The platform emptied, within seconds and I lost sight of them. In my rush to catch up, I bumped into a man sitting in the hallway between the platforms. Looking down to apologize, I realized it was Marcel, a friend, well more of an acquaintance, I hadn't seen in months. He and his friends who lived on the streets had helped me on a case.

"Hey, Danni," he said in a guarded manner. "Remember me?"

The tension in his shoulders eased when he heard my reply, "Of course, Marcel. How are you?"

I faced a dilemma. With an effort, I stopped myself from wrinkling my nose at the rancid smell of old urine, which might have been from the subway or from Marcel. He could be a chatterbox, and I had minutes to spare before I lost Tina and Sammy. On the other hand, if I didn't make time to greet him his feelings might be hurt. I stood waiting for his answer, wondering how long it would be when a raspy voice interrupted him before he spoke.

"How's it hanging, Marcel?" the owner of the voice, a man walking with a cane, and dressed in little more than tatters, said.

Seeing the man, who strode with the elegance of a nobleman, Marcel beamed a smile the size of Rhode Island. He rose to his feet in an instant. As the men shook hands I muttered, "I gotta run," and bolted in pursuit of the sister and brother. I turned back to see if Marcel was upset, but neither of them was interested in me.

I thought Tina and Sammy were headed to the Roue de Paris, the popular Ferris wheel on the plaza. As we approached the area, the empty space reminded me that the wheel was no longer there. I had read in the newspaper that the city had not renewed the permits. Likewise, they had refused to renew the permit for the Christmas market on the Champs Elysées from the same company.

The siblings climbed the stairs between the Jeu de Paume and Musée de l'Orangerie museums and made their way into the Jardin des Tuileries. They were the only ones there, so I waited until they had reached the top to follow.

The weather had turned ugly and a light drizzle began to fall. It was chilly. I was glad I paid attention to the weather forecast and grabbed the raincoat on my way out. They had no raingear or even umbrellas. I feared they might return to the hotel, but they didn't. Instead, they passed the Bassin Octagonal water feature, and sat down on a bench to one side, far from the few diehard visitors who remained there. Once again, they focused their attention on their smartphones, allowing me to select a bench from which to observe them without them noticing me. After a few minutes of rain, we were the only people in that section of the park.

Ten minutes later, just after the rain stopped, two young men about their age joined them. I pressed the button on my badge to confirm what I suspected, they too were Weeia. They chatted for a while, goofing around on the bench until they got up and went to Angelina, a popular café on the nearby rue de Rivoli. I didn't dare follow inside for fear of giving myself away. While they sat in comfort inside, I bought a large cup of hot chocolate and a pastry to go. I waited, drinking the chocolate and savoring the crispy pastry a few steps from the entrance. When I tired of standing there, I paced up and down the covered sidewalk lined on one side with tourist shops for several blocks.

They went to a movie theater on the Boulevard Saint Germain near the Boulevard Saint Michel to catch an original version, not dubbed in French, of an American movie I didn't recognize. I bought a ticket, dreading spending two hours there. I sat several rows behind them and kept my eyes on the group of four.

After the movie, they met two young women, dressed in casual clothes similar to those worn by Tina. The body language of the young men changed. They went from goofy and relaxed to interested and energetic. There was so much flirting I had trouble keeping track of who was flirting with whom. They walked back to the subway station on the Place de la Concorde and returned to the Champs Elysées. From the subway station, they walked along the wide sidewalk, browsing at the large shop windows and chatting. They must have been hungry, when they reached a two-story pizzeria they entered and were seated right away. Once again I waited outside for fear of being seen.

Two hours later when they left the restaurant, I followed them until the group split up, Sammy and the women went west toward the Arc de Triomphe and the other boys scattered. I followed Tina and Sammy for the remainder of the day until they returned to their hotel. Back where I started I sat in the lobby and ordered another cappuccino and waited for several hours. In the early evening, when I saw them go to dinner with their parents, I went to grab a bite of my own. I returned, in case they went out again, but they didn't.

The next two days passed in a similar fashion, waiting for Tina and Sammy in the morning and following them and their friends around town until I was fit to be tied with boredom. My mother left a note to say they would be in touch as soon as possible. In the meantime keeping tabs on the siblings kept me busy.

When I was their age, I had my plate full with work, and when I arrived home there were tons of chores. I was seldom idle for long. If their days in Paris were anything to go by, the Walker children filled their days with little of productive value. Was that the life of the privileged?

On the third afternoon, I decided to take a more direct approach. Once again they went to the Jardin des Tuileries. They sat on a metal bench on the Allée de Castiglione, one of the less popular paths that ran north to south in the park, with their headphones on and their heads down looking at their smartphones. I was pondering how to talk with them without having the siblings blow me off when I noticed Tina walking away, leaving Sammy on his own.

The garden was often crowded, but that day there were few people around. Perhaps because it was unseasonably cold and it had rained for the past week, when I glanced around the only people I spotted were too far away to distinguish their gender with certainty. This was the best opportunity to catch Sammy alone in a private setting since I had been keeping track of their movements. I didn't know how soon Tina would return. She was seldom away from her brother for more than a few minutes. Odds were she would be back before long.

I decided to take advantage of the opportunity. I broke the illusion I had used to surveil them and made my way across from the Allée Centrale, where I had been watching them, with alacrity. I pulled out a one-euro coin I had in my pocket. As soon as I was near Sammy, but before he had looked up to see who was approaching him, I called his name and threw the coin with all my strength at him.

"What the?" he asked when he saw the object headed straight toward his face.

The young Weeia reacted on instinct. Moving with preternatural speed he snatched the coin in the air before it reached him.

"I knew it," I said, sitting on the bench beside him.

Recognition blossomed on his face when he saw me. The annoyance that had been there a second earlier morphed into a shrug of indifference. He didn't even bother to remove his headphones. Anger began to rise within me. I had proven he could move faster than any Weeia or human. He should be contrite.

"You," I blurted in a sharp tone.

Before saying something that might keep him from replying to my questions I stopped, closing my mouth. I needed my wits about me if I was going to make any headway in this case that had so many marshals chasing their tales. He had not reacted to my single word.

"Sammy, I need to talk to you," I said, taking the smartphone away from him and signaling that he should remove the wireless headphones. "This is important."

"It has nothing to do with me," he said, refusing to remove the earpieces and reaching for the phone.

I kept the phone away from him. He scowled.

"I'll be the judge of that once you answer my questions," I said, confident I had struck gold. "I just saw your speedwalking ability. You've been hiding it, but I have proof."

A woman's laugh behind me alarmed the bejesus out of me. At the same time, I got up, tensing, ready to face the threat. I spread my legs in readiness for a fight. I turned to see the source of the laugh, recognizing Tina's voice. She laughed again. My shoulders dropped and my legs resumed a normal stance as I relaxed. Tina's face was full of amusement. Her lips were wide apart showing near perfect teeth in a smile that crinkled her eyes.

"What's so funny?" I asked, annoyed at myself for not hearing her approach.

"You thinking that Sammy is a speedwalker, the speedwalker," she replied.

"Keep your voice down," I hissed. "Somebody could hear you."

Sammy defended his sister, asking, "So what?"

"So what? You're guests in this city and as such you will follow the rules," I said, emphasizing will, in the most authoritarian voice I could muster. "I don't care who your father is back home. Here you're all visitors, and I'm in charge. Do you understand?"

They said nothing, their sullen expressions telling me they remained defiant but didn't dare test my ire. I took two steps back, repositioning myself so I could watch the siblings' reactions to my question with ease.

"Now tell me, what is so amusing about your brother's ability?" I asked.

"It's minor," Tina replied. The smile was gone as she watched her brother, who looked like he had sucked on a lemon. "It only works on small objects. He can't move his whole body at high speed."

"I thought you were keeping it a secret," I said, feeling deflated that my discovery was not as impressive as I had assumed.

"Naw, our parents know," she said. "Sammy's best friend knows, but he doesn't want anyone else to know."

"Why not?" I asked.

"It's lame," he said, looking down at an invisible spot near his feet that had become interesting all of a sudden. "There's nothing to know. I have no ability. Our parents are both major players and I'm a bad joke."

His brows had furrowed and his lips were mushed together in an angry expression. I had once thought my ability was not worth having. I could relate.

"Maybe it will improve with practice," I said, hoping to make him feel better.

"I used to practice every day," he spat. "It's no use."

I believed them, so much for my progress on the case. I doubted there was anything else they could contribute to my findings. I had turned an ordinary day into a bad one. It wasn't fair. Instead of walking away and leaving Sammy in a bad mood, I attempted to mend the fences.

"Is baseball the reason you want your ability?" I asked.

He was quiet for so long I thought he wasn't going to reply until he said, "Why do you ask?"

"Well, you're wearing a t-shirt that looks like a baseball jersey and a baseball cap," I replied.

Tina watched her brother and me wearing a neutral expression. She was not pretty in a conventional way, but there was an air of confidence and cheer about her that I imagined made her attractive to the opposite sex.

"Oh, who are you kidding?" she said, looking at her brother. Then turning to me she said, "He loves baseball." She lingered on the second word for effect, which broke his wooden expression.

I threw the coin so he could catch it and that changed his mood. Ten minutes later, there was no stopping him from telling me all about his favorite tales of the game. I had noticed their friends hadn't shown up that day.

"I thought you had friends in town?" I asked.

"They've all gone home," Tina said. "Michele and Tom speak French. Without them, it's not as much fun. Wish we could go home too."

"Why can't you?" I asked.

"Dad wants to stay here until they resolve the case," she replied.

Sammy seemed pleased when he added, "Yeah, but it's taking so long the old man is about to give in. I think by next week we'll be stateside."

"Can you help solve the case?" Tina asked.

"I'm trying, but it's been a tough case," I said. "Is there anything you can think of that might be important?"

"Like what?" she asked.

"I don't know," I replied. "It could be a detail, something you noticed the day of the attack, someone you saw or heard." She shook her head sideways. "If you think of anything call me."

Tina nodded her agreement. Sammy didn't say a word, which I had grown to interpret as a lack of disagreement. It was better than nothing. At my request, we swapped contact information. After that, we chatted for a while, no small feat when I knew they wanted to go back to their electronic devices, before I made my excuses and left.

Chapter 19

I was distracted when I arrived home, disappointed to have wasted my energy chasing after the Walker offspring. I fished the mail out of my mailbox without paying much attention and climbed to my apartment on the top story. Although Ceri was too dignified to bark, for once she greeted me at the door instead of staying in her doggie bed.

After removing my boots at the entrance, I hung my jacket on the coat hanger and slumped into the couch, throwing the mail next to me as Ceri watched. I would have left it on the tiny table in the entrance foyer, yes I had a foyer, but I kept hoping to hear from my parents. They had said they would be in touch, and I wanted badly to believe them. I sorted through the usual correspondence looking for a handwritten envelope.

"What's this?" Ceri cocked her head to one side. "It's a folded sheet of paper. Someone must have stuck it through the opening at the top of the mailbox. I bet everyone in the building got one." She watched me from the floor. "You can climb on the couch as long as you don't pee on it, okay?" Although the rule was that she wasn't allowed on the furniture I patted the space next to me. She didn't move an inch, nothing. I opened the paper, thinking it was a promotional flyer I would toss. My heart raced as I read aloud: "Want to see MGV in action? Pompidou 8 p.m. tonight. Tell no one. Come alone."

I glanced at my watch. It was 7:15 p.m. If I left soon there was enough time for me to arrive by 8 p.m. I jumped up, excited that I might catch MGV.

"Wow, this is what I've been waiting for, a break in the case," I told Ceri, who was standing and following me with her eyes as I paced around the living room. "Even if he's breaking Weeia rules, he's not hurting anyone. There's no harm in observing him in action, maybe I can learn something new. If I tell the out of town team, they'll steal the collar from under me. Besides, they're so incompetent they'd probably botch it up." Talking about it out loud was helping me think through the issues. "According to Ernie, there's no easy and discreet way to catch a speedwalker without another speedwalker. So I'm tempted to do it." I paused, looking out at the view of the Seine River for an answer. "Yes, I'm going to go. And, I'll bring my smartphone so I can get video of MGV in action."

Five minutes later, I was putting my boots and a dry jacket on by the door. Ceri watched me from across the room.

"Sorry, I almost forgot your dinner," I said to the pooch.

I removed my boots and walked back to the kitchen, where I refreshed her water bowl and poured dog food into her clean food bowl. I knew better than to serve her food in a bowl with leavings from the previous day's meal. If the bowl wasn't clean when I poured her dinner she would sniff at it and leave the food untouched. She was sipping water when I returned to the door. I set several newspapers on the floor near the entrance in case of a doggie emergency.

Before I left I called out, "I'll walk you when I return. If you can't hold it use the newspaper."

I thought of driving, but parking near Pompidou was mayhem. There were private lots, but if there were any concerts or special events I would have to park two kilometers away. A taxi, if I could find one, was the fastest way. To catch a cab in Paris it was necessary to find a taxi stand or *tete de taxi*. I walked to the nearest one, and was delighted to find two taxis waiting for passengers. The driver of the first one lowered his window to ask where I was headed. When I told him, he told me to ask the other driver, pointing at the vehicle behind his.

A middle-aged woman with thinning mouse colored hair sat behind the wheel of a new looking German car. I only knew its nationality because I recognized the metallic emblem on the hood of the black car. As I approached, she lowered her window, "Yes?"

"I need to get to Pompidou quickly," I pleaded. "I'll pay you an extra twenty euros if you get me there in half an hour or less."

I was pretty sure that was doable. The money was an incentive for her to accept.

"You can take the bus or subway and it will be cheaper," she said with little interest.

"I know. I live nearby, but there could be delays in the subway," I said. "I need to get there quickly." I pulled the twenty euro note out of my wallet, showing it to her. "It's important. I'll make it worth your while." In response, she unlocked the doors of the car. "Thank you."

I pulled open the backdoor behind the driver's side and hopped in before she changed her mind. She pressed a button that I thought was to turn off the light atop the car to indicate the taxi was taken. Inside it smelled clean and was spotless. On close inspection I thought the car was a ten year old model. She babied the vehicle. There were magazines and bottled water in a pocket on the back of the seat.

"Canadian," she asked, looking at me on her rearview mirror.

"Yep," I said, guessing my accent had given me away. "I could be American. How did you know?"

"Nope, you have a Canadian accent," she said. "And you're polite."

I was? Nobody called me polite. Grumpy, grouchy, ill-tempered even driven were words I had heard; polite wasn't.

Unlike other taxis I had been in, hers had no global positioning system map device to direct her to our destination. I slid further in as she pulled out into traffic, maneuvering north to cross the river. She called into her dispatcher to announce she had a passenger and her direction.

"No map?" I asked.

"Huh?" she grunted.

"I noticed you don't have a GPS on your dashboard," I said, curious. Taxi drivers in Paris relied on global positioning systems to find their destination. "How do you find the addresses?"

She pointed to her head with her hand, saying, "I have a GPS in here."

I was incredulous, "Really?"

"Yes, in the days before those electronic gadgets you had to find your way to all of the addresses on the test with an inspector in the car beside you," she said. "I learned all the main streets in each arrondissement, and if the address was in a small street I didn't know, we were allowed to refer to a map."

"Wow, that sounds difficult," I replied.

"Meh, if you wanted your taxi license that's what you had to do," she said in a matter-of-fact tone. Her hair was combed back into a miniature bun and she wore a black and white ensemble that reminded me of a limo driver uniform. "Compared to other European capitals Paris is relatively small. What's difficult is all the one way streets and that many of the streets, especially in central Paris, are at odd angles."

"I thought Paris was bigger than London," I said.

"If you include the suburbs it might be, but if you only count the twenty arrondissements that made the official boundaries when we took the test, it's not," she said. "Paris is only six miles wide."

"I never realized that," I said.

"If it wasn't for the congestion and how drivers don't follow the rules, we could cross the city quickly," she said, stopping at a light. She typed into her smartphone. "This website says Paris is forty-one square miles. Compare that to New York City, which is 305."

"That's interesting," I said, meaning it. "It's still

impressive that you can get around the city without software directions."

"If only everything else was so easy," she said, slowing to a halt. "Pompidou is no big challenge. We're here."

I looked around at the dark dead-end street where she had parked, turning her meter off. It was less than twenty euros. I handed her two twenty euro notes and told her to keep the change.

She handed back one of the bills. I nodded my head sideways and handed the money back to her. If I ever needed another ride in a hurry, I hoped she would be around.

"A deal is a deal," I said. "You got me here quickly. I really appreciate it." After I got out, I turned around. "Do you have a number I can call you if I ever need a taxi again?"

She gave me an elegant business card with embossed black cursive letters that said "Maxine Pepin, transport de luxe" above her phone number. I was wondering which way to go.

As if reading my mind, she said, "Take two short rights and a left to the square behind Pompidou. Be careful. It's full of pickpockets."

I arrived at Pompidou Square, an informal gathering place behind the Centre Pompidou, a modern art museum near the site of the city's historic market, ten minutes before 8 p.m. The smell of rain mixed with rancid food filled my nostrils. I circled the plaza, watching for unusual looking characters. There were so many street performers it was difficult to identify particular oddities. There were foreigners, dog walkers, parents walking with a stroller; some sat on the ground, most stood or walked. While people milled around the plaza, waiting for the next impromptu act, I observed them, searching for the speedwalker.

Among the crowd, I recognized foreign petty criminal types I had seen in tourist areas, near banks and automatic teller machines on many occasions. I hadn't seen the individuals themselves, but I recognized their tactics and exotic appearance. Some carried clipboards and claimed to be collecting signatures for a good cause like raising funds for the blind. When distracted tourists allowed one of them within arm's length another one would approach from behind and pick the person's pocket. Others worked in twos, threes or groups, bumping a victim to distract her so that a fellow pickpocket could steal her wallet or phone. They were brazen, fast and efficient.

The children were the ones to watch because they were fearless and faster than the adults. In addition, the police hated anything to do with them because they would feign not speaking French or English. Once in custody, the police faced a mountain of paperwork, and after a few hours, sometimes as little as an hour or two, they would be released and go right back to the same corner.

I was watching a group of those children when I heard a yelp. Turning, I heard another. I pulled out my phone and recorded the scene. The crowd that had gathered around a fire-eater on my side of the square spread apart like water on sand. In the center was a pile of wallets, smartphones, and jewelry. Next to it, like trussed birds ready for the oven, lay several of the con artists and thieves.

A disembodied voice yelled at the crowd, "Watch your belongings. This is not a safe place." Before I could say speedwalker, the Weeia, and I was certain it had to be a superhuman, disappeared. I watched the blurry video on my screen. It was impossible to identify the shadow. It was a slight individual, but beyond that, I couldn't distinguish height, weight, or gender. I waited for MGV to return. In the meantime, the crowd circled the tied and immobile figures on the ground, identifying their belongings from the pile. Before anyone could remove anything, a good Samaritan barred them from touching the stolen items.

"Gypsies," an angry woman said about the dark-haired thieves on the ground.

Grunts and agreements echoed her words. I had suspected as much. A few minutes later, a television van arrived followed by several photographers. The onlookers were circling the petty criminals, looking at their belongings without being able to get them back. The mood soured. By the time the police arrived, a few minutes later, they were worked up, threatening to beat up the gypsies.

One of the thieves had the poor sense to taunt the victims. This made the onlookers anger flare. Someone threw a glass bottle. Two burly men in police uniform lifted the oldest of the thieves, pulling him toward a waiting van before the maddest elements in the crowd got to him. I suspected their reddened faces and swearing were the result of years of frustration. It wasn't clear if they were arresting him or protecting him from the mob.

MGV was gone. There was nothing else for me to witness or record. I headed home on foot. I had reached the Ile de la Cité when I received a call from my boss.

"Hello," I said into the badge that looked like a phone to a casual observer.

"What have you been doing since the team arrived in Paris?" my boss asked, in a voice ringed with annoyance, without any preliminary greeting.

All I managed was a puzzled, "Uh," before he cut me off.

"Never mind," he said. "It doesn't matter. Be at the office at 8:30 a.m. ready to discuss the case." That made no sense, the case they had taken away from me? "The head of the special taskforce has raised several concerns regarding your presence in Paris."

On my way home, I stopped at a new bakery with a view of Notre Dame, picking up a spinach and goat cheese sandwich, a mushroom brioche, two pastries, and one hundred grams of chocolate. The staff wore pristine white uniforms, head covers, and constipated expressions. My neighbor had recommended the place, raving about the mushroom brioche. She had neglected to mention how pricey it was. She must have assumed that because I lived in one of the toniest neighborhoods in the city, I could afford it. The total was more than I usually spent, but I was worried about the meeting the following morning and wanted something to cheer me up. Gourmet food, baked goods among others, was a good start. I knew it would do nothing to slim my figure, but I figured it wasn't the worst habit.

I entered the apartment, eager to take my boots off and plant myself in front of the TV to disconnect for a while. Ceri was standing by the door, reminding me that she needed her walk. I glanced at the newspaper I had left in case of an emergency; it was dry. She was good that way. Still, I knew she must need to go. It had been too many hours since her last walk.

I set the food bag on the foyer table and took her leash off its peg on the wall. As soon as I did, she walked to where I stood, allowing me to clip the end of the leash to her pretty leather and lab created diamond collar. I had convinced Francois to buy a collar with lab created diamonds in place of the one with natural diamonds he had bought her. I was not willing to stroll around town with thousands of euros worth of precious stones dangling from her neck. At least now, she only carried hundreds of euros in coveted gems.

Ceri seemed to smell every lamppost and tree along our way. We ran into a couple of her doggie friends and waited for their usual greetings before moving on. Otherwise, the walk was uneventful.

Less than an hour after I had first arrived, we were back. I refreshed her water bowl and spread my feast on the dining room table. I was glad to be home. As soon as I picked up the brioche to take a bite I heard the familiar ring of a video call. I set down the food and looked at the caller ID. It was Marla.

I swiped the screen to accept the call, saying, "What a nice surprise," as soon as I saw her face.

"Oh yeah?"

"Absolutely, I had a rough afternoon and could use a smiling face," I said, noticing she was grinning. "To what do I owe this call midweek?"

"We talk midweek sometimes," she said in a somewhat defensive tone. I pressed my lips together and inclined my head to one side to disagree. "Okay, okay, not so much."

"We usually talk on the weekends or seriously late at night for me when you're awake and your boyfriend is out of town," I said, amused. "You look like you have something to say. What's up?"

She was pacing around her office with her phone in her hand. The blurry image of her face and the furniture moving out of synch was less than pleasant.

"I have news I want to share," she said.

"Problems at work? Love trouble? Should I worry?"

"No, nothing like that, but I want to tell you in person," she replied, wrinkling her brow in a thoughtful expression. In person meant a problem or something big. Why was she making such a big deal about it? "I was thinking of coming over. Are you free this weekend?"

Thinking about my own issues I replied, "Assuming this case doesn't blow up in my face."

"Exaggerator," she said.

"Not as much as you think," I said. "My boss has called me on the carpet for some weird meeting tomorrow morning at the office with the special taskforce. Anyway, of course you're welcome here, anytime. I'll do my best to be good company. You flying over? When are you thinking of coming?"

"Uh, not sure yet," she replied. The grin returned. "One way or another I'll be there as soon as I can get there this weekend so don't make plans, 'kay?"

"Okay. If you're flying in, let me know and I'll pick you up," I said.

"Hopefully that won't be necessary," she said.

"Is that boyfriend of yours going to transport you? Is he going to spend the weekend here with you?" I asked.

"In answer to the first question, that's the plan," she said. "Even if he does, I doubt he can stay. Besides, I want it to be a girl's weekend for the two of us."

That was unexpected. The last time Marla had come to stay with me had been after Iaen's accident. Since she had found a boyfriend, she had less free hours to talk and visit. I understood.

"What's so special that we get a weekend without the beau?" I asked, curious despite myself.

She was giddy with laughter, replying, "You'll find out soon enough. I'll text you when I know more."

Knowing Marla, she would text me Friday afternoon to let me know she was arriving Friday night. She blew me a kiss and waved good-bye. I waved back, and we hung up.

The conversation with Marla lifted my spirts. I glanced at the food and sighed. I was still hungry, but the nervousness had dissipated. I poured myself a glass of red wine and bit into the brioche. Ceri looked up at me from where she sat by my feet.

"It's better than I thought," I said between bites. Ceri watched me. "Do you want a taste?" She wagged her tail. "As a special treat because I'm feeling happy after talking with Marla I'm going to share some. Don't get used to it. I'm not going to spoil you the way Francois did."

As I tore a chunk of the brioche some of the black mushroom filling spilled. I ripped the buttery bread into small pieces, placing it in her doggie bowl and throwing the filling on top. Once I stepped away, she smelled it and took a tentative bite. She held it in her mouth for a while as if unsure whether she liked it. I walked back to the table and ate the rest. When I looked back her bowl was empty. I had no idea she liked mushrooms.

Knowing I would spend the weekend with Marla turned dinner into a mini celebration rather than the droopy meal I had anticipated when I hung up with my boss. I didn't know what he had planned for the morning. I would cross that bridge when I got to it. In the meantime, I reminded myself that there was more to life than work. Marla was always reminding me of that. I was finishing the vanilla éclair when I had an idea. I picked up my badge and placed a video call to Ernie.

Ernie picked up on the fourth ring, "Hey."

He was at work. I could see the lab in the background.

"I had an idea," I said. "What about using the tracking pebbles to catch MGV?"

"Hello to you too," he said in a mock snarky tone. He continued before I could reply. "If it was that easy I would've suggested it already." Of course he would have. I should have thought of that. "Doubt they could track a speedwalker. Besides they're experimental and their range is limited. Speedwalkers are rare. We may be able to block MGV's abilities when he's out and about, but if he's in public the police would probably capture him before you do. It's risky. Unless you know where he lives and can capture him there away from the public I wouldn't advise it. I haven't had many opportunities to work with speedwalkers, certainly not anyone that moves as fast as MGV."

"It was worth a try," I said.

He was quiet for so long, if it hadn't been for the video I would have thought he had hung up. He was staring away from the screen, his eyes unfocused. That was the look he got when he was concentrating on a difficult puzzle. I knew better than to interrupt him.

"I may know a workaround," he said. "I'll call you later if it pans out."

Chapter 20

I woke up already thinking about the case. Ernie hadn't called the previous night. I waited for a couple of hours, knowing that he wouldn't call in the middle of the night unless it was an emergency. I tossed and turned, concerned about the meeting and wondering what to expect. My sorry tail was tired, but there was no delaying any further. I had to get up.

I went for a run before taking Ceri for her morning walk. My stomach was in a knot in anticipation of that morning's meeting. I couldn't eat anything. Coffee, on the other hand, was the nectar of the gods, at least the ones who wanted to wake up without a headache. Yep, I had what a British friend described as worrying caffeine and tobacco addictions. I indulged in a type of chewing tobacco that involved sucking the brown substance rather than chewing it. Some might add food, but then everyone needed food, right?

On my way into work, I stopped at a bakery near the office, picking up bottled water and a couple of items for Bob and Achilles, street friends I had made just after I arrived in Paris. I walked by the corner where they spent their daytime hours to find Bob alone.

"Hello," I said.

"Hello," he replied, gifting me a wide smile. "Haven't seen you in ages."

"It's been busier than usual at work," I said, knowing he wouldn't pry.

I tended to shy away from humans, because as a marshal my life was complicated and I could never confide in them or explain what I did for a living without lying, a lot. I handed him the bag with the treats. He accepted, mumbling, "Thank you."

I asked after his canine companion, "Where's Achilles?"

"At the vet's," he replied. "I didn't want to leave him overnight. It's expensive, and he doesn't like to be on his own." He forgot to mention he didn't like to be without the dog either. "But he had surgery, and they said he had to stay for observation. They promised no fees. It's a program for people like me, living on the streets with pets." I must have looked worried because before I could ask for details he explained what had happened. "It's minor surgery, nothing to fret over, they said. I call every hour for an update. Simone at the laundromat lets me borrow her phone. She has a soft spot for me, you know. He's fine. They said I should be able to pick him up late this afternoon."

"Give him a hug from me," I said. "I have to go."

That I arrived at the office before Madame Marmotte wasn't surprising. She never sauntered into work early if she could avoid it. No one else was there. I made myself an espresso and sat at my old desk. There were crumbs on the keyboard, and someone had spilled something on the desk and left it. The jerks must assume we have housekeeping service or something. Around 10 a.m. I heard the special taskforce members arrive, moments behind Madame Marmotte. She had grunted what I assumed was a good morning.

Half an hour later, Rupert showed up at my desk, dressed like a member of a SWAT (Special Weapons and Tactics) team and wearing a smug expression. He curled his index finger at me in a motion to follow him. I wished I could turn my back on him and ignore his command. It was too tempting to lash out at him. He had no power and seeing me upset would please him no end. Instead, I smacked my desk hard enough to make a loud noise to release some of my frustration. Startled, he jumped. He said nothing, but at least the smugness was gone from his face. It was petty, but worth it.

"They're in the main room," Madame Marmotte said as we

walked by her desk.

I wanted to tell her that she was stating the obvious, but there was no point in responding. Like Rupert, she had no say in the matter, although she might be enjoying my distress. I felt like a naughty kid heading over to the principal's office, except I was the least naughty person in the building.

The task force leader turned out to be Rupert's father. He was sitting at a desk I had never seen before. While there was furniture in storage, the desk and chairs were modern and shiny new. It was the first time I had seen him in Paris. It was his habit to attend meetings via video, keeping tabs on Rupert. He didn't even look up when we walked in. He was opening his mail. I could see the envelopes. He was playing a power game by making me wait to show me he was in charge.

He was dressed to impress. I could recognize a bespoke suit when I saw one. He wore gold cufflinks and a tie pin with his family crest. Rupert wore one with the same design. I recognized features his son had inherited, except where his father had a firm face to match his political authority, Rupert had a weak chin and shifty eyes that gave away his sniveling personality.

After a long while, he rose to his feet and invited me to sit. Of course, that meant if I wanted to see him I had to look up. I refused to play so I kept my gaze on the wall behind his desk.

"It has come to my attention, Marshal Metreaux, that you have been harassing the Walker family, the children especially," he said.

I should have held my tongue. Instead I blurted, "Oh, really? Did they complain?"

His upper lip twitched a smidgen in an unusual expression that made him look uglier than he was, and he wasn't what you would describe as a handsome man.

"I'm not in the habit of socializing with children," he said in a stern tone. "I spoke with the Elder himself. He said you have been keeping tabs on his family and making outrageous accusations. You have no right and no authority."

"I have every right and all the necessary authority," I said in a louder voice than was appropriate for a reply to a superior. I didn't care. He might have ranked higher than I did in the political strata, but he wasn't my superior. "In case you have forgotten, I'm the acting director of the Paris office. I'm well within my authority to pursue any leads I see fit. Sammy exhibited speed movement abilities. He and his parents withheld that information when I questioned them initially." His brows furrowed in a worried expression, not surprise, but worry. He knew about Sammy's nascent ability. "I had to eliminate him as a suspect."

"We knew about his ability and eliminated him early on in our investigations," he said, walking behind me where I couldn't see him without turning around.

I didn't believe him. I had seen copies of the team's pathetic reports to the head office courtesy of Ernie. There had been no mention of Sammy's ability. Rupert's father might have known about the Elder's son having a speed ability and kept it out of the report as a favor. That was plausible.

"If you had been here doing your job you would have known," he said.

What an ass, they had done everything but escort me out of the building. Anger threatened to bubble out of me like smoke out of a dragon's snout. I drew a deep breath and counted to ten in my head. That allowed me to refrain from telling him off. He circled back around to his desk, picking up an envelope I hadn't seen. With a swagger, he opened it and handed it to me.

"How do you explain this?" he asked.

I stared at a photo of me printed on plain paper. Behind me was Pompidou and the crowd of people from the previous night.

He poked his finger at a blur in the photo. "This doesn't

look good for you. Even a casual observer would realize you're working with the speedwalker you're supposed to be investigating."

I opened my mouth to reply, but he wasn't interested.

"Otherwise why haven't you filed a report about that incident? How is it that you knew to be there at the exact time the speedwalker was there? Better yet why didn't you capture him?"

He waved his arm in the air in a dramatic gesture worthy of a ballet dancer as he continued, "Are you working with the speedwalker in an elaborate hoax to ensure your position here in Paris? Solving the case will make you the frontrunner for the job even though Rupert is by far the better candidate."

Losing my temper, I replied, "Wow, you're living up to your reputation. Only a twisted mind would come up with such a plot. Is that how you rose up the ranks? Yes, I was there last night. But, as I'm sure you know, I'm not in cahoots with him. There was an invitation in my mailbox when I got home. I assumed your taskforce had received one too."

His sideways nod was so brief I might have missed it if I hadn't been staring at him, egging him to reply.

"No? Maybe the speedwalker didn't think much of your men." I left out that I could have told the team, but why should I? They had made it clear they didn't want to work with me. "And as to capturing him, if you know a way to do that without revealing his Weeia identity to humans let me know."

His face turned red and he raised his eyebrows in a startled expression like in the cartoons. I saw Rupert's attempt to approach his father with the corner of my eye, but the man waved the back of his hand toward him, making him stay away. Rupert's father wasn't my boss. I wasn't going to put up with his goading and accusations for another minute. By getting upset and yelling at him I was playing into his hands. No doubt he would exaggerate the interaction in his report. I wasn't going to let him manipulate me like a chess piece off my own board. If they wanted to fire me they were going to have to work for it. I would fight them every centimeter of the way.

I walked out of the office before he could say another word. Ten minutes later when my boss called, I let the phone ring without answering. He called twice more and I did the same, wandering aimlessly around the neighborhood. At first, I was paying no attention to my surroundings. After a while, I remembered spending my first day in Paris in a modest neighborhood hotel near the office, where I had made fast friends with the owner and her son Alain.

He had been my unofficial guide to the city, introducing me, on the back of his motorcycle, to the best known landmarks and attractions. In those days, having no car, I used public transportation as my only means of getting around. Alain had a tiny vintage car repair business and accepted motorcycles every once in a while. I had much more experience than he did fixing vintage cars, so in exchange for lending him a hand in his business, he let me use his scooter.

Although we had been strangers, the owner's welcome had been far warmer than that of my former boss and the office admin. Those first months in Paris had been trying for me. I had dinner at their house on a number of occasions and was grateful to see a friendly face. Their friendship had been one of the reasons I had stuck it out despite Francois and Madame Marmotte's icy reception. Needing to see a welcoming face like theirs, I beelined it to their hotel.

"Danni," a woman's voice bellowed as soon as I entered the hotel. Like a long lost relative, she planted back-to-back kisses on my cheeks. "How nice to see you. Alain's not here. Did he know you were coming?"

"No, I was in the neighborhood and I thought I would pop in," I replied.

"He'll be sorry he missed you," she said. "I asked about you the other day and he said he hadn't heard from you."

I owed him a reply to his last text message. She examined me with her eyes as we spoke.

"My bad," I confessed. "I've been working too much."

She straightened up as if a thought had come to her. She pulled her hair back and glanced at her watch.

"You must stay for lunch," she announced. "It will just be the two of us if you don't mind. You can keep me company with a glass of wine while I whip up our meal."

I instantly felt better. The tension I had been carrying like an extra limb I couldn't see eased.

"How can I help?" I asked.

"By catching me up," she said.

"I meant preparing lunch," I replied.

"I know," she said. "You can set the table, open the wine, and pour us each a glass."

I did as she asked, fishing a bottle of wine from the shelf where she pointed and two glasses from the cupboard. The cutlery and napkins took two minutes to find and place on the table while she sorted out ingredients for whatever she was making, which she said would be a surprise.

"There's leftover bread from this morning," she said, showing me half a baguette. "Will that do or would you prefer fresh bread?"

"That's fine," I said, squeezing the partial baguette to test its freshness.

"How about some country pâté to start?" she asked, opening the refrigerator and glancing back over her shoulder at me for an answer. "My sister sent us some last week made by her neighbor who is in the catering business."

"That sounds special, I um," I said, feeling guilty about dropping in unannounced.

"It's quite good," she said mistaking my hesitation for uncertainty about the quality of the food. "Good enough to share."

"You should eat it with your family," I said.

"This is good for today," she said.

Before I could object she pulled out a glass jar of cornichons and a porcelain container from which she plucked a thick slice of the homemade pâté for us before returning it to the refrigerator. She scooped two large portions of cornichons from the jar and poured them into a small bowl. She cut some celery and carrots into medium chunks and set them in a plate. We chatted while she worked. When she was done, she placed the pan in the oven and sat down next to me. Within minutes, we polished off the pâté, veggies, and bread as well as most of the cornichons.

When she removed the dish from the oven the aroma of rosemary and tarragon with a hint of garlic surrounded us. She served generous portions of chicken and potatoes for both of us and we continued our meal. By then, I felt much better than when I had arrived. Of course I couldn't share anything about my work, but I could tell her in a roundabout way some of the political issues I had been dealing with the past days, those were universal. We had slices of plum tart followed by espresso before she had to leave to run an errand.

As we said our good-byes I was grateful to have such a kind friend welcome me with open arms when I needed it despite a long absence, and she never asked anything in return beyond my friendship. I promised to pop by again soon.

Lunch with her reminded me that I had many accomplishments to my name since my arrival in Paris. I had overcome more than one difficult situation, solved tough cases against all odds, made new friends, and landed on my feet. By the time we parted company, I had gained some distance from the issues. I was still worried about losing my position, but it no longer felt like my world was caving in on me. If Rupert and his father wanted my title it was going to cost them because I was going to fight, and on my terms, not theirs.

Until headquarters said otherwise, I was the acting director.

I was in charge of the office. I lifted my chin and held my head high as I walked down the sidewalk.

Chapter 21

I went to the Ile Saint Louis to check up on Susanna and Mathis. A human man, in his early twenties I guessed, who I had never seen before manned the store. He looked at me from head to toe.

"May I help you?" he asked.

He stood by one of the shelves, dusting a bottle and looking in the opposite direction from me. His stiff stance and body language pointing away from where I stood made it clear he had no interest in interacting with me.

"I would like to see the owners," I said.

"Do you have an appointment?" he asked.

I stumbled for the briefest moment caught off guard by the question. I wanted to tell him his bosses would be interested in talking to me. I wanted to tell him he was behaving like a jerk. I didn't.

"No, are they here?" I asked.

"It's not my place to say," he replied.

I was losing my patience. If I didn't do something my temper would follow.

"Fine," I blurted.

I called Mathis, leaving a voice mail message when his phone company recorder beeped. After that, I called Susanna, who answered on the second ring.

"Hi, Danni," she said. "What a nice surprise."

"I came to check on you," I said. "I'm in the shop, but there's a snooty and unhelpful man here that won't give me the time of day. You here?"

"We had a meeting out of the office," she said as if that answered my question. "I'm across town and Mathis went to buy some supplies. He might be back already. Did you try him?"

"Yes, I left him a voice mail," I said. "Everything okay?"

"As far as I know," she said. "He keeps saying someone is following him, but nobody has approached him again or me. Do you have any news?"

"Not since my last update," I said. I couldn't mention that my parents were monitoring the building around the clock, or that I had hoped to catch a glimpse of them, but hadn't. "Keep me posted."

"Of course," she said. "Let's have lunch next week at the Club. I'll text you."

"Deal," I said, hanging up.

On my way home, I picked up some paper products and laundry detergent as well as dinner fixings and some treats for the pooch at the butcher's.

Ceri's walk was uneventful. When we returned home, I made myself a big salad. I must have dozed off because the sound of a visual call woke me.

"Did I wake you?" Ernie asked when I picked up the call.

I nodded in case my ruffled hair and the marks of the pillow on my cheek weren't enough. He grinned.

"'Sup?"

His grin widened at my question. Ceri, who was curled up in her bed, lifted her head, blinked once, and placed it on her paws.

"You look like a cat with a canary in its mouth," I said when he didn't answer right away. It was early evening. The tension of the day had knocked me out. "I forgot you were going to call."

"Remember how I said I would get back to you?" he asked.

"Yes, you always do. I know," I said. "You were going to look into a way to track the speedwalker."

"I have good, no, excellent news," he said, grinning like a little kid.

"Oh? What is it?"

"I may have a solution," he said.

"What's the solution, smarty pants?" I asked.

"You'll find out soon enough," he said.

"Now would be good," I replied.

"Can't," he said.

"You're not making any sense," I said. "Your lips are moving and words are coming out, but I have no inkling what you're trying to tell me. What is up with you today?"

"You'll see," he said, the grin back.

It was starting to annoy me. Ernie was a straight shooter. It wasn't like him to beat around the bush.

"When will I see?" I asked, hoping we might make progress with a direct question.

"Not sure exactly," he replied.

"Are you trying to annoy me?" I asked. "Because if you are, it's working."

"No, really, I don't know," he said, amusement written all over his face. "I'm not joking. Bear with me, and all will be revealed. Well, maybe not all."

"Cut it out, Ernie," I interrupted him. "Do you have helpful news or not?"

"Yes," he said.

Frustrated I straightened, raising my voice so that Ceri took notice. "You're the boss. What the hay?"

"I don't have permission to tell you anything else," he said. Although his grin was gone, he still appeared pleased with himself. "Be prepared for a meeting at any moment within the next twenty-four hours. It'll be worth your while. I promise. Will you do that?"

"Yeah, sure," I said.

"Excellent," he said. "Don't discuss what I've told you with anyone, not even Marla."

"You haven't told me anything," I blurted. "What?" I began and stopped. It was Ernie. I trusted him. "Oh, never mind. I'll go along. Don't have to dress up do I?"

"No, though you might want wear something other than

pajamas," he said. "I've got a meeting in ten minutes. We good?"

I nodded, and we hung up. If I hadn't seen him with my own eyes, I might have wondered what was going on with Ernie. He looked like his normal self, a bit more playful and self-confident than usual, but otherwise there was nothing that jumped out at me as out of the ordinary beyond his mysterious responses.

"That was weird, right?" I asked Ceri who had lowered her head, but was watching me. "I wonder what's going on with Ernie. Maybe he needs to get approval from a muckity-muck at the Marshals Academy for some new technology thingy."

I set my clothes on a chair next to my bed in case he called during the night. What were the chances? I was still curious about the meeting Ernie had mentioned when I turned off the light and went to sleep. It seemed like five minutes passed by when an unfamiliar bell woke me. Alert, I glanced around to see my badge on the night table lit. I reached for it, noticing there was a message, "Press button when ready for transport." It was 2 a.m. There was a button in the center of the badge between the two short lines of text. Must be what Ernie was referring to, I thought.

Getting up, I went to the bathroom and changed my clothes. Unsure of where the meeting would be or with whom, I loaded my shoulder bag with some basic gear. A girl could never be too prepared for a fight. It was chilly outside, so I grabbed my jacket. When I was ready. I took a deep breath, letting it out slowly before pressing the button.

Chapter 22

I almost dropped my badge when the space in front of me shimmered. My badge vibrated drawing my attention to a new message, "Cross through." When I moved my hand in front of me I felt a pull. The closer it was to the shimmer the stronger the pull. It was unsettling. I could decide not to go. That wasn't going to happen. I was too eager to capture MGV and secure my job. And, I was curious about the portal or whatever that was. Maybe it was true that curiosity killed the cat, except I was no feline.

I stuck the badge in my pants pocket and adjusted the bag on my shoulder before taking two steps straight into the weird space. A powerful energy dragged me through. It was the oddest sensation, like moving at high speed while standing still. I blinked and it was over, but I was no longer in my room in Paris. It reminded me of being transported by a Weeia like Marla's boyfriend, yet not like that at all.

I was woozy and teary eyed. I reached out to steady myself, placing my left hand on the nearest wall. Around me was a bedroom with wood walls, ceiling, and floors. A night table separated two queen beds each with its own private night table on one side. Where the heck was I?

Before I had much time to wonder, Ernie walked in, greeting me with a quick hello as if we met that way on a regular basis. He seemed to be in a hurry.

Curiosity got the better of me and I asked, "Where are we?"

"That's easy, Moosehead Lake," he said, glancing at his badge.

His badge? He never wore his badge, saying only active duty marshals needed to wear them. I followed his eyes to a button identical to the one on my badge, which he pressed. In an instant, the air shifted into an unfamiliar vibration similar to the shimmering at my apartment.

"After you," he said, motioning with his hand with a flourish for me to step in. When I hesitated he added, "It's safe. I promise."

"Fine," I mumbled as I braced myself for another sharp pull. There was a tug and I stumbled. I had braced myself against a force like the one I had felt in Paris. The one at Moosehead Lake was far gentler. With little effort, I recovered my balance.

Having exchanged my room in Paris for one in Moosehead Lake, I had expected another room. I was surprised to find myself outdoors, in a garden to be precise. I use the word garden because it's the closest I have. Yet, it doesn't describe the place with accuracy, not by a mile.

It was unlike anywhere else I have ever been. It was well lit as if from the sun, but there were shadows indicating directional lighting. When I looked heavenward the orb was nowhere to be seen in the clear blue sky. The grounds appeared to be tended by human hands, while also wild and impossibly ancient. Statues and buildings, also old, stood out for their odd designs. Huge wood and stone slabs melded together as if made of an identical substance. It was so quiet, my normal breathing sounded loud to me. As I waited and watched, I heard unfamiliar birdcalls and insects clicking.

I was alone. I had assumed Ernie would follow me. It hadn't occurred to me that he might stay behind. Why hadn't he warned me? Or given me instructions of some kind? In an effort to regain my calm, I began to observe my surroundings. Perhaps there was a clue there I had missed. The hues of the flowers were vibrant and their scents heady. I was admiring the colors of a rosebush near me when a kind of whooshing behind me made me turn around.

"There you are," I blurted in a much louder tone that I meant. I was relieved to see my friend. "I thought you weren't coming."

"I should've warned you," he said. "Time feels different

here than back home. I was right behind you across the portal."

He sat at a bench I hadn't noticed a few steps from where we stood, indicating with a sweep of his hand that I should join him.

Once seated and unable to contain my curiosity, I asked, "Where the heck are we?"

"I don't know what it's called," he said. "I've heard people refer to it as Gardenly."

"Clearly, it's much more than a garden," I said, admiration seeping through my voice. "Are we on earth?" He nodded. "You sure?"

"To the best of my knowledge," he replied, amused.

"If you grin again I'm going to smack you," I said only half joking. The cloak and dagger tactics were starting to annoy me and I was cranky, probably tired. "You dragged me out of bed in the middle of the night with no explanation, all mysterious and secretive. Why am I here? What is going on?" I emphasized the first word in each question.

"You told me you wanted to catch MGV, right?" he asked. I nodded my agreement. "That's why you're here. Before we go any further you have to promise you will keep everything about tonight to yourself. You can't tell anyone, not Marla, not your family, no one."

"Uh, okay," I said, sounding dumb to my own ears.

Turning serious he said, "I vouched for you."

"I said okay, no need to beat me up about it. I already agreed to keep the secret, whatever it is."

That appeared to satisfy him because his face turned serious as he spoke, "Have you ever wondered where our badges come from?"

"There have always been wild rumors about that," I replied. "I asked some of my instructors at the Marshal's Academy years ago about the origin of the badges and how they were made. Their answers made no sense. I suspected they didn't know."

"Very few know where and how they are made," he said. "Have you ever heard about The Descendants?" I shook my head from side to side. "How well do you know the story of the Unelmoija and our people?"

"I know the school story I learned when I was a little girl," I replied. "What does that ancient history have to do with where we are today and our badges?"

"A lot. The Unelmoija was the most gifted and powerful Weeia in our history as well as our forbearer," he said.

"Yeah, yeah, she was all knowing and wise," I said. "She sacrificed everything so that we might blah, blah."

He raised his hand, asking me to be patient. The long go around in what was the middle of my night, regardless of the sunlight wherever we were, wasn't improving my mood.

"Everything you said is true and more," he said. "She has been the only Weeia with all four henkis and an infinite number of abilities. Did you know she lived in modern times?"

History wasn't a favorite subject. I cared about the present and the future more than the past. I cared about abilities, who had them, and what they could do.

While The Elders are powerful and almost always have two abilities, Weeia in general have no abilities or Lowes abilities. Medius and Maximus are much less common. Weeia with two abilities, like my parents, are exceptional.

"No, she was our ancestor," I said.

"Yes, she was, after a fashion. Yet, before that she lived in our era," he said, watching me for a reaction.

"I always thought she was more of a myth than a real being," I said. "Four henkis and infinite abilities, are you kidding me? For starters you would need significant fuel and immense concentration."

"Yes, I agree," he said with some enthusiasm.

"Assuming you're right and there was such a woman, where is she now, why haven't we ever heard of her or seen her?" I asked.

"That's what I was explaining. She had to live in the past because of some problem," he said. "That part of the story is a bit murky. I'm not sure what happened."

"Let's say I believe it, which I'm struggling to," I said. Ernie was a nuts and bolts guy. It was unexpected to see him going on about the legend of the Unelmoija. Then again he loved superheroes and comic book characters and role playing. "That stretches the limits of my credibility, but even if we do that why are we talking about her again? What does she have to do with our badges?"

"She doesn't have anything to do with them herself," he said. I scrunched my nose in confusion. "Wait, before you blow a gasket hear me out. There's a group of Weeia who are direct descendants of the Unelmoija. Very few Weeia know about them. Those who do, like me, and now you, are sworn to secrecy. They are known formally as Ihmiset from old Finnish, meaning people. We call them The Descendants. The women descended directly from the Unelmoija are known as the Daughters of the Descendants."

"Really? Are you making that up? It sounds made up," I replied.

He ignored my snippiness and continued, "They're unlike anyone you've ever met. They remain outside Weeia politics and seldom interact with Weeia except those designated by them for particular tasks."

"Like you?" I asked.

"Yes, at first I didn't believe it," he said. "It took some adjusting to understand that they're Weeia, yet they're more than superhuman, think of Weeia abilities times ten or more, times one hundred. This place we're in. They made it so we can be comfortable when we come to see them, so that we may interact with them without freaking out."

"What does that mean?" I asked.

"As far as I can tell their environment isn't concrete enough for us to grasp," he said.

"I understand the words. I don't get what they mean in a tangible sense," I said. "Is it real? Who is they?"

"It's definitely real in that it exists, but not in our universe, or the way we perceive it," he said. When had Ernie become so, so knowledgeable? "A powerful dreamshifter made it." He looked around and back to me. "Have you noticed our badges are limited?" I pressed my lips together and looked up above his head, thinking. "That they don't track all abilities?"

"What do you mean?" I asked.

"Well, for example, they don't track speedwalkers or dreamshifters," he replied.

"They're both very rare," I said, unconvinced that was a good answer. "It's probably not worth the effort."

"The badges have limitations few marshals even know about," he said.

"Why?"

"I have no idea," he said.

"How is it that you know so much?" I asked.

"It's my job. I'm the go-between," he said.

I had never given much thought to the badges or the technology that made them possible. Ernie always added software to mine before other marshals. I was his superhuman guinea pig when it came to improvements and new features.

"When we met, your job was all things techie. How did you go from that to meeting The Descendants?" I asked.

"In part, it was because the weapons master was busy with weapons development and I was next in the office," he said, shrugging as if to say it was no big deal.

While Ernie loved to be admired and praised, he could also be modest. The former was more common than the later. Could it be that he was maturing? One of our instructors at the Marshal's Academy had drilled into our heads that people didn't change, except under duress or trauma. I was learning to keep my red hot temper in check.

"I don't believe for a moment that it was by accident," I

said. "This role is important and requires someone able and trustworthy. There are loads of marshals and Weeia leaders who would give their right arm for an opportunity to work with the badges and the super superhumans who make them."

"I suppose," he said, mysterious again. "I'll tell you the rest of the story another day, maybe over dinner."

"Oh, was that you asking me out?" I asked.

The invitation caught me by surprise. Ernie and I had a budding romance during my last year at the Marshal's Academy. It fizzled to a friendship when I was assigned to Paris and we were an ocean apart. A hectic work schedule and six-hour time difference did nothing to improve matters. I met and fell in love with Iaen, and through it, Ernie and I stayed friends. When Iaen died, I was devastated. Ernie bent over backward to be there for me. He was a good friend. I would always be grateful to him for that. It was thanks to him, Marla, my family and work that I had recovered.

"And if I was?" he asked in a small voice.

"I'm not sure," I replied. I hadn't gone out with anyone since I had lost Iaen. "I don't know if I'm ready to date. What's more important is our friendship. It means the world to me. I wouldn't want to do anything to risk it."

"No risk no reward," he quipped. Before I could reply he went on, "I'm kidding. I wouldn't, you know, well." He went silent for a moment before speaking again. "I'm your friend no matter what. We can have dinner between friends until you're ready for more."

"Ernie, you know I'm a straight shooter," I said. "I don't know how long it might be before I'm comfortable seeing anyone romantically. I don't want to mislead you in any way."

"Understood," he said in a brighter tone of voice than a moment earlier. "Friends first, and there will be no strings attached to dinner or anything else unless you ever want them."

I didn't want to think about dating, but I didn't want to hurt his feelings either so I replied, "Uh, okay." With luck, it would signal to him how much I preferred to focus on just about anything else.

Chapter 23

Ernie started to say something and stopped as his eyes focused behind me. I turned to see an orange-clad figure approaching quickly. Ernie rose to his feet. I did the same.

"We'll talk later," he said, distracted as he watched the other person, his voice trailing at the end.

Ernie's face relaxed and the corners of his lips spread out, forming a smile showing teeth and reaching his eyes. I recognized the expression. Whoever was coming was someone he liked. I glanced at my badge, pressing the button to see if it was Weeia or human.

"He's human," Ernie said when he noticed what I was doing.

As the figure reached us, I saw it was a man. He had no hair on his head. He was dressed in a dark yellow robe rather than an orange one as I had thought. His robe, the color of old mustard seeds I had once seen in a spice stand in the Latin Quarter organic street market, wrapped around and over his left shoulder, leaving his right shoulder and part of his chest naked.

The man returned Ernie's smile and raised his hands, setting his palms together and lowering his head while saying, "Namaste."

"Namaste," Ernie replied, returning the gesture.

I estimated the old man to be in his eighties. As he turned to me the smile on his wizened face faltered for an instant. There was an air of calm about him like an invisible cloak. He reminded me of Buddhist monks I had seen in photos and on television. The robe reached his ankles above bare feet. Faded tattoos in a language I couldn't read or recognize covered the exposed skin on his arms and shoulder.

Facing me, he joined his palms together and repeated the

greeting, "Namaste."

Unsure of what I should say or do I mumbled "Uh, hello." Articulate and responsive, that was me, not. Despite how calm he was, I had no idea who he was or why we were meeting him, not to mention what I was supposed to reply. Turning to Ernie, I asked, "Does he speak English?"

I was thinking about the translation app on my badge. Before I had a chance to look for it both men laughed. It was a gentle, kind laugh.

"Yes," the man replied for Ernie, his bright eyes on me. "I graduated from Berkeley."

He had a minuscule accent. If I had only heard him without seeing him, I might not have noticed it. It was somehow charming while inconsistent with his exotic appearance, like watching a snake charmer pull out a smartphone mid-charm. Plus, I hadn't expected a university man.

As he extended his arm, he said, "I've heard much about you, Marshal Metreaux."

We shook hands. His palm was dry, callused, and firm. He was no stranger to manual labor.

"You have?" I asked after he released my hand. "I've never heard about you."

When I turned to Ernie to ask why he had not prepared me for the meeting the man said, "That was my doing. I'm afraid Ernie wasn't permitted to tell you anything. We have strict protocols here." His arms spread out at mid-chest level. "I trust you understand."

Before I could reply, he began to walk past the bench where Ernie and I had been sitting. As if waking from a dream, Ernie and I rushed to catch up with him. When I looked ahead, I noticed a gazebo that had not been there when we arrived. At the edge of the gazebo, we removed our shoes and followed the old man's footsteps. A tatami mat covered the floor. The material was neither soft nor coarse on my feet.

Questions swirled through my mind, but movement caught

my eye beneath the roof of the gazebo, where a long-haired woman sat straight backed, her eyes closed. A tiny brown bird landed on her shoulder as I watched. She remained impassive.

"She's meditating," Ernie whispered. "What should we do?"

The old man shrugged as he replied, "Her instructions were clear. As soon as we arrive, we're to let her know."

Her crossed legs were visible beneath the linen white fabric of her clothes. I couldn't tell if it was a skirt or pants. Once we stood five feet away, the old man cleared his throat twice, thrice until her eyes opened.

The old man and Ernie bowed, joining their palms and greeting her in a soft reverential voice, "Namaste, Daughter Celeste."

Now that we were near her, I realized she was a teenager or a young adult. Her skin was blemish free and perfect as if she had never spent too much time sunbathing and never had a pimple. Her shiny brown hair was striking in its beauty. It was so pretty, the color so vivid, I wondered if it was a natural. I stared and my mouth opened of its own accord. Playful blue eyes zeroed in on mine, making me feel awkward under her scrutiny. Where the old man had an air of calm about him, hers was intimidating in its intensity.

She responded in the same way saying, "Namaste to you, too. Stop calling me Daughter Celeste." She had a clunky British accent, as if English wasn't her first language. There was an unexpected squeakiness to her voice, like an old vinyl record playing at the wrong speed. She moved with such speed and grace, one second she was facing them, and the next she was facing me without my seeing her turn. "Welcome, Dannielle Metreaux. You will excuse me for leaving out your hard earned title. Here we have no use for Weeia titles. In this space—" She glanced at the men.

"In this plane," the old man completed the sentence in the same gentle tone of his greeting.

"Yes, in this plane we are independent of Weeia authority.

The Elders, the marshals have no say here," she said.

She spoke without contractions, enunciating every word and lingering on them as if they brought her pleasure. She was self-confident, and although no one had said as much, I had the feeling I was there at her invitation.

"If we have no titles—" I began.

She interrupted me, asking, "Why do I?"

"Exactly," I replied.

"Dannie," Ernie said as if I had committed a faux pas at a fancy banquet.

I wasn't going to be pushed around. I was tired of following stupid rules without asking why.

"I have every right to ask," I replied.

The old man spoke up, bowing from the waist down as he watched her, "If I may?" As soon as she nodded her permission he continued. "The Descendants and the Daughters of the Descendants are the closest Weeia get to religious devotion. They deserve your deepest respect."

"While I appreciate your devotion where I come from respect is earned," I replied to him in a not unkind voice. "As far as I'm concerned and until I know otherwise, we're all equals." From the corner of my eye, I saw a smile without teeth expand on her face. The old man nodded an acknowledgment without replying. A slight frown marred his otherwise calm features. "You're welcome to call me Dannielle. What should I call you?"

"In this plane you may call me Celeste," she said.

The old man's frown grew deeper as he asked, "Daughter Celeste, are you sure that is wise?"

She waved his concern away with a flick of her wrist. She extended her hand palm up in front of me. Wondering what she wanted, I glanced at the men.

"Give her your badge," Ernie commanded.

"What?" I asked. With the exception of Ernie, no one was allowed to touch my badge. "Why?"

"Do you trust me?" he asked.

"Of course," I replied. "But, what's the point? It's inert in the hands of strangers anyway."

I pulled out my badge and studied it. "It's working fine."

"It will be better," he said.

"Rather cryptic that," I replied, uneasy about handing my badge to the young woman. "How about I hand it to you and you hand it to her?"

"You must make the request in person," Celeste said.

I showed off my fast thinking by replying, "Huh?"

"Protocol requires that you appear in person and ask a Daughter of the Descendants for her assistance," the old man said. I must have looked as confused as I felt because he went on, "You must stand before her, hand her the badge, and request humbly that she assist you."

I was starting to understand that Celeste was more important than I had at first assumed. To allay my nerves, I blurted, "Whoa, this doesn't involve any kind of animal or human sacrifice, does it? I'm not promising my firstborn to a devil worshiping cult, right?"

Under normal circumstances Ernie laughed at my jokes. But, he was stiff. I had the feeling he was grinding his teeth. If the old man's frown grew any deeper it would form a permanent groove on his forehead.

"Okay, okay loosen up a bit," I said. "Celeste, is that true?"

"Yes, Danielle," she said.

The old man closed the space between us with two steps. He leaned near without touching me, so close I could smell rice and tea on his breath.

"Bend on one knee, hand her the badge, and say these words: Daughter of the Descendants I ask for your assistance," he said.

I'm not the bend on a knee type. Instead, I took two wide steps, placed my badge on her palm, and said, "It would be good if you do whatever it is you do to my badge."

I was a tad nervous and the words were less smooth than I would have liked. That didn't pose a problem. She moved her chin down a smidgen before lifting the device from my hand. As soon as I felt the weight was gone, I stepped back to the spot where I had been standing.

The old man remained silent although his brows knitted together in a slight frown. Ernie winked at me. Celeste closed her eyes and hummed. She remained that way for a short while, ten minutes perhaps. The old man placed his index finger over his lips when I parted my lips to ask a question. Ernie shrugged. I had the feeling he would have been more relaxed if the old man hadn't been with us.

When she opened her eyes, she searched for me, saying "It is done. Your badge may now find speedwalkers and portals. Use it wisely, young lady." I accepted the badge from her hand, mesmerized by the energy she radiated. "Oh and be aware."

"What?" I asked, shaking a little.

"There is uncertainty right now," she replied without missing a beat. "These new features may not last."

I turned my badge around in my hand. It didn't look any different than when I had given it to her. After all the mystery and what-not the added apps might be duds? I hoped I had misunderstood.

"What does that mean?" I asked in a loud voice.

I hadn't realized that while I was studying my device, Ernie had approached Celeste. They were speaking in whispers. The old man had taken several steps back and stood with his head bent as if praying. I was about to repeat my question when she handed him a small parcel and he returned to my side.

"Ready?" Ernie asked.

"No, I didn't understand. What did she mean?" I said, miffed at the cryptic comment and dismissive attitude.

"Don't worry about it," he replied. "It's like when you get new software that may have glitches, you know, like when you beta test new stuff. I'll walk you through the new features, think of them as apps." I made a face, to which he replied by adding, "Well amazing apps you can't tell anyone about."

"That's more like it," I said. "How difficult will they be to use?"

"Not too bad," he said. "The hardest part will be keeping a low profile while you track and capture the speedwalker around a densely populated city."

"You forgot paranoid," I said.

"What?" he asked.

"Around a densely populated, paranoid city," I explained. "Between the state of emergency, the bombings, and stabbings the city has seen lately the police are on high alert for anything and everything, and Parisians, who usually don't let much get in their way, are on edge."

"I see what you mean," he said. "And, the speedwalker, has become a sort of hero around town. They better not see you taking him down or who knows what they'll do. I don't envy you." I grinned. "Okay, maybe a bit. I'll admit I have fantasized about being a marshal."

Seeing my grin widen, he smiled back. When I turned to look for Celeste she was gone, the old man too.

"Now what?" I asked.

"We return to my office and get you home," he replied.

"You say it as if it was the most normal activity in the world," I said.

"It wasn't so bad," he said. "The way back may be bumpy." He pressed the button and the air shimmered once more. He motioned with his hand for me to go through. As I did, I heard his voice trailing behind me. "I'll see you there. Wait for me."

There was no bumpiness on the return to his office. On the contrary, I didn't feel much pressure at all. Seconds after I arrived I began feeling queasy. The room kept moving and my stomach followed. I fell to my knees and wretched without warning. I sat on the floor until it passed then I rinsed my mouth and found paper towels to clean the mess.

It was an hour before Ernie arrived. I was fidgety and drained. It annoyed me that he looked fresh as a daisy.

"Hiya," he said. "You look awful." In response, I punched his arm hard. He winced, but didn't step back. "You need to rest."

"Marla is coming to spend the weekend, I need to get my place ready for her," I said.

"There's time," he said. "This is more urgent. Besides, it won't take long, but you have to sleep."

"I don't want to sleep," I said. He bobbed his head once to indicate he didn't believe me. "Well, maybe I do want to sleep, but in my bed. Just show me how to use the new apps and I'll be on my way."

"No can do," he replied in an annoyingly calm tone that told me he would brook no arguments. "I didn't want to pull rank, but you're forcing my hand. You're in no state to do this. There's a guestroom you can use, with a shower. When you have slept at least two hours we can discuss this."

"Two hours?"

"At least," he replied. "I'll know when I see you. This is serious business and you need your rest to learn it. I won't be in Paris when you use it to hold your hand."

"Fine," I conceded with little enthusiasm.

"Follow me," he said.

Chapter 24

The guestroom was spotless, if Spartan. There were no electronic devices to distract me. The bed was firm and comfortable. When I turned off the night table lamp, darkness filled the room. I was wicked tired and as soon as I closed my eyes, I must have fallen asleep.

I woke up on my own, stretching in my horizontal position for a few precious minutes before looking at the time. I had slept for four hours without stirring. Remembering Marla would be visiting me and I hadn't done anything to prepare my apartment for her arrival, I bolted out of bed. I showered and felt refreshed although I had to wear the same clothes.

Ernie was at his desk hard at work on his computer. He turned in my direction before I could surprise him.

"Feeling better?" he asked.

The instant I opened my mouth to reply, a young man, perhaps a student, walked in and handed him something. I couldn't see what it was from where I was standing. Ernie looked at the object and signaled with his hand for the man to wait.

"Tell her I'll be in touch as soon as I have news," he said to him.

"When?" the young man asked.

"It might be tomorrow, but it could take me three days or more," he said, fixing his gaze up and to the right as he spoke as if he was calculating when it would be ready. "Better tell her it'll be a week."

"She'll be unhappy," the young man said.

Ernie shrugged. The young man waited as if by staring at Ernie it would speed the process. Ernie turned back to me. By then, I was standing in front of him, but I waited for the young man to leave before speaking.

"I had no idea you were in such high demand," I teased.

"Everybody waits until the last minute and then wants me to drop everything to fix their crisis," he said, sounding frustrated.

"You should get some help," I said.

"I've tried, believe me," he said.

"And?"

"They never last," he said. "They think they know everything when they really know nothing. They arrive late, take long lunch breaks, and leave early. Oh, and they want to get paid more than I earn and have three months off in the summer, plus time off for other holidays twice a year."

I had no idea what a Pandora's box I had opened with my suggestion.

"If that wasn't enough they're slow learners and want to solve everything with an app or 'machine learning' that will make them millionaires overnight. So, I have more work every day. I do my best, especially when it's for marshals like you who rely on the tech to stay alive." He set a box he had been holding on his desk. Inside, I could see part of a badge. "You manage fine without your badge for most situations. These new functions are exceptional because without them it's almost impossible to catch a speedwalker in a city without arousing suspicions."

"You know me so well," I said.

It was true. I used my badge as backup, where other marshals relied on their badges for most of what they did. I had learned to be self-reliant early in life and it worked well for me. My aunt and uncle had taught me to make the effort to do things right instead of rushing and always searching for short cuts. If I needed to go somewhere, I studied a map instead of reaching for a GPS. If I wanted to know the time, I relied on my internal clock and glanced at the sky before looking at my watch.

He smiled as he said, "Yep. Speaking of knowing you well.

You look much better. How are you feeling?"

"Great," I said.

"Are you hungry?" he asked.

"Not really," I replied. "I think my stomach is confused since I left Paris in the middle of the night. I need to get home. You know Marla. She'll give me a ton of notice or none. Can you walk me through the basics?"

"Sure thing," he said, standing next to me and extending his hand for my badge. I handed it to him. "You have to use the sub function key."

"Which one is that?" I asked. He showed me how to find it. "And now?"

"You press that key and the on button at the same time," he said, inviting me to do it. "To follow the speedwalker's movements on a pop up display you use the usual pop up function key." He pressed the function key and the display opened before us. He pressed the function key again to close it. "I assume you might be in public, so it's best if you learn how to observe the movements directly on the badge."

"There—"

"I know what you're going to say," he interrupted me. "I have a speedwalker simulation ready so you can try the feature now. It's not exactly the same, but it should be close enough to give you an idea of what to expect."

"You're a genius," I said, meaning it. I swear he stood taller and his eyes shone brighter than before my compliment. "And, I don't even have to wait three days."

He laughed. The happiness on his face reminded me of how much we used to enjoy each other's company when I had been at the Marshal's Academy doing my advanced training before I was assigned to Paris, before I had met Iaen. It seemed like a lifetime had passed. An hour later, we hugged good-bye, and I went home the same way I had arrived. The method wasn't my favorite, but it was fast.

I had been gone less than twenty-four hours, but my

apartment seemed empty. The instant I made noise, Ceri came to greet me, wagging her tail and looking up at me. I was happy to see her. I lifted her off the ground unsure of how she would react. Although I had seen Francois carry her that way on a number of occasions, we didn't have that kind of bond. Or maybe we did because she snuggled up against me and let me pet her, closing her eyes when I ran my hand over her head.

"It's nice to be home," I said, noticing night had fallen. "I bet you're hungry."

I carried her to the kitchen and set her down so I could rinse out her bowls. As soon as I placed fresh water in her bowl on the floor she walked over to it and drank her fill. She did the same with the food.

"I'm sorry I wasn't here to feed you sooner," I apologized as she ate. "I'll take you for a walk when you're done."

When we returned from her walk I showered again and climbed into bed. I was exhausted. No sooner had I fallen asleep than the ring on my badge woke me. A second later, the doorbell rang. I was half asleep, but I grabbed my bathrobe and went to the entrance, assuming one of the neighbor's children's friends was at my door by mistake. It happened every so often that they knocked on my door. Ceri followed me.

Eager to return to my slumber, I opened the door as I asked, "Who is it?"

Marla, grinning from ear to ear, replied in a half song, "It's me."

That woke me up. I hadn't had the energy to clean. The apartment was a mess.

"Hey, you, what a nice surprise," I said, mustering a smile of my own to welcome her as she embraced me in a giant hug. "Come in."

"You look tired and sleepy," she observed as she bent down to greet Ceri. The poodle had wagged her tail fast and circled around Marla's feet as soon as she had seen my friend. "It's not that late." Glancing at her watch, she added, "It's just after midnight. Did you get my message?"

Rubbing the sleep from my eyes I struggled to wake up. It felt like 3 a.m.

"Uh, no," I said. "I was out most of the day yesterday for work. I must have missed it. When did you send it?"

"Right before I arrived at your door," she said, the grin back in full force like a too bright sun.

"Now I don't feel bad for missing it," I said, striving to keep from becoming annoyed at her. She had told me she would be visiting over the weekend, even if she hadn't pinpointed the day and time. That was an effort for her. Left to her usual approach she would have shown up unannounced at my door. Except for work, where she had little choice, Marla was impulsive and never planned far in advance. "I'm thrilled you're here. Is Mike joining us?"

"No, he dropped me off and had to head back right away," she said.

"I don't have much to offer, but we can have a glass of wine," I said.

"Don't worry, I know your fridge is usually empty," she laughed. "I came to see you. Mike is always rushing, you know. It wasn't a wasted trip though. We had a romantic dinner in that gourmet place with the woman chef you told me about. Remember?"

"Vaguely," I replied, not wanting to dwell on the restaurant memories. It had been a while back when Iaen had been alive. He had been friends with the owner. He had sold her several modern art pieces. She had prepared a special menu for us one night. A pang of sadness threatened to take over my mood. I shook it off, focusing on Marla's evening instead. "How was it?"

"Dinner was fantastic," she said, her eyes widening. "The décor is kinda dowdy like something my grandmother started and never finished." I remembered the dark red walls and muted colors. Before I could ask about the menu, she went on, "The service was hot and cold. As long as the food is nice I can forgive uneven service. Plus, they were friendly. Mike walked with me to your building, but you know him. That was a lot of hours in one place. By then, he was ready to burst with the need for speed. He said if he can, he'll pop in over the weekend."

Great, I thought, another last minute arrival to look forward to. My face must have shown what I was thinking because Marla squeezed my shoulders and said, "Don't worry about it. And, don't worry about tidying up your place. I don't care about that. I'm full of energy. I'll give you a hand."

I kept a clean home, but when I was busy, most of the time, it got messy. It was common for laundry to sit unfolded until I pulled it out when I needed it. I piled dirty clothes in the hamper until I had nothing left to wear. Recycling bottles accumulated, too, until I had no choice but to drop them off at the city's huge bins a few blocks away.

Marla started picking up empty cartons from the table as she made her way into my home. Ceri, who had been watching her, and I followed her inside. I was glad she was back. She was like the offspring of a ray of sunshine and an energy drink, full of optimism and spunk. Ceri's tail wagged.

Once she cleared the living room, dining room and kitchen, she opened the refrigerator and gasped. Hadn't she just had dinner? Ceri stood by her feet as if waiting for a treat. Marla glanced down at the canine saying, "The only food is yours, sweetie. How does Danni manage?"

"All right already, I've been busy," I said. "I eat out or buy takeout. I was going to go to the express grocery store before you arrived, but you beat me to it."

"The one that reminds me of Las Vegas?" she asked.

"That's the one," I said. "If you're hungry, I'm sure there will be something open. I'll go get you whatever you want or better yet come with me. We can even take the pooch. What do you feel like?"

"A snack would be fine," she said. "Let's go to the supermarket."

I dressed and grabbed money and my badge. No sooner had I thought of Ceri's leash than she stood by the door wagging her tail. The first minimarket was closed, but ten minutes later we found an open express market on the Boulevard Saint Germain. I imagined the nearness to the university campuses ensured customers at all hours.

The three of us walked in. Sometimes I was forced to leave Ceri tethered at the entrance, but at that hour nobody noticed her. The aisles were empty, except for a shaggy-haired man with a strong urine smell that made my stomach turn, who was staring at the potato chip section as if his life depended on the choice he made. Marla walked ahead while I picked up napkins and paper towels.

Marla's voice made me turn in her direction. It was the enthusiasm more than the words that attracted my attention.

"Perfect," she said as if she had discovered a new continent.

When Ceri and I reached Marla she was cradling three bottles of expensive champagne in her hands. That would blow my budget for the month, nay longer. The express marts had the highest prices. They knew people paid little attention when they were shopping at the last minute or under stress for finals.

"Who knows how long they've sat on the shelves. Besides, I know a place with fresher products and better prices," I said in the gentlest tone I could muster. "There's even a shop that specializes in champagne. Their prices are probably just as high, but they have lots of choices. We can go there tomorrow."

"I want some bubbly tonight," she announced, placing two bottles in the shopping wheelie we had brought from home. I had grabbed it at the last minute not expecting we would be buying that many items at that hour. Seeing how it was almost full, I was glad I had. "I'll get these now, and we can go to the other places tomorrow. Some chocolate and strawberries. Do you have bubbly glasses?"

I shook my head from side to side. Marla picked up her pace until she found a package of six champagne glasses, which she placed in the shopping wheelie.

"We can pour it in wine glasses," I said. She scrunched her nose in disapproval. "Remember we'll have to carry anything that doesn't fit in the cart."

That didn't slow her down. When two young men entered our aisle, moving in slow motion, I pulled Ceri out of their way. Marla continued browsing the shelves while we waited.

"Yeah, I know," she said without getting upset by my reminder. "I've been down this street, literally, before."

"Okay then, get whatever you need and we'll figure out how to get it home," I said, hoping she would be satisfied soon.

Marla was wealthy, her parents were anyway. I was on a budget, less so since I had a salary bump from my acting head of the Paris marshals office job, but still a budget, but I still felt obligated to cover all her expenses while she was my guest. I wasn't sophisticated or knew about high society etiquette like she did, but I had learned good manners as a child with my parents and later at my aunt and uncle's home. With most people, I couldn't care less. Marla was my friend so I made a special effort. Although I didn't want to cramp her style, I also couldn't afford to eat and drink the way she did.

"We're getting married," she blurted from where she was standing in front of the wines.

"Who?" I asked in a less than brilliant moment.

She laughed, giving me precious seconds to think.

"Considering what you do for a living you seem rather clueless," she replied. "Who do you think?"

Marla and Mike had been together for more than a year. It shouldn't have surprised me, except she had never given me a single clue as to the progress of their relationship. Some days, she was head over heels for Mike, and other days I wasn't to mention his name in front of her. And, I was too focused on my own life to give it any thought. I recovered as best as I could.

"That is wonderful," I said, speaking slowly and emphasizing the final word; walking to where she stood and hugging her. Hugging was her style more than mine and I figured she would welcome the embrace. Although I was tired I made myself express interest and enthusiasm. She hugged me back tighter than I would have expected given her thin frame. "Congratulations. Did you set a date? Will you have a big wedding? Tell me everything."

That made her smile return. Ceri wagged her tail, looking up at the two of us.

"Yes, we're getting married at my uncle's French villa," she said. "I want you to be my maid of honor."

She stopped, waiting for me to answer. Although I was surprised and touched, I doubted I was the right choice.

"Me?" I asked. "I don't know the first thing about being a maid of honor. Are you sure?"

"One hundred percent," she said, nodding and circling me in a small dance. "You're my bestie. You'll figure it out. I know you will. When you set your mind to a task, you give it your all."

Her eyes had a fierce expression I knew well. It was the one she wore when she had made up her mind, and nothing shy of a hurricane would sway her.

"This isn't about my willingness to do the job," I said, knowing she wouldn't change her mind easily. "I would bend over backward for you. You must know that. But—" I searched for the right thoughts so that I could find the matching words to explain that I wanted to be there for her. "I don't know anything about that girlie stuff you like so much."

She squinted in response as if to question what I was saying.

"Yeah, don't give me that look. You know what I mean. For

example, I don't know anything about wedding dresses, don't care, don't want one."

She squinted further until her eyes were narrow slits.

"I think they're a huge waste of money, a dress you spend a small fortune on only to wear once in your life. I don't even wear dresses, period. The only item of clothing I care about at all are my boots, and that's because they're comfortable not because they're fashionable."

She held her head at a stiff angle. She was undeterred, but I continued making my case.

"And, I've never organized a bachelorette party, never been to one. Weddings aren't my style. Shouldn't you have a friend who is wedding-oriented at least?"

"I don't want anyone else," she replied as if that took care of the questions I had raised. "Tell me you'll be there, by my side, on the single most important day of my adult life."

The thought made me uneasy to say the least. I wanted her to have the best marriage ceremony possible. What if I messed up? What if I wore the wrong clothes, invited the wrong friends to the bride to be events, made poor menu choices?

Her shrieky voice startled me, "Danni, please I need to know that if I freak out the day of the wedding you'll be there to hold my hand. You're the only one I trust."

"I'll think about it," I said, letting out a breadth I had been holding.

"Yay," she said, her eyes moist with tears.

She hugged me. I was too startled to hug her back. Ceri barked, drawing my attention down. I had been so absorbed I had stepped on her foot. I lifted my boot and pulled her up into my arms, rubbing her tiny toes to make the hurt go away. Marla pet Ceri and cooed. In the end, she insisted on carrying Ceri home while I drove the grocery cart. It was just as well because when we left the shop it was drizzling. That kind of rain was common in Paris. It seemed to be so light as to almost not be wet, but after a while of walking in it I found myself soaked and cold.

Chapter 25

Marla tucked Ceri inside her leather jacket so she traveled home in comfort and style. Happiness beamed out of her as if she radiated it from her pores. It made me glad for her. I hoped life with Mike would be everything she wanted. She yakked the whole way back about how wonderful he was, how she couldn't wait to be married and other marriage related nonsense until I tuned her out.

When I heard her say, "Tomorrow we're meeting my uncle for breakfast" I turned to her.

"It's 2 a.m. now. Do you mean this morning or tomorrow morning?" I asked, hoping for the latter.

"Does it matter?" she asked, flashing me a devil may care grin. "Now, we're going to open one or both bottles of bubbly, the chilled one first, and toast until the sun rises. Then we'll figure out the rest."

I was beaten. There was no way I would turn her down. I kept quiet in the hall of the building. Given the late hour, I wouldn't put it past my neighbors to complain if we were loud.

"Whatever you want," I said once we were inside my apartment.

"Don't sound so defeated," she said, setting Ceri on the floor. The prissy poodle was dry. The two of us were not. We removed our wet shoes, leaving them by the front door. "It'll be fun. You'll see. Being a maid of honor will be—"

I interrupted her, "Whoa, I haven't said yes yet. I agreed to think about it, that was all."

"We both know you'll do it," she said in an upbeat tone, slipping her free arm around my arm. "Take your time, but later this morning when we meet with my uncle, I need you to focus and take charge. I don't want his wife, who doesn't like me much, to highjack my wedding. Okay?"

I nodded, knowing she was right. I would help plan her big day as best as I could. She had been such a good friend to me for many years. She had put her life on hold when Iaen had died unexpectedly to be with me. She never asked for anything. The least I could do was repay her by agreeing to her one small, well ginormous, request.

"You have family members like your mom who would do a fabulous job," I said. "Why me?"

Marla's mother owned an events company. She orchestrated gatherings to celebrate wealthy people's special moments for a living.

"Because you're my friend," she said. "My mother would turn my wedding into an opportunity to drum up business and she would make a big splash."

"I thought you wanted a big splash," I said.

"Not really," she said. "I want to share our special day with my friends and family and Mike's. I want beautiful memories, not a commercial event filled with a bunch of my mom's clients." She was talking a mile a minute. "I know you'll have me at heart. And before you ask, yes it helps that you're in France. Wait until you see my uncle's chateau."

"What? A chateau? I thought it was a villa," I said, convinced the task would be daunting no matter how sweet she sounded.

"Tomato, tomato," she said, pronouncing the words with American and British accents. "He calls it a villa. I call it a chateau. It's a stunning property that used to belong to one of the king's advisors back in its heyday. He has poured a ton of money into restoring it authentically, hiring the best artisans, buying original furnishings whenever he can find them and period pieces if he can't. I met the guy who was in charge of the project. He's an art historian. It has a moat and everything."

"Oh boy," I said, making her smile show teeth. Eager to think about something else I asked, "Want to change into dry clothes? I can lend you a pair of pants and a t-shirt while yours dry."

"Yeah, thanks," she said, following me to the bedroom. She opened my dresser and pulled out one of my sleeping T-shirts. It was extra-long with a tiger on the front. "This is perfect. I'll pour us some champers while you put away the groceries."

Twenty minutes later, we were sitting in the living room in low light, toasting her upcoming marriage to Mike and nibbling on cheese crackers and olives we had bought at the mini supermarket. As soon as the pale yellow liquid dropped to half a glass, she reached for the bottle she had chilling in an ice bucket and refreshed it. I had forgotten I had an ice bucket.

"Did I show you my ring?" she asked, extending her ring hand in my direction.

It was difficult to make out details in the low light of the room. When I leaned in to admire it, she removed it from her finger and gave it to me.

"Wow! It's the size of a small kingdom," I said, knowing she loved jewelry.

"It is, isn't it?" she said as I handed it back to her. "We chose the stones together and had the goldsmith make the design similar to a ring Mike's grandmother lost during the war. She was delighted. She liked it so much I started to worry." I made a face, rolling my eyes up to the ceiling. "I might be exaggerating, a little. The center stone is colorless and near perfect."

"I don't know much about diamonds, but aren't colorless stones outrageously expensive?" I asked.

She almost glowed with pride when she replied, "I haven't seen the final bill, but yes, Mike got carried away. His mother ordered a matching bracelet as a wedding gift to me. She said she wants to spoil me."

Our conversation meandered from her wedding plans, Mike, and her parents to her uncle's villa and back. Iaen came up more than once, and I changed the subject to avoid the sadness that usually followed any thoughts of my deceased boyfriend.

Chapter 26

I'm not sure how, but we drank two bottles of champagne before dawn. While Marla showered, I took Ceri for her walk. When I got back, I showered.

"We have twenty minutes to get to the Club," I said in a loud voice so she could hear me in the bedroom. "You ready?"

"Just a minute," she yelled back. "I'm covering the bags under my eyes with concealer. Want some?"

"No, thanks," I said, dreading arriving late even though it was Marla's uncle waiting and not mine.

Twenty minutes and many more attempts to leave on my part later, we headed to the front door, where Ceri watched us leave. Of course, we were late.

Her uncle was seated at a table for four, facing away from us. Marla placed her index finger over her lips, indicating her plans to surprise him.

"Uncle Archie, sorry we're late," she said, bending down to hug him. "It was Danni's fault."

Her mischievous laugh during a rare moment of quiet in the posh dining room, filled half the space. When he turned in our direction, I saw a phone in his hand against his ear and neck.

A smile without teeth split his lips apart. He held on to the phone with a tight grip.

"Hello, ma chérie," he said, extending his cheek for the customary double cheek greeting between close friends and family members. She obliged. He pointed at the vacant seats. "Sit, sit."

"This is my friend Danni, who I told you about," she said, attempting to introduce us, but he had resumed the phone conversation and wasn't listening to her.

She turned to me and was about to say something when our

server arrived. After he set down the two glasses of unsolicited bubbly, he had brought he greeted me and I introduced Marla. He had been on vacation on her previous visit to Paris.

"I heard about you from your uncle as well," the server said. He was good looking and fit. His uniform was a smidgen too tight compared with other servers. I couldn't be sure, but I had the feeling he was flirting with her. "Welcome to Paris. The champagne is brut from Epernay, on the house. Here is the menu. The day's specials are listed on the small loose sheet."

She paid no attention to the leather bound menu. As she watched, the server and then her uncle, I fished the list of specials out of mine, handing the paper to Marla, who covered her smile by appearing to study it. Seeing her on the edge of laughter made it difficult to keep my composure. I coughed to mask my mirth.

"I recommend the smoked, wild caught Alaska salmon," he said. "I understand you're celebrating a special occasion." She nodded her agreement. "In that case, I propose some French caviar."

She glanced at her uncle for his input, but he was still on the phone. She turned to me.

"Will you have some?" she asked.

"Sure," I said, unwilling to rain on her parade by turning down her caviar offer.

I had tried caviar once and found the salty fish eggs icky. Archie's voice had risen so much, I wondered if someone would ask him to lower his voice.

"Don't look so excited," Marla teased.

"I've only had caviar once, but it was really salty and fishy," I replied.

"I promise this will be completely different," the server said. Addressing Marla, he asked, "We have Beluga in 250 gram and 125 gram tins, 800 or 400 euros. Which would you prefer?"

"Hmm, I don't know if my uncle likes caviar," she said. "As soon as he's off the phone, I'll ask him." She glanced at her uncle, whose voice had dropped to booming from supersonic. He was so engrossed in the conversation he paid no attention to her. "That might be a while. Go ahead and bring the small tin. If we eat it, we can order another one."

We toasted Marla's future nuptials while we browsed the menus. When the server returned with the caviar, served on a bed of ice with bite size mother of pearl spoons and tiny pancakes, we were ready to order. Marla had Belgian waffles, and I had a vegetable frittata. Her uncle had ordered before we arrived. It was another ten minutes before Archie hung up.

"I'm glad you went ahead and ordered," he said. Eyeing the caviar, he smiled and reached for one of the spoons, piling it high with dark gray caviar. I was surprised it wasn't black. "Excellent idea." Marla got a spoonful before he pounced on the remaining fish eggs. She mouthed sorry to me when the server took away the empty dish. "Bring another one," her uncle said to the server as he was walking away. To Marla he said, "Tell me all about the wedding."

"Uncle Archie, meet my friend Danni," Marla replied. He accepted my extended hand, his eyes boring into me. "Danni, meet Uncle Archie."

"Archie. It's a pleasure," he said. "Marla speaks highly of you."

She did? Given my family name, I had no idea she spoke of me to her family at all. I felt a rush of heat and was certain I was blushing. I didn't recall Marla ever mentioning him. I wasn't sure what to reply, so I mumbled something that might have sounded like thanks.

"You're the marshal, right?" he asked.

Marla answered for me, "Yes! She's the head of the Paris office."

"Acting head," I corrected her.

"I'm very proud of her," Marla said. "She's my best friend."

Oh boy, there was more blushing. I wanted to say she was my best friend too, but it seemed lame. As I was at a loss for words, I said nothing.

"That's nice," her uncle said. If he knew of the blemish on my family's reputation, he didn't mention it. What a relief. "Is Michael joining us?"

"He prefers Mike," Marla replied. "No, he couldn't make it, but he says hello. We love the idea of having it at your cha-villa. Can we pick any dates we want?"

"Of course, we'll close it to the public so you can have the place to yourselves for the day," he said. "Better yet, Beatrice suggests you spend the night before and the night of the wedding there. She, we think it will make things easier for you."

"Beatrice is my uncle's wife," Marla explained. "He went to school in the US. She's one hundred percent French. She couldn't be here because she has an opening this weekend in Italy. She's a sculptor."

"Would you like to see it?" Archie asked.

"Absolutely," Marla replied for both of us. "We would love to."

"You've never been?" I asked Marla.

"I was there when I was a little girl, but I don't remember much," she explained. "It was closed for renovations for years. After that, I was busy at the academy. I couldn't make it to Beatrice's birthday party last year. Visiting France from California is harder than I thought."

"It looks a lot like it did when you were a little girl," Archie said. "We've done our best to restore it to its glory days." Turning to me, he added, "We used to live there. It was built before Versailles, and it's been in our family for generations. The government considers it a historic chateau. The costs of preserving it as an earmarked building, combined with socialist taxes were so high, we decided to open it to the public to produce revenue for the upkeep."

"Will it be full of tourists?" she asked.

"Although visitor traffic peaks on the weekends, I doubt it will be too crowded," he replied. "This time of year, there are fewer travelers than in the summer because of the chilly weather and rain. It won't matter. Visitors are allowed in only sixty percent of the buildings." I thought that was a lot. At that moment, the server brought our breakfast, including the additional caviar. "Of that, they may visit fifteen percent independently. To see the rest, they must book a guided tour in advance. The private tours generate additional revenue and help us protect the antiques and reproductions from occasional acts of vandalism."

The smell of food reminded me I was hungry. Before I could take the first bite of my frittata, Marla handed me a mother of pearl spoon filled with caviar. The temptation to turn it down faded when I saw the eager expression on her face. I took a deep breath before placing the tiny and perfect eggs, not a single one was broken, in my mouth. The flavor was not what I had expected.

"Nice, right?" she asked. "I think of it as the flavor of the sea."

That was a more poetic description than I would have come up with, but it was apt. And it had just a hint of salt. I still felt bad for eating the eggs of an endangered fish. I kept my thoughts to myself.

As if hearing my thoughts Marla said, "Don't worry. The caviar comes from a farm."

Before I could ask about it her uncle spoke, "I arranged for us to have lunch on the estate. You can drive down with me and stay until tomorrow if you like. There are plenty of rooms and I'll be spending the night."

"We would love to stay, uncle, but we can't today," she said.

"I thought you might say that," he said. "I would've done the same when I was your age. You can catch a train back tonight. I have a meeting with some elected officials I can't miss. You can have the run of the place while I'm gone. When I return, we'll have dinner together. After that, my driver will take you to the station."

Many, if not most, Weeia were well-off and some were filthy rich like Sébastien, so I had seen a fair share of upscale homes because of work. Some of Iaen's friends lived in great comfort, and we had been invited to dinner at several tony homes. I had never visited a friend's private family chateau.

Whatever had upset Archie earlier didn't disturb him during breakfast. He kept his voice at a normal volume, asking about Marla and her relatives, Mike and his family. I didn't mind that they did the lion's share of the talking. I took advantage of the opportunity to observe Archie. He wore a suede jacket in khaki over a collarless shirt in the same color. He also wore black pants and loafers in similar color leather as my boots.

Although there were no famous brand labels on his clothes, I could tell from the fabric and the style they were custom made rather than off the rack. He had medium brown hair, thinning in an uneven pattern on his crown and was clean-shaven. Fine lines ran around his mouth and his eyes. I guessed he had been a handsome man in his youth.

When he rose to his feet, I confirmed my estimate of his height. He was about six feet tall and fit. I guessed he jogged or played a sport. I caught a whiff of his cologne as Marla and I walked past him on our way out of the dining room. It was subtle yet masculine. I wasn't a big fan of commercial perfumes, but his I liked. Although it was unlike Iaen's for some reason it reminded me of him. I gulped, pushing away the thought before it saddened me too much.

When the valet brought Archie's car around, Marla climbed into the front seat of the most elegant car I had seen close up. It was a Bentley. I walked around to the seat behind Archie so I could see her face during the drive. The valet chased after me, opening the door before I could reach for the handle. Inside the car was spotless. It smelled of leather. I sat down, distracted with the vehicle. Marla was texting so I was alone with my thoughts.

As we left the Isle Saint Louis where the Club was, I watched to see what road he took out of the city. If I wasn't mistaken we were heading south.

When she noticed me looking at the highway signs she said, "We're going to the Seine-et-Marne Department." My blank expression made her elaborate. "It's named for the Seine and Marne rivers. The most famous landmark is Fontainebleau, as in the forest and castle of Fontainebleau."

"I've heard of the castle," I said.

Since Marla and her uncle began discussing family members I didn't know I tuned them out. I wanted to enjoy the drive and the car, watch the scenery out my window. Despite my good intentions, my eyes wouldn't stay open. I leaned back in the most comfortable car seat I had sat on and fell asleep.

Chapter 27

I woke up annoyed. Marla's gentle shake roused me from a deep slumber. I had been dreaming about her wedding and her uncle's estate. For some strange reason in my dream gnomes were hell bent on crashing the party. Marla's smile was wide.

"You slept the whole drive," she said.

"Sorry," I said. "I hope you're not embarrassed that I fell asleep in your uncle's car."

"Only a little," she said. After an awkward pause, she continued. "Besides, it rained. On the plus side, it was the first time in years we chatted without interruptions. He's an interesting guy."

"How so?" I asked, regret at having disappointed Marla and missed out on the scenery during the drive, mixed with curiosity about her uncle, waking me up.

"I'll tell you later," she said. "My uncle is waiting to show us around."

I stretched my arms and neck and got out of the car. The sky was gray and the ground wet. Puddles peppered the gravel parking area. There was no sign of her uncle. A uniformed man approached us.

"Where are we?" I asked.

"In Nancy, a village in the department I mentioned to you earlier, remember?"

"Seine-et-Marne," I said.

"Yep," she said, sounding distracted.

When the man reached us, he handed each of us an umbrella before removing one of several suitcases from the trunk of the luxury vehicle and taking it with him. That was when I noticed it was drizzling. Around us there were several buildings. It was the back of house rather than the main gate.

A sign pointed to the museum entrance, public bathrooms, cafeteria, golf cart rental, and gift shop. I wondered which building housed the private rooms reserved for the owners.

"Ready?" Marla's voice interrupted my thoughts.

"Sure," I said, stretching my calves.

Moments later, we were in the main building, where we caught up with Archie who was dishing out instructions to several staff at what appeared to be the museum front desk. Somewhere along the way, he had added a green scarf to his ensemble, which he was removing as we arrived.

The drab gray of the worn and wet exterior was a sharp contrast to the beauty inside. Although ornate high ceilings, carved wood doors, fine fabrics, and period furnishings weren't in my wheelhouse, with Iaen, I had learned to appreciate history. I wanted to see some of the details, but Archie moved faster than I would have liked. After passing through five rooms at the speed of a bullet, I lost track of what was what and its historic significance. I stopped listening, because I couldn't keep up. That was the king's room, next the queen's room, the library and on it went. As best as I could follow in previous centuries landed nobles were required to have accommodations worthy of a king and queen at the ready in case the royals wanted to overnight on a whim. Only one monarch had ever spent the night there.

Two hours later, my feet were beginning to ache and I was numb with the chateau minutiae. I couldn't care less which pope, minister or royal had spent time there in what year. Where I was getting crabby Marla was full of energy and enthusiasm, listening to Archie's every word and asking questions.

"This would be a perfect location for the reception," she announced as we entered a marble rotunda with expansive views to the estate gardens and water fountains.

"You could have the reception in the garden if you like," Archie said.

Marla's eyes focused on the exterior view. I followed her gaze. Muted green stretched as far as I could see. There were manmade ponds, statues, water features, and elaborate gardens in every direction. Narrow paths, where a few open golf carts roamed, meandered through the estate. There were countless puddles in the paths like the ones in the parking lot.

"What if it rains like today?" I asked, causing Marla's smile to fade.

"We'll move it here," he offered with the ease of a practiced salesman. He placed his hand on her shoulder in a reassuring gesture. "We rent the grounds for special events during the warmer months. Our staff supervises everything. They even organize some of them. I'll personally make sure we have back up plan in case of showers."

Another hour of high speed walking, interspersed with inspections by Marla of a room she liked or a feature she didn't, passed by. I was ready to pull my hair out or better yet pull someone else's if I didn't get a cup of coffee and somewhere to sit soon. To my chagrin, we had stood in the same location for a long while and neither of them showed any signs of slowing down. My feet screamed for a break. Before I took any drastic measures I would regret, I leaned against a wall.

"Don't, please, don't touch that wall," Archie said in a commanding voice. "That wallpaper was carefully restored by expert artisans at great expense."

Of course it was. Everything in the castle was valuable, historic or both. The entire place might as well be made of sugar.

"Sorry, I didn't know," I mumbled, afraid I would say something I regretted. I breathed deep and let the air out in bits before speaking again. "I could use a cup of coffee. Is that possible?"

Archie responded in an amiable tone, "Certainly."

He removed his smartphone from his pocket and ordered

coffee. Ten minutes later, when we turned a corner to yet another hall of historic significance and I saw a bare wood table with a pot of coffee and three fancy cups and saucers, I could have yelped for joy. There was also a tray of dainty butter cookies. I could have eaten them all, but I didn't. Score one point for me.

Our short stop allowed me to recover my good mood. I was thankful for the rest I had when we paused in the kitchen to meet the chef. In general, I was more interested in meals than in history. I was only willing to dedicate so much attention to food preparation, details about ingredient sourcing and characteristics, and serving styles.

Marla, on the other hand, appeared riveted when the chef explained his fondness for local sourcing. Once he began describing the pains he took to purchase mushrooms from a community expert who foraged in the Fontainebleau woods I zoned out. Archie's phone rang and he stepped out to answer the call. I armed myself with a bland smile and sat in the nearest chair until they had exhausted their conversation. Marla sounded so excited. I was happy for her, although, I remained convinced I was the least ideal friend for the task at hand.

Ninety minutes later two staff members served us an elaborate lunch in a private dining room with antique dinnerware. I felt better after the meal although the wine pairing did little to keep me awake. We spent the rest of the day visiting more of the chateau inside and out until I was ready to scream. Even in the light rain the grounds were as impressive as the interior was pretty. By the time we returned inside, our clothes were wet. Dinner was even more elaborate than lunch and with two additional courses, I counted. After dessert, we moved to a cavernous room with a huge stone fireplace where we had after dinner drinks and petit fours.

I was dreaming of going to bed when Marla announced we were ready to head back to Paris. Archie must have heard my sigh because he offered espressos. I said yes to a double espresso before he finished the sentence. Marla had one too.

"Call if you need anything," Archie said as we climbed into his pristine Bentley, handing me his business card.

His driver took us to the train station. While we waited in the warmth of the luxury vehicle he bought our tickets. I was too tired to protest when he escorted us onboard the Paris bound train. Only once we were seated did he leave. Marla's energy seemed boundless.

I heard her say, "Off white and peach would be perfect colors for—" just before I leaned my head against the seatback chair and closed my eyes to nap. Every so often I opened them, looked at Marla, around our compartment and closed them again while she rattled on, "Mike will like—"

I felt like I had dozed off seconds earlier when she shook me, saying, "Our station is coming. You're not sleeping, are you?"

"How can you think that?" I asked, rubbing the sleep out of my tired eyes.

She laughed. At least she wasn't mad at me.

"I doubt you heard anything I said the whole way here," she replied. "We settled on fall dates." I raised an eyebrow. "Before it gets too cold. When we get back to your apartment I'm going to write it down on your wall to make sure you save the date."

The train was almost empty by the time we got off past midnight. It was raining again and the dim night lights cast an eerie glow on the train station.

"While you were in the arms of Morpheus, Archie texted me that he had organized a transfer," Marla said as we made our way down the platform.

"That was nice of him," I said. "It shouldn't be difficult to find a taxi at this hour, but you know when it rains there are no cabs."

Marla greeted a woman, dressed in a black suit with a white

blouse and flat shoes, who held up a sign with my friend's name. The woman said her name, but I didn't catch it all, something like Sandrine. I couldn't hear her last name. She asked if we had luggage, taking the bags of goodies the chef had gifted us from Marla's hand and leading us away from the central hall.

"Please wait here," she said. "I will bring the car around."

"We can walk. Is it far?" Marla asked.

"Two blocks away," she replied, popping open an umbrella I hadn't seen and walking away at a fast clip. "I'll be back in two minutes."

True to her word, she returned before we could miss her. Beads of water fell off the polished black exterior of her new looking luxury sedan. I braced myself for the smell Paris transport vehicles always had, a mix of colognes, food and body odor. Inside it smelled like nothing. The interior was spotless.

"I can offer you water, coffee, champagne," the woman said before taking her place behind the wheel.

"If it's chilled, champagne be would great," Marla said. Marla laughed when I stared at her in amazement. "A glass for my friend too."

"I'm humbled by your staying power," I said. "I don't think I can."

"Of course you can," she said. "We're celebrating. Besides, we don't have to drive and we don't have to be anywhere tomorrow morning. We can sleep in."

The woman opened the trunk of the car and within minutes handed each of us a crystal glass of sparkling pale liquid. She also set plates of nuts and tiny pieces of deli meats in a tray between us. Marla took a sip.

"It's perfectly chilled," she said to the driver. "I've never seen that brand."

"I buy directly from a family producer," the driver said. "Do you like it?"

Without hesitating, Marla replied, "Yes, it's better than nice."

"I guess I have no choice," I said before taking a sip of my own. "It's delicious."

The ride was slow and unhurried. Every so often the driver would point to a famous landmark. I was enjoying the bubbly and snacks so well and listening to Marla's incessant chatter so it took me longer than it should have to notice we were across town from my apartment. When she pointed out the Eiffel Tower I brought it up.

"There's no universe in which this is the way to my apartment," I said. "What are we doing all the way here?"

"I was asked to show you the best of Paris by night," the driver said. "To do that I'm circling around the city and at the end I will drop you off at the address of your choice. I thought you knew. Would you rather we do something else?"

I looked at Marla, who was chugging the champagne and had polished off the tray of nuts. She was riding a wave of happiness.

"What would you like to do?" I asked her. She shrugged. "I'll take that as you're happy to continue doing what we're doing."

"Do you have more nuts?" she asked the driver before answering.

"Yes, but it will be necessary for us to stop," she said, waiting a moment for Marla to nod her agreement, she turned onto a quiet one-way street.

It took her moments to retrieve a box from her trunk. She refilled our glasses and refreshed the trays with more of the same. After our stop, Marla took photos with her smartphone at every opportunity and of every monument or landmark we passed, posting some on social media and sharing a handful with Mike.

"That was a fun surprise," Marla said as we arrived in front of my building an hour later. Although she was under the influence of the bubbly she walked unaided. She handed the driver a tip adding, "I love Paris at night with the lights twinkling. You made my night special, thanks."

I didn't see how much she handed the woman, but it must have been a generous tip and in cash because the driver wore a bright smile when she thanked my friend. She hadn't smiled during our drive. As she drove away, she was still smiling.

Once we got upstairs, Marla lay down to rest. I took Ceri for a much deserved walk. It felt like only minutes had passed when Marla woke me up by playing loud music with a repetitive beat I didn't recognize and didn't care for. She swayed to the rhythm like a fish swimming in a typhoon.

"That is so annoying." I said as I rose. "Shut it off, please."

"Not a chance," she replied, dancing and singing somehow to the unintelligible lyrics. She raised the volume. "You're capable of going back to bed. Don't you need to walk Ceri?"

"Yes, I need sleep," I moaned. "I just walked Ceri."

"That was hours ago," Marla said above the music.

"Okay, okay," I said, pushing the sleep away from my eyes with my knuckles while searching for the source of the music without success. "I'll get up, but please lower the music before my neighbors knock the door down and call the police."

"I've heard their loud music many nights," Marla said. "How come they can have it and we can't?"

"One," I began and stopped when she scrunched her nose and raised her lips together in disagreement. "Two or three of the neighbors play music loud enough to hear inside the apartment. It's not fair to the others to make them suffer."

"It's not suffering," she replied. "Upbeat and innovative, is what the music reviewer of some publication you have never heard of said about the band and their sick beats."

"Whatever you say as long as you turn it off," I begged. She wasn't giving in so I offered another solution. "How about you play it, softly please, when I take Ceri for her walk?"

"Agreed if you take her within the next five minutes," she

said, grinning at her victory. "You jogging?" I shook my head. "We can have breakfast somewhere when you get back."

I dressed and was out the door with Ceri in tow in seven minutes. Marla started playing the music again as I closed the door. She was waiting for us when we returned.

"I talked to Archie and everything is set," she said as soon as we entered. "He set aside the entire chateau for our wedding for the Thanksgiving dates we picked." She twirled like a ballerina in her socks. "Mike is onboard, you're confirmed, all close family members said yes. The only answer remaining is Mike's best man and we're pretty sure he'll be available. Wee!" She twirled again. "Oh, and Archie recommended a great place for Sunday brunch. He made reservations for us already. It's in a five-star hotel so you might want to change." I nodded, surrendering to the request and heading to the bedroom to do as she suggested. She and Ceri followed me. "Hurry up! I'm starving."

"How about you do something useful while I change?" I said.

"Sure. What do you need?" she replied.

"It would be great if you give Ceri fresh water, clean her bowl first or she won't drink it, and a couple of scoops of her doggie breakfast," I said. "You need to clean the breakfast bowl with soap or she won't touch the food."

"Really?"

"Yep," I said, pulling black pants on and searching for a clean top that would pass Marla's inspection.

I opted for a basic black t-shirt with a designer scarf I had bought at a consignment shop sale. I was hoping the scarf would distract her from the plain ensemble. It worked like a charm.

I'm not a fan of buffets and brunch was in part a buffet so I was doubtful about the meal. We could have gone to the Club, where we were almost guaranteed great food, service and privacy.

"What is it with you and buffets?" my friend asked as we neared the restaurant.

"They tend to be noisy and crowded and the food is more about quantity rather than quality," I explained in a neutral voice.

I hadn't asked why she liked them. It was annoying that I had to explain why I didn't.

Parking was a nightmare in central Paris and I didn't want to spend an hour circling the building in search for a parking spot so I handed my car keys to the valet with trepidation. As we entered, I caught a quick glance at the lunch and dinner menu posted in a glass covered display case. The set menus cost three hundred and fifty euros per person not including beverages. Based on that, I estimated our meal would be pricey. Brunch would have to be on me as Marla was my guest and we were celebrating. I always paid in cash to avoid overspending. I had a feeling the cash I had on me would not be enough. I was glad I had a credit card for emergencies.

The restaurant, elegant and refined, was on the ground floor of a former private palace. The dining room walls and ceiling were covered with pretty al fresco paintings from the nineteenth century. Since there were few tables, it was quiet in the dining room. A uniformed woman greeted us with much deference and escorted us to our table.

Looking around the dining room and its frescoes Marla exclaimed, "It's beautiful." I couldn't disagree although it wasn't my kind of place. "The tablecloths and napkins are perfect, like they pulled them out of the wrapper this morning. The silverware and crystal ware are lovely." She touched the petals on the two exotic orange flowers in a crystal vase on our table. "I think these are hibiscus flowers."

"My name is." I couldn't make out what the man in his fifties, who I hadn't seen until he spoke, said as soon as Marla stopped speaking. "I'm the manager. I'm pleased to welcome you. May I offer you a beverage?"

"Black coffee," I said.

"I'll have a cappuccino," Marla said after a moment.

An instant later, a young woman appeared with a silver tray with both coffees and a variety of sugars and sugar substitutes.

"There is a buffet and you may also order from the a la carte menu," she said, handing each of us a leather bound menu the size of a digital tablet and setting a large tome on the table. "There are several champagnes, tequilas, and sakes on offer as part of the buffet as well as mimosas made with fresh squeezed orange juice. The wine list is here should you prefer to order a bottle of wine or a cocktail."

Marla was lost in her menu for what for her was a long while. I browsed both pages of the printed menu, skipping the extensive wine lists.

"Do you know what you're having?" she asked. I shook my head. "Let's check out the buffet."

She waltzed over like a princess who had a restful night. Tired, sleep deprived, and hungry I followed feeling more like the ugly frog. There were breads and pastries, cereal, yogurt, cold meats and fishes, caviar, cheeses, salads, fresh and dried fruit, champagne and alcoholic drinks.

"I'll have my appetizer from the buffet and mains from the menu," she announced as she picked up a plate and served herself. "Not sure what I'll do about dessert."

I followed her example, piling my plate high with bread, cheese, and every other item that looked appetizing. I headed back to the table, assuming she was behind me. When I looked toward the buffet, she was speaking with one of the staff. Moments later, she returned.

"Everything okay?" I asked.

"Perfect," she said. "I don't know much about sake so the server is picking a sake for me, for us."

"No way am I having sake for breakfast," I said, meaning it.

"It's not breakfast, it's brunch," she said, ignoring my

refusal.

I was about to answer when a staff member arrived with two small glasses, setting them on the table. I let my head hang in frustration.

"Come on, at least taste it," she said. I took a sip as she watched so she would leave me alone. "And?"

"It tastes like alcohol," I said. She took a sip of her own. "And?"

"Not bad," she said, but her facial expression told me she wasn't sold on the beverage. She took another sip. "I would rather have more champagne."

She pushed the glass an inch away from her dish. As if by magic, the same server reappeared.

"May I take those away?" he asked.

"Yes, thank you," Marla answered.

"Would the ladies like some champagne instead?" he asked. "I would be only too glad to bring it for you."

Marla beamed at the offer, responding the instant the man asked his question, "Yes, please, one for each." I widened my eyes at her. Turning to me, she said, "Oh, come on. I don't want to drink alone."

"Fine," I said.

"Make that a bottle," she said to the waiter. "Very cold."

"Of course. Which champagne would you like?" he asked. "Shall I bring the wine list?"

"That won't be necessary," she said. "It would be helpful if you or the sommelier pick."

"Very well, ma'am," he said.

After ordering salmon for mains, Marla made another trip to the buffet. I ordered a ham and cheese omelet and resisted a return to the buffet with all the self-control I could muster.

When I thought she had finished she asked, "Cheese?" and headed back to the buffet. I succumbed to temptation and sliced a generous piece of Roquefort for myself.

"Well?" Marla asked while we awaited our espresso

coffees at the end of the meal.

"Uh, not bad," I said.

"It was better than that," she said. "You can't possibly find fault with any of it."

I could when I saw the bill, I thought. I would suck it up and deal with the overpriced treat after she had gone. I wasn't about to tell her it would throw my budget off-balance for more than one month.

"I'll admit I was hesitant when I saw the buffet," I began.

"But," she poked.

"Only cold items were in the buffet and the staff kept it clean," I said. "The hot dishes were made to order the way I like it."

More prodding followed, "Go on."

"I see you're enjoying this. They clearly used top drawer ingredients. It was delicious," I said.

"I'm not surprised," she said, grinning. "Archie's a gourmet. He doesn't just like to eat. He likes to eat well. He knows the restaurant manager, which is how we're in the best seats and how he got a table for us at the last minute."

"Great," I mumbled, still worried about the dent it would make in my wallet.

"Oh, and it was Archie's treat," she said. "We don't have to pay a cent. He even took care of the tip."

Relief flooded me and I let out a breath I hadn't realized I was holding. Marla was more relaxed than I had seen her since we had graduated together at the Marshal's Academy.

"I'm sure it wasn't inexpensive," I said. "That was nice of him."

"Meh, he has money to burn," she said. "It wasn't what it cost that I like. It's that he made the effort to organize it."

His assistant probably took care of it. I kept the thought to myself to avoid spoiling the experience for her.

Just after the coffee arrived, one of the staff rolled a trolley with sweets next to our table. There were caramels, hard candies, marshmallow like *guimauve*, and bite size chocolates. We each selected four items. They were exquisite.

"Your taxi is ready whenever you are," one of the staff informed us after we had polished off the espressos and sweets.

"We didn't order a taxi," I said.

"Perhaps there is a mistake," Marla added in a diplomatic tone.

"I'll find out," the server said.

Before he could leave the table the manager returned to ask if we had a pleasant brunch and explained the situation.

"Your uncle ordered a private transfer for you," he said. "You may leave your car here as long as you like."

"Outstanding," Marla said. "In that case, let's go."

Later that afternoon, once brunch had settled in my stomach, and taking advantage that Marla was napping, I went for an extended jog along the Seine. When I returned, she was still crashed out, so I left her a message and took Ceri for her walk.

We were at the butcher buying food for her when I received a text from Marla saying Mike had arrived early. He was in a hurry, and did I mind if she left before we returned. And, just like that, the exciting weekend ended.

Chapter 28

My apartment seemed empty with Marla gone. Even when I pretended not to care, her enthusiasm and joy of life were contagious. Although I dreaded my duties as maid of honor, I was happy for her and Mike and wished them the best.

To keep from feeling lonely, I decided to practice using the new speedwalker tracking feature on my badge. First, I had to learn how the feature worked in a safe place. Under normal circumstances, I would have practiced at the office. But, I had been avoiding my boss. He had called several times, but he had only left one voice mail message. He didn't sound like he was on my side. The best I could hope for was that he was neutral.

Given the open hostility of the out of town task force toward me, it would be best to stay away. If Sébastien had still been a marshal I would have called him, with permission from Celeste. Considering that I lived in one of the toniest neighborhoods in a historic building, my apartment was large. For training purposes, it was less than ideal. I couldn't think of a safer or more private place so I decided to begin that very evening.

Once I knew where the speedwalker was I could open a portal using the new app to get to the location in a hurry. It was easier said than done, because while I could traverse the city that way, whoever was on the other side of the portal could see me and my apartment. It sure would be embarrassing to have to arrest myself for exposing the Weeia.

I tried opening and closing portals in places where there would be no people or cameras at that hour. As a safety, the portal wasn't supposed to open in solid matter. I attempted to get it to do just that to make sure it wouldn't. It didn't. I had to be careful to stand back or the momentum of the portal would suck me to the other side right away. That happened twice before I figured out to stand to one side. After a half dozen trials, I thought I had the hang of it.

I liked that with some finesse on my part, it was possible to adjust the height and exact location of the opening. That meant I could check out a location before jumping through. It was possible to place the doorway in a barren alley, empty corner of a park or another safe spot. When necessary, I could use my illusion to cloak my arrival so no one would see me.

I slept well that night, knowing that even if the odds were against me by a huge margin, with the aid of the Daughters, I had a fighting chance. As I fell asleep I thought about my parents. I had resisted the temptation to find them, as my father had asked when we had last spoken. It was heartbreaking to know they were out there and I couldn't see them. It was better than not having parents, I told myself as sleep took over.

I continued avoiding my boss. Monday morning while I was jogging, rather late on the United States East Coast where he was, he left a message letting me know he had heard about my argument with Rupert's father. Since he sounded unhappy, I decided to wait as long as possible before calling him back.

I wondered how things were at the office. I took a chance and called Madame Marmotte. I figured there was a fifty-fifty probability she would tell Rupert about my call.

"Marshal Metreaux," she answered. "You're smart not to come in. The task force members are rude, crude, and useless. You're not missing anything, believe me."

"Oh?" I asked, surprised at the less than hostile reception.

"They haven't shown their faces in here yet," she said, sounding self-satisfied as if she had predicted they would fail. "MGV is making an appearance nearly every day. It's as if he's laughing at them. A birdie told me they were out late drinking last night. Before you ask, I can tell you they haven't found anything useful, not a single clue. They're becoming irritable, and that's putting it mildly. If they continue this way, I may arrive late on purpose."

When I heard the part about arriving late, I almost laughed out loud. Since I had been in Paris, she had only been at work on time once or twice when she wanted to impress Francois.

"I'm–" I began.

"Never mind the situation here," she interrupted me. "Are you making any progress?"

"Not yet," I said, anticipating a tongue lashing she never delivered, better to quit while I was ahead. "Call if you need me."

I was fooling around with my badge, still testing the new feature, when the light indicating the speedwalker had been detected lit up. I was nervous. I wasn't ready to use the feature. I wasn't prepared to capture him.

Pushing aside my insecurities, I figured out the location, the Place de la Concorde. It was a busy intersection near the United States Embassy and the Jardin des Tuilleries. In the middle of the day it would be crowded with tourists and Parisians, not ideal.

"Where could I drop in unnoticed?" I asked myself.

When she heard my voice Ceri perked up. After a minute, she settled back down. As I was watching her, it occurred to me that there could be a way to pass by unseen. As I observed the plaza through a pinhole opening high above the street I saw multiple police vans with lights flashing enter the traffic circle in the center of the Place de la Concorde. Figures in military garb, armed to the teeth, poured out of the vehicles. They took control of the area, blocking access to cars and pedestrians.

While everyone was focused on them I created an opening large enough for me to traverse behind a cluster of trees in a construction zone that had been cordoned off and was vacant. To be double sure I cloaked myself invisible. I concentrated so much on the place and remaining unseen that I didn't pay enough attention to the actual spot. I tripped over an ankle level mound of debris, falling into the mud.

I was brushing off the mud when I noticed a black-clad figure with a balaclava covering its head heading toward the place from the opposite side at high speed in a motorcycle. After an unexpected loud crunching noise, the figure flew over the handlebars, landing on a pile of garbage that hadn't been there when the figure ran into the obstacle. Out of nowhere, MGV appeared and looked over the fallen person as the police arrived. In the blink of an eye, MGV disappeared. Before he did, I locked my app on him, hoping it would work. As I watched, a red dot zoomed across the map on my badge, making its way across miles of the city in a flash until it stopped.

Chapter 29

While the police arrested the motorcycle rider, I stayed hidden watching the dot. It was moving at a normal speed like a person walking. Using my app, I opened a viewport high above ground level at the new location. There was a small park with a traffic circle around it. There was something familiar about it. I had been there before. It was near Kate's place. Sure enough there she was, carrying a bag and drinking out of a takeout cup. There was no one else in the area yet the dot kept moving. We had all assumed MGV was a man, but we had never seen a face. Was Kate MGV?

I made my way to the park, keeping invisible and watching where I landed to avoid falling into another mud puddle. Fifteen minutes later, I rang the buzzer to Kate's apartment.

"It's Danni," I said when she asked who it was.

"What a lovely surprise," she said. "Come on up."

The few minutes it took me from the building entrance to her floor stretched out. A million questions and doubts crossed my mind. Was it possible that my app was malfunctioning? I didn't think so. As much as I didn't want to arrest Kate the more I reflected on the possibility of her being MGV the more it rang true.

I raised my hand to ring the bell, but before I touched the button she opened the door. Her face was flushed like someone who had just exercised. She welcomed me in with a warm smile. The expression on her face was relaxed and open. The scent of dried lavender in her home reminded me of my previous visit. There were fresh yellow and blue flowers in a vase in the living room behind her.

"Is everything okay?" she asked.

"Not exactly," I said, searching for the right words to accuse her of the crime and not finding them.

"Have a glass of wine and tell me how I can help," she invited.

"It's not a glass of wine sort of visit," I replied.

"Oh?"

I hated to be there. For once, I didn't want to do my job. I didn't care about getting credit or the one-upmanship of beating the taskforce, none of it mattered. One of the few Weeia friends I had in the city was in trouble and I was going to confront her. I decided if she made a run for it I wouldn't pursue her.

Once I made the decision I relaxed and the words stumbled out, "You sure had me fooled. I never would've guessed in a lifetime." Her brow furrowed and her mouth opened a bit in a puzzled expression. "You're MGV."

She took two steps back, watching me with concern. I remained where I was. I didn't want her to get spooked or worse yet hurt.

"What are you talking about?" she asked. "Why would you say that?"

"I watched you at the Place de la Concorde," I said in a neutral tone. She didn't deny it. I had hoped she would. I took a deep breath and let it out slowly. "You took down the guy in the motorcycle, moving so quickly I could hardly see you." A shy smile spread over her lips. "Wow, it's been amazing every time. And all the while I never suspected. I thought MGV was a man, how silly of me." Her shoulders sagged. "I followed you here."

"Are you a speedwalker?" she asked. I shook my head sideways. "How did you find me?"

I wasn't supposed to discuss the app with anyone so I didn't mention it. As silence enveloped us concern spread over her face, fine wrinkles formed around her eyes and her lips tightened.

When the tension became too uncomfortable I said, "The details don't matter."

"Does the taskforce know?" she asked.

"They will," I said.

"I don't want anything to do with those goons," she said.

"You know them?" I asked, surprised.

"I've watched them," she said. "They're a disgrace."

Anger threatened to take control. To keep it in check, I forced the tension out, counting to ten.

"Why did you do it?" I asked in a louder tone than I wanted to use.

"I didn't mean to," she said, looking at the wall behind me, remembering. "I was so sad and full of rage. It was such a senseless death." I noticed she hadn't said her husband's name. "I didn't know what to do with my life. I couldn't return home. Some of my happiest memories are here. The days we spent in Paris are among the best in my life. Coming here was a dream come true for both of us and we lived in a haze of joy. Leaving meant abandoning all that. The night he died it was as if someone ripped my heart out of my chest. I couldn't breathe, I couldn't eat, I couldn't sleep, nothing mattered." She focused her eyes on me. "You know. You understand."

I nodded. A long while passed. Neither of us moved.

"One day in the midst of my pain I discovered I had a new ability," she said. "At first I didn't want to use it. Curiosity and boredom drove me to try it." She shifted her feet. I let my weight rest on my left leg, eager to hear more. "The speed made me feel something. When I used my new ability the darkness receded. I didn't know anything about my skill and I didn't dare ask anyone, but every run improved my mood. I kept at it until I got good. It didn't take long. I had lots of hours to burn. I became convinced that fate gifted me a fantastic ability way past the usual age for new Weeia abilities to develop for a reason, to help others. I could say I happened upon a victim by accident. The truth is I went in search of one, knowing where I might find bad guys." She looked me in the eyes. "For the first time since my husband was taken away from me so violently, I felt alive. And, I've helped people. People who would've been hurt without my intervention are safe. As a marshal you must understand what that's like. You lost Iaen so you know that feeling of being adrift."

I broke my gaze away. I did of course. I also saw the problems she was causing, and I felt sorry for her. I was tempted to tell her to leave Paris. I could lose my job if anyone found out I had MGV and allowed her to go.

"Yes, but I trained to be a marshal," I said in a soft voice, avoiding the subject of Iaen. "It's my job." She opened her mouth. Before she could speak, I went on. "More importantly I don't make it easy for humans to discover our secret by running around in public rescuing them from criminals. That's the first Weeia law, you know that."

She nodded and glanced toward the door. If she used her ability I could track her and she knew it, but I didn't want to. I had a feeling she had guessed that.

"I'm in a very awkward situation," I said. "I want to help you, I do. You have made it difficult with your public appearances. All the hero worship you have fostered may seem good, but it places knowledge of our people at an awful risk. What were you thinking?"

"I wasn't thinking too much," she said. "I knew in the back of my mind it couldn't go on forever, but I was on top of the world. Helping others with my ability feels wonderful, and I've never been found. That has to count for something."

"You've been lucky," I pointed out.

"Yes, and it helped that the taskforce is useless," she said. She sighed. "The rest you know. Everyone assumed I was a man. That worked to my advantage."

"Did you drop off the note in my apartment, telling me where MGV would be?" I asked.

"Yes, I hoped it would give you an advantage and make your boss send the taskforce back," she said. "I'm sorry it didn't work. What happens now?"

"I'll have to take you—" an urgent text interrupted me before I could finish. I pressed the buttons to read the message as I said, "Hang on. I need to read this."

The origin of the message was unknown. It said I shouldn't report finding MGV to anyone and wait for instructions.

"That's odd," I said more to myself than to Kate.

"What's that?" she asked.

"Someone knows I found you and doesn't want me to turn you in to my superior," I said.

"Who?" she asked.

"I, uh, I'm not sure," I replied, feeling as baffled as I sounded. Although it could be Argus, I had a feeling I knew the source. "The ID display was *unknown*. I've never seen that before. I didn't tell anyone what I was doing. It's not as if it's easy to hack a badge. I don't even know if that's possible."

"Maybe I should leave," Kate said.

"I don't think that's necessary," I said, sounding way more confident than I felt. I was torn about following the instructions. "Whoever it is knows what's going on. They may even know our location. If they meant you harm, they would already be here."

I was anxious, wondering what it all meant. Kate looked like a cat about to jump off a ledge. The beep of an arriving text startled us. I almost dropped my badge trying to punch the command to read it. When I did I was somewhat relieved and also uncomfortable.

"Oh no," I moaned. "Not again."

"What?" Kate asked, her face twisted with concern.

"I can't explain other than to tell you we have received an important invitation," I said. "It's a good thing."

"If it's such a good thing why do you look like you might throw up?" she asked.

"I'm feeling a touch queasy," I said.

"Are you nervous?" she asked.

"No," I said. "Queasy. Anyway, I think we should accept."

"We? Is it for both of us?" she asked.

"Yes, I think so," I replied. "It's definitely for you and I'm to come along." A portal opened behind Kate. We wouldn't have the leisure of many minutes to discuss it. "Okay?"

"You're a good cop, Danni," she said. "I trust you. If you think we should go—"

Seeing the portal shimmer, I interrupted her, "Sorry, but we have to go now. Brace yourself."

"For what?" she asked.

"It's hard to explain," I said. "I can tell you, it upsets my stomach in a big way." Worry lines appeared on her forehead. "We can hold hands if you like."

I offered my hand and she took it. I pointed behind her and as she turned she gasped.

"Okay, here we go," I said, taking a step toward the portal.

I heard a swoosh at the same moment that we were sucked through. When we landed in Maine, I tumbled. Seconds later, I spilled my dinner.

I wiped my mouth and turned away from the mess to rise to my feet. The first thing I saw was the old man's bare feet and robe. I waited a moment to make sure the world had stopped circling around me.

I heard a voice in a familiar British accent say my name, "Danielle Metreaux." She may have said something before that when I was busy emptying my stomach.

It was Celeste. Kate stood next to her, watching the woman. Her expression was unreadable. I imagined she was as surprised as I had been on my first visit.

"In this plane we are independent of Weeia authority. The Elders and marshals have no say here," Celeste said.

Once again she spoke without contractions, enunciating every word and lingering on them as if the act of speaking brought her pleasure. When I got to my feet Kate turned to me.

"Are you all right?" she asked.

"I will be," I said, still wobbly. "You?"

"I was a touch uncertain when we arrived, but I'm okay now," she said. "Celeste kind of introduced herself and was just explaining where we are."

"We have been following your progress," Celeste said, looking at nothing in particular and making me wonder if she was talking about Kate or me.

Kate's eyes were fixed on Celeste. I understood. I had been the same way the first time. There was an ethereal quality about the Daughter of the Descendants. When she moved she glided rather than walked. I had been expecting praise, but there was none.

"It is not safe for you to remain in Paris," Celeste said.

If Kate found it offensive that the stranger was interfering in her life it didn't show. She seemed calm.

"Except for Danni, Marshal Metreaux, no one knows who I am," Kate said.

"There are many searching for you," Celeste said. "Had Marshal Metreaux not found you today, it would have been a matter of hours or days before they found you."

I had a feeling she wasn't referring to the taskforce only. I shrugged in response to Kate's glance.

"In the nicest possible way, why do you care?" Kate asked.

Kate was much politer than I was. She reminded me of Sébastien, who moved in elite circles and managed to be serene and say pleasant things when I didn't. Some days, I wished I had that polish and patience.

Celeste's answer was not helpful, "We seldom interfere in matters of The Elders or the marshals."

"I get that, but why are we here?" I asked, emphasizing we at the end of the sentence.

"Yes, I see what you mean," Celeste replied. Turning to Kate, she said, "If you continue your unsanctioned activities in Paris, you are almost guaranteed one of two results; Argus will capture you or the marshals will. Your ability is uncommon, if not rare, and you have become proficient at using it. Allowing the marshals to punish you or allowing Argus to press you into their service would be a great loss. In the case of Argus, it might tip the balance in their favor. We do not support that outcome."

"I understood part of what you said," I said to Celeste. "Kate, did you follow all that?"

"Not entirely," she said. "How can I help you?"

"It is I who can help you," Celeste said, waving her hand in the air.

"Okay, I'll bite," Kate said. "How can you help me?"

"On behalf of the Daughters I am offering you asylum," she said.

Kate and I looked at each other. She appeared as confused as I was.

When it was obvious Celeste was done talking Kate asked, "I appreciate your offer. What does that mean exactly?"

"It means you will be safe from all parties who wish to capture you," Celeste said.

"Where?" Kate asked.

"We will provide a place for you to live," Celeste replied. "Rest assured it will be comfortable and well beyond their reach. You may continue to use your abilities within your abode."

"And in exchange what will you want from me?" Kate asked.

"We have no particular requirements, except that you keep knowledge of your new home to yourself and your abilities away from the parties who currently pursue you and their allies or representatives," Celeste said.

"I could leave Paris," Kate said.

Her complexion was pale, her eyes guarded. She was beginning to realize she was cornered. I felt bad for her.

"You can, but now that they know of your existence, they

will not rest until they capture you," Celeste said. "It may take years. You will have to remain vigilant always. Their reach goes far, and Argus respects no rules."

Kate began to pace. I couldn't blame her.

"I've heard rumors of Argus," Kate said. "I thought it was nonsense. Are you saying they're true?"

"I do not know what you have heard," Celeste replied.

"I heard Argus is a conservative wing of Weeia," Kate said. "That they believe they should rule the world and will stop at nothing. That they hire mercenaries, human and Weeia. Is that correct?"

"That is a rather fanciful description," Celeste said.

"Is it true?" I asked.

"It is partly accurate," Celeste replied. "Do you have an answer?"

Kate's calm appeared to fray. She opened her mouth and closed it without uttering a word.

"Won't they follow me here?" she asked.

"They cannot reach you here," Celeste said. "However, you may wish to close any affairs you have pending. You may not discuss this offer or your new residence with anyone other than Marshal Metreaux."

"I see," Kate said in a sad tone. She was silent for a while. When she spoke it was to me. "Danni, do you know Celeste well?"

"Not really. I met her recently," I said. "A friend introduced me to her. It was only with her aid that I was able to track you. I trust him so if he trusts her than I do, too. I believe her when she says you're in danger."

Celeste stood so still that for a nanosecond I wondered if she was a mannequin or a digital projection. I pressed down my desire to touch her to make sure she was a living breathing being.

"This is what I want to do," Kate said, her color returning to normal. "I want to go back to Paris to wrap up my life cleanly. Once I do, I'm willing to move here and accept your generous offer."

"Very well," Celeste said. "When you are ready, let us know."

"How will I do that?" Kate asked the question that was on my mind.

Celeste handed her a black sphere that resembled a marble. Kate rolled it in her fingers, turning it this way and that until she found a latch and pressed it. When we looked up Celeste was gone.

"Wow," Kate said.

"Totally wow," I said, wondering how we would return to Paris.

"Why didn't you warn me?" she asked.

"I swore not to discuss the Daughters or this place with anyone," I replied. "I had no idea—"

Before I could finish speaking, a portal opened in front of us. Kate stared at it and back at me.

"We better go," I said.

"Where will it lead?" Kate asked.

"Not sure, back where we were, I hope," I said.

An hour later when I stopped heaving, Kate and I sat down to talk. Her apartment was an odd mix of high end furnishings and flea market buys.

"Sit, please," she commanded. "Would you like a cup of coffee, a glass of water or something to eat?"

"Water," I croaked.

As she handed me a glass of chilled water she said, "I'm going to make one more public appearance before accepting Celeste's offer."

The cold water soothed my throat, which was sore from throwing up twice in less than two hours. It hurt a bit to talk, but not as much as I expected.

"Based on what she said it could be dangerous," I pointed out. "Are you sure?"

"Yes," she said in a confident voice.

"I can cover you," I volunteered.

"Naw, it would put your job on the line if anyone found out," she said. "I'll be fine though I really appreciate you offering."

"When are you going to do it?" I asked.

"I'm not sure yet, but soon," she said. "Don't worry, I'll say good-bye before leaving town."

Sure enough, two days later there was a report on the news about MGV. She had stopped saved two Japanese tourists from being mugged by knife wielding attackers. After that, she had given an interview to a well-known journalist. The interviewer was certain it was MGV because she had witnessed the superhuman's arrival and departure. MGV had only responded to questions submitted in writing prior to the meeting and posed for a single photo. She had to move on, she said, because she was ill. She would not be back in Paris, she announced at the end of the interview.

The next morning, I received a text from her suggesting we have lunch. I agreed right away.

Chapter 30

Perhaps because I was exhausted, when I arrived home I didn't notice right away that Ceri didn't greet me at the door. I turned on the light. She wasn't in her doggie bed either.

"Ceri, Ceri, where are you?" I called.

"Danni, don't be frightened it's your mom and dad," a woman's voice said from the living room.

My tiredness evaporated when I turned on the living room light to find my parents sitting on my sofa. The cushion prints on their cheeks and messy hair told me they had been napping. My exhaustion was replaced with elation.

"I promised we would do everything possible to see you again before leaving," my father said, setting down a digital reader and rising to greet me. "Sorry about breaking in."

"You can break in anytime," I said, grinning like a little girl. I had been sad for days, thinking I wouldn't have a chance to see them again. Having them both there was better than I had expected and a huge surprise. "If I can find it I'll give you my spare key before you leave."

Ceri jumped off my mother's lap when she got up. Considering she had never met my parents she was cozying up to them well.

"She's fussy," I said after we exchanged hugs. "I'm astonished she snuggled up to you so easily."

"She's been a delight," my mother said, bending down to pick her up. "I think she's lonely when you're out."

I could have kissed my father when he said, "I hope you don't mind that I took her for a walk."

"That's perfect," I said, meaning it. "Now all I have to do is give her water and feed her."

"I took the liberty of cleaning out her bowls and giving her fresh water," my father said. "I wasn't sure what she ate so I gave her some of my hamburger." My eyes widened. "She ate the first piece so I gave her more. She ate almost a whole one, minus the bread."

"She's going to be your friend for life," I said, feeling giddy to have my parents in my apartment. "So much for a guard dog."

It was a bonus that they and Ceri liked each other.

"I bet she would sound the alarm," my father said. "I heard your old boss is settling in well in Maine."

I was ready to reply that I wouldn't know because he hadn't asked about Ceri. Instead, I nodded. I didn't want to spend our precious time together discussing Francois. I had so many questions, I didn't know where to begin. My heart felt like it might burst out of my chest with joy.

I managed to ask the most pressing question first, "How long will you stay?"

"Through the night at least, longer if we can," my mother said. "Let's make the best of it. Do you have plans?" I shook my head. "Wonderful. We bought some food. If you don't like it, we can get something else. Your father and I will take turns keeping an eye on the perfume maker's house on the Ile Saint Louis."

Her eyes filled with tears, threatening to make mine do the same. She caressed my cheek as my father watched. Ceri looked up at us.

"Talking with you is so easy," I said to my parents a short while later. I was dreading their departure. "I would never have guessed we would get along so well."

"Nor I," my mother said. She turned toward my father. She straightened her stance. "Thierry, I'll take the first shift."

"Already?" I asked. "I had hoped to have you both with me for a little while longer."

"The danger for your friend is very real," my mother said. "We have been watching and it's clear someone is keeping an eye on his place. We've asked some colleagues to help with the shifts. Until they get here, we don't dare leave the perfume maker unprotected. The late night is too quiet for them to attempt a break in. That will give us a respite."

"I didn't know," I said, feeling guilty. "I can take a shift."

"Nonsense," she said. "You look exhausted. You can spend the off shift hours with us here."

"On condition that you two take my bed so you get some sleep," I said.

"Okay," she said.

I was thankful that she didn't ask where I had been or why I was spent. I appreciated that she respected my privacy. Even without knowing me, she could tell I needed rest. With that, she planted a kiss on my forehead and headed out.

The concern must have shown on my face because my father said, "Don't worry. She's tougher than I am."

The hours flew by as we talked. I was tired and wired at once. I remember falling asleep and my father covering me with a blanket before tiptoeing out of the room with Ceri on his heels. I heard my mother return and go to my room. I almost followed her to make sure she was staying. When I woke up hours later, my father was already awake. He took Ceri for her walk while I had a cup of coffee.

"I'm going jogging," I said when he returned. "Want anything?"

"I'll go with you, if that's okay," he said.

"Better than okay," I said.

I suspected he was being protective, but it didn't matter. I was thrilled to be with my father even if it was only for a short while. We took the stairs down to the river's edge. There were far fewer people in the lower level than on the street level and it was quieter. I wasn't a fan of chatting on the run and it seemed he wasn't either. I also liked the wide sidewalk there. We ran side by side in silence. Although my father's hoodie protected his identity and blocked me from seeing part of his face, every so often I noticed him studying me.

"Will you have breakfast with me?" I asked as we completed the final segment.

"Yes," he answered. "It's better if we stay at your apartment. We didn't see anyone watching it, but I prefer to be safe. I'll join you for a bit before I take the next shift. Your mom plans to spend the morning with you."

"Great," I said. "I have coffee and sugar, but otherwise my fridge is mostly empty. I thought we would pick up some groceries on our way back. We can get some bread and pastries, food for Ceri, and today there is a street market near my apartment."

"Lead the way," he said.

Remembering I was supposed to have lunch with Kate that day, I texted her asking to reschedule. She replied offering the following day as an option and I agreed.

We carried a ton of groceries between us. As we entered my apartment, leafy greens and baguettes stuck out of the top of the bags. My mother and Ceri greeted us at the door.

"Claire, we brought enough food for three meals and for the pooch," my father said after kissing her good morning.

"More like enough to feed an army," I said, laughing. "The only thing we're missing is Ceri's treats because the shop was closed." On hearing her name, Ceri's ears perked up. "And, he refused to let me pay for anything."

"Well done," she said. Turning to me, she took a bag that threatened to drop. "Let me take that for you."

I handed her two bags while I removed my shoes. Somehow, my father managed to remove his shoes without releasing any of his bags.

"I'll get breakfast going while the two of you shower," she announced.

At my father's insistence, I went first. I took my usual quick shower and returned to the kitchen to give my mother a hand.

"How can I help?" I asked.

"Keep me company," she replied. "Make yourself a cup of coffee if you want. Do you like eggs?" I nodded. "Is an omelet okay with you?"

"It depends," I said. "What's in it?"

"Eggs, ham, cheese, and some chives," she replied. "Okay?" I nodded my approval as I sipped my coffee. "Breakfast will be ready in ten minutes."

"I'll set the table," I said.

"Your dad did that already," she said "He tidied the kitchen, cleared the dishes from last night, took out the trash, and unloaded the dishwasher."

"Wow, he doesn't waste time," I said, admiring him.

"Given our lifestyle, we tend to be speedy and organized," she said, gifting me with a lingering glance. "We want to enjoy our day with you as much as possible."

"What time are you leaving?" I asked, dreading the answer.

"I'm trying to convince our colleagues to fill in for us so we can stay with you a little longer," she said. Her brows furrowed forming three fine lines on her forehead. "If that's not possible, we'll have to move on after your father's shift ends."

That was at the end of the day. My heart sank. My disappointment must have shown because she placed her hand on my arm in a comforting gesture.

"Let's make the best of today," she said. "I promise we'll find a way to stay in touch." I widened my eyes in disbelief. "It's dangerous, but now that you're a grown woman and a very capable marshal, we'll make it work."

I opened my mouth, intending to challenge her, to ask her not to make promises she couldn't keep, to remind her of all the years we hadn't seen each other, to accuse her of leaving me behind. The words died before they passed my lips.

As she was putting the finishing touches on the omelet she turned serious. She pushed a rebel strand of hair away from my face.

"Danni, we weren't exaggerating when we told you Argus is formidable," she said. "The most important part of our visit with you is to make you understand that. They're ruthless zealots who will stop at nothing in the pursuit of their goals. They lie, bribe, blackmail, torture, steal, kidnap, and murder all in the name of their sacred mission. Anyone who stands in their way is erased without hesitation. They're powerful and have ample resources. They have eyes and ears at top levels."

My mother had been so intense, I hadn't heard my father enter the room, so his voice startled me, "They're convinced as Weeia they're superior to humans and entitled to rule the world, literally. They have no respect for Weeia who side with humans. You're either with them or against them. There is no middle ground for Argus."

"They're also chauvinistic at their core," my mother said. "It's like we've regressed to the dark ages. According to their social mores, women, including Weeia women, are inferior to men. While they stop short of forbidding women to work, they say openly that women should obey men in all matters. What's even more surprising is the number of women among their ranks."

"It's so dated it sounds like something from a movie. What do they want?" I asked.

"World domination," my father said in a serious tone of voice.

"Surely, the marshals are dealing with them. How much of a threat can they be?" I asked.

"You would think that, but as we discussed already the marshals are compromised," my father said. "We're convinced Argus's influence among The Elders and the marshals reaches the highest levels. It's impossible to know who to trust. Be very careful, especially of strangers."

I wanted to mention Celeste, the Daughters of the Descendants and how she had mentioned Argus, but I had given my word. Although they were strangers, Ernie had introduced me to Celeste and the old man. He wasn't a stranger. I trusted him.

"I have to go," my father said after glancing at his watch.

He kissed my mother and then me and headed to the door.

Curiosity made me ask, "How do you know if someone is a member of Argus?"

"It's surprisingly easy and difficult simultaneously," he said, smiling. "That's why we're here."

"I know, to help me steer clear of the bad guys. I'm a grown woman," I said in a snarkier voice than I intended. "I can take care of myself. Besides nobody can be everywhere and hear everything, and no one is as evil as you make them sound."

Instead of insisting they were right my mother conceded, "Perhaps you're right. We have been after this particular boogeyman so long we might have convinced ourselves that it it's worse than it is."

We chatted a few minutes longer, but I felt guilty for snapping at her. She kept looking at her watch and seemed to only be half listening when I mentioned being a maid of honor at Marla's wedding.

"Sweetie, I need to go out," she said, getting to her feet. "I have to find out if our colleagues can cover for us. I'll be back as soon as possible."

I felt alone in my apartment. To avoid the emptiness, I decided to take Ceri for her walk and swing by the butcher shop.

"Life is good," I told Ceri as I got ready. "I caught MGV. Thanks to me she met Celeste and will be leaving town. Marla is getting married, and I'm happy for her. And best of all, my parents are alive and visiting us."

She looked up at me. As soon as I touched her leash, she wagged her tail.

"Let's go get you a treat to celebrate," I told Ceri, walking toward the Ile Saint Louis.

After we left the butcher shop, having escaped with the

most affordable order possible I whispered to Ceri, "Let's say hello to dad."

No sooner had I finished speaking than we heard a van speeding away down the center of the island neighborhood.

"How far can that guy go before the police stop him?" I asked no one in particular.

Ceri began barking, which was unusual. The vehicle threaded around parked cars until it slowed to a crawl and stopped next to where we stood, giving me a chance to see it in detail. The driver, a middle-aged man with black hair and a beard was sweating. The van itself had a coat of paint so thin I could see the logo for a local plumbing company beneath the white paint. That was odd.

The ringing of my badge made me jump. I was tempted to ignore it until I saw it was Madame Marmotte. She never called. Curiosity more than anything drove me to pick up.

"Are you near the perfume shop?" she asked without any greeting.

"You mean Mathis's shop?" I asked, wondering what she wanted.

"Drop whatever you're doing and go there immediately," she ordered, hanging up before I could ask why.

I thought of calling her back, but the shop was so close it would be faster to go there than try to convince Madame Marmotte to explain what was up. She might not answer if I called back. As usual the main street was crowded so I took the smaller side streets, which was easier and faster. The door to the shop was torn off its hinges and thrown aside. My heartbeat sped up. I didn't like taking Ceri inside, but what else could I do?

"In here," a familiar woman's voice called from inside. "Hurry."

As I approached, the voice I recognized belonged to Madame Marmotte. The figure lying flat on the floor was my father. Madame Marmotte was crouching down in an impossible position, holding his wrist in her hand. She pierced me with her gaze. In the back of my mind, it occurred to me that she seemed out of character, but my father's condition drew my attention.

"He was shot, in the liver I believe," she said in a matter-of-fact voice. "He's bleeding profusely." I looked around as if the pool of blood beneath him wasn't proof. "There's no time for an ambulance to arrive. If he doesn't receive care right now he's going to die."

"Get Danni," he moaned. His features were twisted in pain and his voice was a shallow rasp. The tanginess of the blood reached me. "She can help."

She turned to me, saying "You have a healing ability."

"What? No," I said before thinking about his words.

"He wouldn't say it if it wasn't true," she said. "Are you sure?"

"Uh, pretty sure," I said.

"Your father's life is on the line," she said. The intensity of her gaze belied her neutral voice. "I'm sure you have it in you. Can you feel it? Before you say it's not true, you must be completely sure."

I stared at her. She matched my stare and upped the ante. My father moaned again.

"How exactly can I do that?" I asked in a pleading tone.

"Take a deep breath," she instructed me. I did as she asked. "Count backward from ten, slowly."

As I counted, she took my hand and placed it on my father's while holding the other hand. I felt a drain on my energy like turning on a light switch. I knew the pull was real. In the same way I could read a book, I realized she was right. It was his liver, and the life was draining out of him. I also knew, by instinct, what to do, where to direct my thoughts to heal him. I repaired the artery and sealed the opening.

Chapter 31

I'm not sure if we were there a minute or an hour. I observed my father hoping for signs of improvement. Until his pallid color warmed Madame Marmotte remained silent. He didn't talk either. When his condition became better, I knew that, too.

"How?" I asked her.

"Did I know you're a healer? I can detect latent Weeia abilities," she said, her uncommon smile showing teeth. "It's not useful for much, but in this case it saved your father's life."

"How did you know he's my father?" I asked. "Are you one of the white knights I heard about?"

She scoffed. Shifting her weight, she jumped to her feet, surprising me.

"Since when do you have such agility?" I asked.

The Madame Marmotte of that day was unlike the woman I knew at work.

Ignoring my question, she said, "They took Mathis. It's lucky Susanna and the kids weren't here. Sometimes when she's working late if she can't find a babysitter on short notice they spend the night upstairs. They fled in a white van. Did you see them? Do you have any idea how we might catch them?"

"I might," I said, stepping away for a private conversation. I dialed Kate's number, willing her to pick up. "Someone I know is in trouble and I'm calling to ask for your help."

"Not a friend," she said.

"No, but I know him and I feel responsible because I'm in charge," I explained. It was more than that. Following a series of out of control freak incidents by Weeia, caused in part by Mathis's abilities, he had held his abilities in check, by order of the marshals. That was why he was still free and in Paris.

If Argus had taken Mathis, they could force him to do their bidding and that would be a huge disaster. I hated asking, but couldn't think of any other way to rescue Mathis. "He was kidnapped by bad people. I have to get him back."

"I've never dealt with kidnappers. What can I do?" she said.

While my mind raced to find an answer silence filled the room. In the distance, I heard an ambulance and children playing during their break from a nearby school. I became aware of the strong odor of perfume around me. I rubbed my nose without thinking. It wasn't a single fragrance. Bottled perfume in a variety of options was displayed in elegant boxes on cases against two walls. Testers sat on a glass topped table.

"I saw what could be the getaway vehicle a few minutes ago, less than an hour," I spoke the words as the solution occurred to me, halting while I strung the thoughts in my mind. "They couldn't have gotten very far in the heavy Paris traffic. Once they leave the city, I have no idea where they might take him or what they would do to him." My voice was louder than I wanted, but I couldn't spare the effort it would take to calm down. "The vehicle is distinctive. You may be able to spot it if you hurry."

Urgency ringed her voice as she said, "Tell me quickly then. I'll do what I can."

I did as she asked, mentioning details about the logo and the van I wasn't aware I had noticed until I told her. She asked a couple of questions before falling silent. Behind me, I heard Madame Marmotte talking to my father. I couldn't make out the words, but I could distinguish their voices.

"I'll be in touch if I find them," Kate said, hanging up.

I called her back. She answered right away.

"Wait, can you come here first?" I asked.

She sounded annoyed when she replied, "What for?"

I lowered my voice to make sure no one heard me, "So I can track you. That way, if you find them, I can catch up with you and take Mathis off your hands." She began to object and halted mid-sentence. As soon as she went quiet, I explained my plan. I wanted to scream at her to do what I told her, but she didn't work for me. I took a deep breath and let it out in several slow small exhales until I was calmer. "It's my job to rescue Mathis. You're supposed to stay out of sight. I'm not asking you to make a public appearance, just to find them. I can take it from there."

She didn't sound convinced, but she agreed. I sighed with relief. She was the best chance I had to locate Mathis. I would deal with her grumpiness later if I had to. For the moment, I went back to check on my father, hoping he was all right. He was sitting half upright against the wall with his eyes closed.

"How's he doing?" I asked Madame Marmotte.

"He's hanging in there," she said. "I made him as comfortable as I dared, and called your mom." Unlike the Madame Marmotte I knew, this one was businesslike, efficient, and moved with speed and confidence. Gone were the frail appearance, sluggish steps, and condescension. She showed no sign of seeing my jaw drop. "She's coming to get him. Let's hope she arrives before the police. There's no time to waste answering stupid questions. More importantly, we don't dare trust him in their custody. Argus has pawns within the high ranks of the French police."

"You called my mom?" I asked, too stunned that she knew my parents and had heard of Argus to ask a better question.

She walked to the door and looked out. She shook her head to say there was no one there.

"What was so urgent that you walked away from your father?" she asked in an accusatory tone.

"I don't have to explain anything to you," I replied in a harsh tone. In lieu of responding, she stared at me. She might have saved my father's life. She knew my parents and cared about them. The least I could do was answer her. The words rushed out of me, "I did everything I could for him. He seemed to be recovering." The door was open. Anyone who walked by might hear us. Taking a long breath, I continued in a lower tone of voice. "The kidnappers have Mathis. I called for help."

"Who?" she asked.

Before I had a chance to answer Kate, dressed in full MGV gear, appeared. I saw her eyes widen as she took in the broken door, pool of blood, my gravely wounded father and Madame Marmotte. Madame Marmotte stared at MGV. I signaled for her to hold any questions. MGV stepped to one side so that a casual observer passing the open space where the wood door had stood wouldn't see her. Her eyes focused on my dad. She showed no sign of recognizing him. I was relieved that she didn't know who he was.

"I think he's okay," I said to her, my voice shaking. I held my hands tight in an effort to calm down. It worked. The shaking was all but gone as I spoke again. "I'm dealing with this. You focus on finding the van. Remember, it's been recently painted white with the logo—" Her open palm toward me made me stop. She pointed to the door to let me know she was leaving. "I know the chances are low that you'll find them. Thanks."

I followed her out into the sidewalk, pulling my badge out and pressing the button to track her. I glanced around to see if any concerned citizens had gathered wondering why the door was missing.

"You would think someone would notice that the door is gone," I said as I stepped back inside.

"There's always a renovation project underway somewhere around here," Madame Marmotte replied. "People don't pay attention anymore unless something gets in their way. That's good for us today otherwise the police would have already arrived. If a neighbor did call, which is possible, they probably think it's a break in and they're taking their sweet time. Only terrorists and gunshots get priority these days."

My shaky voice returned when I pointed out, "They shot

him."

"I suspect they used a silencer," she said.

"Why bother?" I asked.

"Until they had their target they didn't want the police to show up," she replied in the same confident manner as before. "Your mom is here. She won't be able to park. While I tell her to wait find something to cover the blood. Use more of your, um, skills again in case it makes a difference. Between us we can get him up and out."

I did as she asked. I leaned down and touched his arm with my hand. As soon as I made contact, I felt his pain and distress. It freaked me out a bit, but I pushed down the anxiety and pulled on my new ability, seeking the best way to aid him by instinct alone. Navigating through his body, passing his arteries, veins and vital organs was like making my way through a room full of glass furniture without any light whatsoever, a false move and I could hurt him, kill him even.

"I'm better," my father said, startling me. "You're a healer. Did you know?"

It looked like he was going to make it. Joy and relief filled my heart.

"Not a clue," I said, tears streaming down my cheeks. "We were lucky that Madame Marmotte could tell. If it hadn't been for her—" My voice broke. I couldn't imagine losing him again. "We need to get you out of here. It's not safe. Think you can get up?"

He winced as he tried to move. I pulled my hand away to give him space. Madame Marmotte, followed by my mother arrived minutes later. Her face tightened at the sight of my father.

"Thierry, can you walk?" my mother asked.

"I, ah, I think so," he replied.

Leaning on my mother on one side and me on the other he got to his feet. I knew he was in pain, yet except for an initial grunt he made no sounds.

"Give me a second," I said as we neared the front door. "I'm going to create an illusion around us to make it appear normal."

Taking a deep breath, I concentrated until I could visualize the illusion. It would be easier to cover two of us in illusion than three.

"Open the back passenger door," I instructed Madame Marmotte. "Mom, you and I will get him in while I cover us in my illusion. Keep your voices normal. I will muffle them, but it's best if the tone doesn't stand out to passersby. I'll keep the illusion up for as long as I can while you drive off."

"That should do it," she said. Strain showed on tight fine lines around her eyes and lips. She pressed her upper arm over her face. It was the same motion I used to remove sweat when I jogged. I imagined she was removing tears. She lowered her voice as she spoke again, "Odile told me you saved him. Thank you."

"Don't thank me yet," I said, unsure of how much I had done. "Do you have someone to help?"

"Yes, if I can get away from here before the police arrive," she said, looking around.

Getting him into the car was faster and easier than I had expected. He sat upright, leaning his head back against the seat. He was pale and his breathing was uneven, but I thought he would recover. The acrid smell of blood made me gag. I wanted to get in the car and go with them. The thought of staying behind when I could protect them tormented me.

"Honey, Madame Marmotte tells me you want to go after them," she said. The strain, which had eased once we got my father in the car, returned to her face. There was no point in arguing. "They usually hire out the riskiest parts of the job to thugs. Are you packing?"

"Packing what?" I asked.

"A weapon to defend yourself," she said in a low voice.

"Uh, no, I just went out for a walk with Ceri," I said.

"Besides, I don't normally carry weapons."

Pulling a gun out of her pant leg, she said, "Take mine. You might need it."

With that, she hugged me tight for a minute before walking around to the driver's side and climbing in the car. I bent down and gave my father a kiss on his right cheek, the one facing me. As soon as I stepped back, Madame Marmotte closed the car door.

From inside, my mother said, "Be careful," before driving away. Tears poured out of my eyes as I watched the car move away. I wiped my face while I watched them inch forward to the intersection and out of my sight. I kept the illusion for as long as I was able.

"You look tired," Madame Marmotte said. Handing me a chocolate she ordered, "Eat this."

I took it, but didn't eat it. I pulled out my badge and stared at it. I was relieved to see the dot that indicated Kate's whereabouts was moving.

"We need to go inside so you can take down the illusion," she whispered.

"Okay," I replied, walking into the building. "Ceri, where is she?"

"She's fine," Madame Marmotte said in a soothing voice I had never heard. "She's in one of the bedrooms. Don't worry. I'll take care of the police and Ceri. Now, eat the chocolate. You've been using your ability a lot in a short period. You need to refuel before you head out."

All of a sudden I was tired. Although there were no chairs near us and blood stains littered the entrance I wanted to sit on the floor. It took a great deal of effort to move. I held the chocolate in my hand. She took the bar from my limp fingers and unwrapped it, handing me a large piece and taking a small one for herself.

"Her food," I said, not sure why.

"I have it," she said.

"It tastes like cardboard," I said.

"It doesn't matter," she said, placing her piece in her mouth. "The sugar and carbs will make you feel better. Trust me."

She was right. It was like air blowing into a balloon and making it expand. After a minute or two, I felt energetic, and my movements returned to normal.

"Better?" she asked.

"Yep," I answered, more confident than minutes earlier.

"Good girl. Now go," she said.

"Are you sure?" I asked, hesitant to leave her to face the cops on her own.

"Yes, I've got it under control," she said. "Once I clean up the blood all that will be left will be signs of a break in. I can deal with that easily. Thefts are everyday occurrences in Paris. There will be no reason for them to linger. They'll write down some information, give me a case number and be on their way. Go find Mathis."

I took two steps toward the door and turned back. She was already heading further inside.

"Madame Marmotte, please don't mention MGV to anyone," I said. "No one, not even my parents, know. You're the only person in Paris who knows I'm in contact with MGV or that I've solved the case."

I avoided using any pronouns on purpose. If I said "he" I was lying and if I said "she" I was giving away her gender. Kate's secret was her own. She had gone to great lengths not to speak. I wasn't about to tell Madame Marmotte that MGV was a woman, not a *mec* after all. She wasn't known for her discretion. It was a tall ask. I was bracing myself for an argument that never arrived.

She hunched down about a head in height and returning to the voice I knew well from work she asked, "MGV who?"

Relief flooded me. She was going to keep the secret.

"Thank you," I said over my shoulder as I left.

Chapter 32

I noticed the flashing lights before I saw the police vehicle as I headed around the corner. With more effort than I would have expected, given how mean Madame Marmotte had been to me since my posting in Paris, I resisted the temptation to return to face the cops at her side. I picked up my pace, walking north toward the Right Bank. Being familiar with the island was proving handy. Once again, I glanced at my badge, assuming Kate hadn't had any luck. To my surprise, the dot that represented her on the screen was stationary. I was wondering what that meant when she called.

"I sent you a photo. Is that the van?" she asked.

"That's the one," I said. "I'll be there as soon as I can."

Wondering where I could find a quiet place, I descended the stairs to the river level, which on the Ile Saint Louis was for pedestrians only. On weekends it was busy, but during the week and at that hour there were few people, save the occasional dog walker or homeless person. I walked until I reached the nearest bridge, praying none of the regulars who squatted under makeshift card box homes was around. To my relief, the space was vacant.

I crawled under the bridge and using the new feature on my badge opened a tiny portal to Kate's location from which I scouted a safe arrival spot. I wanted to call Kate, but I didn't want to give away my hiding spot to anyone who heard me. I took a deep breath and crossed over to the alley I had selected after double-checking I was alone. As soon as I arrived, I called Kate.

"I'm in the alley. Where are you?" I asked.

"I'm watching the van," she said. "It's not going anywhere soon. I'll find you. It will be quicker."

She found me in the blink of an eye. It didn't take long to

reach the van. I opened the back doors, hoping to find Mathis. Instead, it was full of painting supplies, dirty brushes, ladders, and buckets. I stuck my head inside. There was nothing else. The driver stuck his head out the door in protest.

"Sorry, wrong van," I yelled, shutting the doors and walking away.

"It looks like the van you described," Kate said.

"Yes," I said, unable to keep the disappointment out of my voice.

"I need something to eat," Kate said, heading toward a bakery.

I followed her into the shop. We bought several sandwiches, pastries, and fresh squeezed orange juice and sat on bar stools facing a tiny counter to eat. On a normal day, I had a good appetite. When I used my abilities, my appetite doubled. Within five minutes, we had polished off everything.

"That's better," Kate said. "Gotta go. I'll call if I find anything."

I wanted to know how my father was doing, but I had no way to reach my mother, so I called Madame Marmotte. When I got her voice mail, I left a message asking her to call me. She was notorious for not picking up messages, so I wasn't holding my breath that she would. Judging by the piles of garbage strewn around the streets, the graffiti-covered buildings and cars and the pungent smell of old urine I was in a seedy neighborhood. It wasn't an area I knew well, but it seemed to be near the red light district.

I walked south toward the center of town, searching for a café to wait for my mother or Madame Marmotte to call me with news of my father, or for Kate to ring with an update. I found a tiny place, which brought to mind the term hole in the wall. It had two tables for two inside an old butcher shop and three plastic stools in a wedge of sidewalk. I sat down inside, sharing a table with a woman wearing headphones, engrossed in her smartphone and nursing a cup of black coffee. I was so lost in my thoughts, worrying about my father and Mathis that the ringing of my badge made me jump a little.

"Found it," Kate said as soon as I answered. "Come quick."

"I'll do my best," I replied, hanging up.

I needed somewhere private to open a portal in a hurry. I studied the woman who had sold me my coffee. She wore her black hair in a no nonsense style and had elaborate tattoos on every piece of exposed skin. There were letters in foreign languages that I didn't recognize, buildings, people's faces, and animals. She wore a neutral expression and headphones attached by white wires to some device I couldn't see. I doubted there were public bathrooms, but it was worth a shot. To my surprise, the tiny café had a unisex bathroom and she explained how to find it. It was around the corner, past a faded green door and down a long narrow hallway.

Although she had said it would be unlocked when I turned the handle the door was locked. I heard muffled sounds and moments later, a young couple pressed by me into the hallway. Once inside, I locked the door behind me. It was half the size of the café and clean. After I took advantage of the opportunity to use the facility for its intended purpose, I opened a portal near Kate's new location, scouting the best place to arrive. Once I was ready, I unlocked the door and crossed over. Two minutes later, I tapped Kate on the shoulder, making her jump and yelp.

"It's a good thing there's nobody around," she said. I laughed. "It's over there." She indicated a parked van I hadn't seen. "I walked around several times. Unless someone is hiding in the back where I couldn't see, it looks empty."

She was right about nobody being around. It was a short one-way street without any traffic. I checked my badge. We were the only two Weeia in the vicinity. I walked up to the van and opened the door. It was empty, but I recognized Mathis's scent.

"I never thought I would be glad to come across that smell,

but today I'm so happy I could hug him," I said to Kate, who had followed me to the van.

"Do I have any idea what you're talking about?" she asked.

"I forgot you've never met Mathis," I replied. "He smells awful. It must have something to do with his body chemistry. I've never asked him."

"What? I thought he was a perfume expert," she said.

"He is, and more," I said. "Scents are his super power. And yet, he smells foul. Stick your nose in here, and you'll see what I mean."

She did. As soon as Mathis's odor reached her, she reeled back and winced, scrunching her face in disgust.

"How tragic for him," she said.

"I'm not sure he's aware of how badly he stinks," I said. "I've never discussed it with him in detail."

I shut the door as quietly as I could. We walked back toward where Kate had been earlier. "Any idea how long ago they parked?"

"Not sure, but I don't think much," she said. "The engine is hot. I haven't seen anyone else drive down the street since I arrived."

"Unless they're on foot there is nowhere to go but back," I said. "They could be changing vehicles around here."

"I can take a look," Kate offered. When I placed my hand on her arm to stop her, she turned to face me. "What are you thinking?"

I took another look at my badge, adjusting the setting for a wider range than before. There were two Weeia around the block. The upgrades were wonderful. I made a mental note to thank Ernie and Celeste.

"Sweet," I said. She gave me a puzzled look. "There are two Weeia and two humans a block from us."

No sooner had I spoken, than we saw a sedan pulling out of a garage into an alley, open at both ends. We could see it well from where we stood.

"Wait," Kate said, disappearing.

Seconds later, some old construction scaffolding that had hung at the far end of the alley, fell blocking the exit. The vehicle was too large to turn around, leaving two choices, return into the garage or reverse out of the alley toward me. It reversed. I waited, my mother's gun in hand, for it to reach me. As it did, I heard the sound of glass breaking near the car. Almost in the same instant, I saw the driver pulled out of the car by invisible hands, Kate's I assumed, and hogtied.

The car kept rolling backward until it swerved and smashed into the wall at the side of the alley, crumpling the back fender. The engine stalled. The only sound in the alley was the pinging of the motor and the car settling. My heart beat faster when the door of the car smashed open and a figure got out. My badge told me it was a Weeia.

All that noise would draw attention. Soon someone would come, call the authorities or worse yet, their Argus bosses. I didn't have the luxury of time. I sprang into action, reaching the figure as fast as I could and subduing him with two kicks. As soon as he dropped to the ground I collared him, dampening his Weeia abilities. While I was doing that, Kat must have disabled the second human. He was unconscious in the alley, his hands and feet tied.

"They're no amateurs," she said. "They're carrying military weapons and gear."

"The other one?" I asked.

"He ran away," she said, pointing to the back of the car. "Try there."

I hoped Mathis wasn't injured. I fumbled with the lock for a couple of minutes, my heart beating fast.

"You should go," I said.

She nodded and disappeared. I would have to leave her out of my report.

"Finally," he grumped when I managed to open the trunk and he recognized me. No it's nice to see you or thanks. "I thought they were going to get away."

"Are you okay?" I asked.

"I've been better," he said, his pungent odor reaching me as I helped him out of the back of the car.

I grinned for a second. For once, I was so glad to be close to the source of the stink.

"We need to leave," I said, striving to stay calm. "Can you walk?"

"I think so," he said, making a poor show of it for the first few steps. He pushed me away when I reached out to help. "I...I can manage."

It took us about twenty minutes to walk two blocks until I found another alley, where as soon as we were out of sight, I covered us in an illusion. He was out of breath and sweating.

"Sit there," I ordered him in hushed tones. "I need to make a call and then we can get out of here."

"I want to go home. Can't it wait?" he asked, sounding annoyed.

"No, it can't," I replied. "I'll get you back as soon as I can. You'll be glad to know I captured one of the men who took you."

He grunted something unintelligible, closed his eyes and leaned his head against the wall. Given recent events, I would give him some leeway. He might have a headache or be ill. I crouched down and studied him. His body odor was strong and I wanted to step away from him. Instead I told him I was going to touch his arm. He opened his eyes for a millisecond. There were no outward signs of injury. I rolled up his sleeve, exposing the flesh, and placed the palm of my hand on his arm, reaching inward with my healing ability. Like a grumpy bear he growled, but didn't open his eyes or dislodge my hand. He was stressed, but otherwise seemed in good health. I removed my hand and got up almost in a single movement, seeking odor free air to breathe.

I pressed down the anger that threatened to bubble up,

reminding myself that it didn't matter if he showed his appreciation. It was my job to rescue him. Whether or not he thanked me, I felt great. I wouldn't have been able to do it without Kate. I owed her big.

"It's Marshal Metreaux in Paris," I said to my contact at CUT, short for Clean-up Team, marshals who took care of emergency situations, as soon as he answered.

Although I had turned down his job offer, he had given me his direct number the last time we had spoken. He was the team leader.

"What's up?" he asked.

"I have a situation that requires your expertise," I said, texting him the address. When he gave me his number he had emphasized the importance of discretion when calling from a public venue so I kept the description vague. "There are packages ready for pick up, the sooner the better."

"Do any of them require shipping stateside?" he asked.

"At least one, I think," I said, unsure of their procedures.

"Are you nearby?" he asked.

"I am, but I have a time sensitive package of my own to return," I said.

"Can you wait fifteen minutes?" he asked.

"Make it ten and come alone," I said, giving him a new location near us.

"Understood," he said and we hung up.

I trusted him, but preferred to be cautious. I would go alone and watch him before approaching him, cloaking myself so he wouldn't see me until I was convinced it was safe. I waited five minutes, estimating it would take me a couple of minutes to reach the address I had provided him. Turning to Mathis, I braced myself for a grumpy outburst.

"There's something I have to do before I can take you home," I said. "Stay here no matter what. I'll be back as soon as I can. Okay?"

"Yeah, fine," he said, looking at me. As I took several steps away from him. "Don't forget me."

"I won't," I promised.

For once, everything went according to my plan. When the CUT leader arrived, I outlined the basics without revealing Mathis's identity or location. I was relieved when he didn't ask for them. He also didn't ask why I had no back up. He was a man of few words.

"What do you need from us?" he asked.

"There is a Weeia and two humans in the alley," I said in a soft voice so only he could hear me. "I was hoping you would take the Weeia into custody back to Moosehead Lake. He will need to be charged for kidnapping and other actions in the course of the crime that violate our prime directive."

"Do you mean he risked revealing the existence of the Weeia by his actions?" he asked in a whisper.

"Yes," I replied. "He and his partner, who got away, hired human criminals to capture a Weeia citizen. Anything they learned, saw, or heard as part of their actions could be problematic."

"You want us to wipe clean the human's memories of their interactions with the Weeia," he said.

"Correct," I said.

"And you're unable to assist because you have the victim in your custody," he said.

"Yes," I replied, hoping he didn't ask to see him.

"I assume he's willing and able to testify when called up," he said.

"I'm sure that can be arranged, although as you can imagine he is a bit shaken given his experience today," I said. "If he cooperates and identifies his accomplice, I can assist here to find him or her."

He nodded his understanding, adding, "I'll be in touch, soon if we have questions."

We shook hands and he walked away in the direction of the alley where I had left the prisoners. I sighed with relief. To be safe, I waited ten minutes and walked in the opposite direction from where I had left Mathis until I found a dark place. Once there, I cloaked myself in an illusion, appearing as someone else, and circled around to where the perfume maker was waiting.

Chapter 33

"What took you so long?" Mathis asked as soon as he saw me.

Now that the meeting was behind me, I was beginning to feel tired. I remembered my father.

"My dance card was empty," I replied in a snarky tone. "Do you think I was goofing around? I came back as quickly as I could."

"Not fast enough," Mathis said.

"Believe me I want to get back as much as you do," I said.

"Can we go now?" he asked.

"Can you stand up?" I asked. In answer he got to his feet and walked in my direction. I saw fear in his eyes and my anger faded like a burst balloon zigzagging out of control. "Great. I'll get you back to your house now."

"How?" he asked.

"In a taxi," I replied. He watched me for the longest while. "I'll go with you."

"You promise?" he asked.

"Yes, I'll see that you're home safely," I said. "I'm not going anywhere before that."

It was an hour before I found a taxi willing to drive us back to central Paris. I had to promise to pay in cash and I had little cash on me. Mathis insisted on paying.

I was relieved to find Susanna was waiting inside when we arrived. Her lips were tight and worry lines crossed her forehead.

"Mathis," she yelled as soon as she saw us. "Are you okay?"

After an initial check to make sure the house was safe, I walked in behind Mathis. He slumped into a chair without answering. She glanced at me. I shrugged.

"Danni, thank you so much for getting him home safely,"

she said, hugging Mathis in his chair and then me.

"How did you find out?" I asked.

"Madame Marmotte called me," she said. "I've been worried sick. By the way, she said to tell you that he's better. Don't ask me who. She just made me repeat the words, said you would know."

Before I could reply, she turned to where the perfume maker sat. She stared at him as he held his head in his hands.

"Mathis, are you all right?" she asked her partner.

He rubbed his temple as he replied, "I've been better."

She released her breath. I understood her relief. I felt the same way or more about my father. A second later, she started pacing around the room. She was always the take charge half of the partnership. He was the take cover half.

"What now?" she asked.

"I'll file a report with the head office, but regardless of their reply, you need to stay off the radar," I said.

"What do you mean exactly?" she asked.

"Someone went to a lot of trouble and expense today," I said. "I'm convinced they won't stop." Her eyes grew closer as if she was struggling to process the words. "They want Mathis, maybe both of you. We were lucky. We might not be as lucky the next time."

"Are you're saying we need to leave the house?" she asked.

"No, you need to leave Paris," I replied.

Her mouth opened and closed. Mathis looked at me and then at Susanna.

"This is the only home I know," he said, but his slumped body belied his words. He had reached the same conclusion on his own. "Where would we go?"

"I can ask the marshals for an official relocation," I offered.

Susanna's eyes bore into me. Mathis followed her gaze.

"You don't think that's what we should do," she said after a while. "Tell me."

Susanna's journey as an immigrant had been arduous to say

the least. She had survived, among other reasons, because she had learned to pay attention. I imagined she could tell from my micro expressions what I was thinking. I wasn't one to mince words and in the months we had known each other I had come to care for her and her kids. So I told her what I thought.

"The fewer people who know where you are the better," I said. "If you can disappear on your own." I let the words hang. "Quickly."

"Mathis, we should do what she says," she told him. He looked pained. "Come on. Would you rather they take you again?"

"No," he blurted.

"Then it's settled," she said.

"It's me they want," he said. "You and the children can stay in my house."

She turned back to me. I shrugged.

"If you're gone they might take me," she said. "Or they'll use the children to force me to do whatever they want. It's not safe for us to stay either. Right, Danni?"

"It's possible that they would try to coerce you by threatening Susanna and the children," I said. "I wouldn't rule it out."

Susanna and Mathis were business partners, not a couple. And the children were Susanna's, but in the months they had been together they had developed a close bond. Susanna was a survivor and a capable chemist. Mathis was a loner and a gifted perfume maker with a unique Weeia ability. Each could find success on his or her own. As partners, they were better than on their own.

Susanna had a sunny personality. Despite Mathis's grouchy nature they got along well. On his part, Mathis had become attached to her son and daughter. If I asked him, I imagined he would deny it, but I had seen him with Susanna's children and he had never looked happier.

Mathis was pale and haggard. He made me think of the old story of the ostrich sticking its head in the sand. She drew a breath, staring out the window for a while. He studied his shoes, giving me the impression he didn't want to think about it let alone discuss it.

"We can start from scratch," Susanna said in a tentative voice. "The important part is to be alive, free and together."

Silence engulfed us for a couple of minutes. It wasn't my decision to make so I waited.

I was thinking of leaving them to discuss it when Mathis got up. He looked at Susanna, his eyes swollen, red and fearful like a man haunted by ghosts only he could see.

"I only speak French. Paris is the only place I know well. Where would we go?" he asked.

"You can learn other languages," she said, sounding relieved. "We can discover other cities together. There are many francophone places where we could live."

"If that is what we must do," he said, letting the last word hang.

"Yes," she said. Turning to me, she went on, "Danni, can the marshals help?"

"I'll put in an urgent request," I replied. "In the meantime, is there somewhere you can go?"

"I have some relatives in Normandy," Mathis said. "I'll ask if we can stay with them for now."

"Don't tell anyone where you're going, not even the children," I said. "Once you get there keep a low profile. Let me know when you're settled."

Mathis sat unmoving when I said good-bye. Susanna walked me out and we hugged. Wherever they went, I had a good feeling about them.

Chapter 34

The following morning after jogging and taking Ceri for a walk, I decided to go to the office. I arrived at 9 a.m., having popped by to see Bob and his faithful hound on the way. It was quiet inside the building, the first good sign.

My desk was untidy, strewn with half empty mugs of coffee and candy wrappers. The break room was worse. I made my way to the workout room, and as elsewhere there was no one around, yay. I tidied as best as I could and returned to the break room to make myself a cup of coffee. I had just sat down at my desk to enjoy the silence when I heard someone arrive. I braced myself for a confrontation with one of the taskforce members. Instead, it was a familiar face.

"You're back," Madame Marmotte said when she entered as if I had returned from a lunch break instead of being absent for several weeks.

"The taskforce?" I asked.

"Gone," she said. "Since MGV announced he was leaving, they packed up and left with their tail between their legs. They were such jerks. I couldn't be more pleased."

She had her nose up in the air as usual. She walked with greater speed than I remembered. Otherwise, she acted as if she had never called me to Mathis's house and we hadn't seen each other the day before.

"Do you know anything about," I began.

She put her index finger to her lips and interrupted me, "Not a darn thing."

"You don't know what I was going to ask," I protested.

"Pretty sure I do," she said, handing me a scrap of paper folded in half while still indicating I should let it go.

"All righty then," I said, and walked back to my desk where I unfolded the paper. "Forget I said anything."

It had three numbers. It took me all of three seconds to recognize them as the beginning of the address where I had met my parents.

"Got it," I said out loud.

She raised her eyebrow, signaling with her hands that I should destroy the paper. After I did, she took the pieces and ripped them into smaller bits. She walked away with them in her hand toward the bathroom. I assumed she was going to flush them down the toilet.

"I need to run an errand," I announced as soon as she returned. "Call me if you need me."

I took an indirect route in case anyone was following me. It took me an hour and three quarters to reach my destination. My mother opened the door, letting me in and hugging me once I was inside. Her scent surrounded me. It was familiar and unfamiliar at once. I could have remained like that forever.

"Danni, I'm so glad you're safe," she said breaking her embrace.

"What? No, I'm fine," I said. "It's Father I'm worried about. How is he?"

"Much better," she said, turning her attention to the interior of the apartment. "He's napping."

A man's hoarse voice said, "I'm awake. Let her in, Claire. She's here already."

My mother's shoulders slumped as if releasing a heavy weight. For the first time, I noticed fine lines around her eyes. In that instant, I had a glimpse at her anxiety for my safety. She gestured with her hand for me to walk in front and I did.

"Dad," I blurted as soon as I saw him lifting a suitcase. "Take it easy. You were at death's door yesterday."

His smile warmed my heart. My mother watched beside me.

"That might have been, but my very talented daughter healed me," he said, setting the load down and opening his arms.

I ran into his embrace like a little girl, giving no thought to his injury. He made an involuntary grunting sound. When I tried to pull back, he held me.

"Sorry, I didn't mean to hurt you," I said.

"It's fine," he said, holding me at arm's length and glancing at me like a detail-oriented inspector. "Odile said you found Mathis?" I nodded. "How? Never mind. How are you?"

"I'm good," I said. "A bit sad because they're going to have to leave town."

"I didn't realize you were friends," my mother said.

"I wouldn't say I'm friends with Mathis, but I'm definitely friends with Susanna and the children," I said.

"Of course," she said. "You're the one who convinced the powers that be to allow them to stay and give them Weeia status."

"You're well-informed," I said.

"We do our best to keep up to date about you, Danni," my father said. "It's not always easy. We have to be very careful."

"How did you find out we were here?" my mother asked.

"Madame Marmotte handed me a note with part of the address," I said. "She made me tear it up and I think she flushed it down the toiled afterward."

"Odile has always been a careful agent," she said. "Did she tell you anything about us?"

"No, I left as soon as I realized where you were," I said. "I came right away."

"Did you come directly here from the office?" my mother asked, concern marring her features.

"No, I circled around the city, changing buses and subways eight times, then I circled around your neighborhood twice, making sure there wasn't anyone following me," I said, proud of myself.

"Well done," my father said, his eyes softening.

"What about you?" I asked.

"We're leaving," my father said.

"That's why you were lifting the suitcase," I said, pain

filling my heart. "But, you're not fully recovered."

"We don't dare stay any longer," my mother said, placing her arm around my shoulders. "We don't want to leave, especially now that we found you, but it's not safe for us to stay."

"And, more importantly, it's not safe for you if we stay here," my father added. "You being here today is a risk we shouldn't be taking."

"We would never forgive ourselves if anything happened to you," my mother said.

I thought I saw tears in her eyes, but she turned away before I could be sure. Tears filled mine, and I didn't care. I let them fall where they may. My father's gaze lingered on the two of us.

"We'll be in touch as soon as we can," he said.

"You shouldn't carry heavy objects," I said, anything to delay the separation. "Let me help you get ready. I'll get my car and drive you wherever you need to go."

My mother turned down my offer, "Absolutely not."

"It's not safe for us to be out in public together," my father said. "Someone might recognize us."

"What can I do?" I asked, pushing the despair away as far as it would go.

"Nothing, sweetie," my father said. "You've done so much already. You saved my life yesterday."

"The transport will be here and we won't be ready," my mother said. "Since you refuse to leave, you can give us a hand by taking the bags to the door. I'll double-check that we have everything."

She walked out of sight to the back of the apartment. My father began lifting the suitcase again until I took it away from him.

"Sit. I'll do it," I said.

Without a word, he let me take hold of the bag and roll it to the entrance next to another suitcase I hadn't seen when I entered their apartment. It was killing me that they were leaving. I reached out to him for a final hug. Out of nowhere, I began to sob.

"Stop that," my mother's voice ordered in a kind tone. "We'll see you soon. We can't be late. Thierry, will you see if the taxi is here?"

As soon as I let go of my father, she gave me a hug. When we parted, my hands were wet with her tears. My father and the driver had loaded everything into the trunk. All that was left was to watch them drive away. They were both looking at me when the car turned. I'm not sure how long I stood rooted to the spot, hoping they would change their minds yet knowing they wouldn't. It was past noon when I wiped the tears from my face, angry I couldn't stop them, and headed back to the office. Halfway there I decided I couldn't face Madame Marmotte, and went home.

I was restless in the apartment, wanting to go out and wanting to stay in. I had no appetite so it was only when I went to refresh Ceri's water bowl and feed her that I saw the envelope. It was heavy linen paper. I wouldn't have known what to call it except I had seen paper like that on an invitation for a party Sébastien received when he was still working as a marshal with me. My name was written in cursive handwriting like something from an eighteenth century novel.

I wondered who had been inside my apartment. The envelope appeared harmless enough, but after all the warnings my parents had given me I decided to be cautious. I used protective gloves to open it rather than touching it with my bare fingers. Inside, folded in half was a single sheet of the same type and color of paper. We would be pleased if you brought your friend Kate to Gardenly in two days was written in identical handwriting. As soon as I read it, the sheet of paper and matching envelope disintegrated until nothing remained.

It was then that I noticed a baseball on the table with a

second envelope leaning against it. I wasn't a baseball fan. Wondering why Celeste had gifted it to me I picked it up to discover it was covered in signatures. A note explained they were from the team members who had won the last World Series. It also suggested it never hurt to have an Elder on your side.

As I watched the paper fade into thin air, I remembered that the Walker Family was leaving Paris. Picking up the baseball, I ran out. When I arrived at their hotel, they were in the lobby, surrounded by suitcases and staff. How could four people on vacation have so much luggage, I wondered.

Amid the flurry of activity, Tina saw me followed by her brother. When I caught his attention, I threw the ball at him. We were about a meter apart so he caught it with little effort. A puzzled expression grew on his face when he saw the writing.

"Are these what I think they are?" he asked.

"Yep," I said. "Keep it. It's my way of saying I'm sorry for almost accusing you of being MGV."

"You were only doing your job," Amanda, who I hadn't seen approaching, said.

Stunned, Sammy stared at the object in his hands and back at me. Tina's attention was on her smartphone again.

"Are you sure?" Sammy asked me.

"Yes," I said.

That won me a huge grin that showed his teeth. Without another word, he went to show it to his father who nodded his approval. I couldn't hear their conversation, but Ted turned to me, making eye contact.

"Do you need help getting to the airport?" I asked Amanda more to make conversation than anything.

"It's nice of you to offer," she said. "As you can see we have more luggage than we can fit in one vehicle, and nearly as many staff assigned to us. They'll sort it out. I heard on the grapevine that you're getting a promotion, congratulations."

"I am?"

She winked in response, gifting me a warm smile.

"I haven't seen Sammy smile so brightly in months, thank you," she said. Her whole face lit up. "If you're ever in Texas look us up."

"I will," I said and we shook hands. "Bye, Tina."

She had her earbuds on and didn't hear me. When I left, Ted and Sammy were still dealing with the hotel staff.

Chapter 35

It was Friday morning, five days since I had last seen my parents and three days since I had taken Kate to Gardenly. Work had been quiet, so quiet that I was bored to tears. Madame Marmotte had returned to her usual self, although I noticed she hadn't paid much attention to her manicure and her walk was a smidgen less rickety than it used to be.

She arrived in her usual tardy fashion, waltzing into the break room in search of coffee and pastries. She was in luck because on my way in I had gone by the bakery, dropping off goodies for Bob and Achilles, and bringing her a pain au raisin, one of her favorites. On her way back to her desk with her coffee and pastry, she stopped by my desk.

"I guess you're the new boss," she said.

"Technically, nothing has changed," I said, wondering why she had brought up the subject before I had my second coffee. "I'm the interim head of the office the same as last week."

"The taskforce is gone," she noted.

"Yes, I'm aware of that," I said, trying not to show my annoyance. "They left because MGV left. It had nothing to do with me."

"Maybe, maybe not, but you saved Mathis and collared all but one of his attackers while they were sitting on their hands," she said. "And, the only person in Paris MGV communicated with was you."

"I suppose," I said.

"Rumor has it Rupert has no chance," she said. "You're the de facto boss."

"His father is well-connected," I said, turning around to make sure he hadn't arrived. "He's going to keep pushing."

"I don't doubt it," she said. "I had the displeasure of meeting him and watching them in action. They're ill-mannered oafs, bullies, and a disgrace to the marshals service. I was glad to see their collective backsides. I only wish that little squirt had gone back where he came from with his father."

"How do you really feel about it?" I asked in a light tone, hoping to stay away from controversy regarding my direct report and his powerful father.

She smirked. I couldn't blame her. From what I had observed, they had been ghastly to her during their Paris sojourn. On the other hand, she had sided with Rupert when he arrived, thinking he would be her ally. It wasn't until he showed his true colors that she took my side or at least didn't take his. It was curious that my mother had referred to Madame Marmotte as an agent as if she was on active duty rather than an office admin. It made me wonder if she worked for them.

"So, do you have any fun plans for the weekend?" she asked as if we made small talk all the time.

"I'm doing maid of honor stuff for Marla," I said. "And Ernie said he might come for a couple of days if he found seats on a really cheap flight." I was crossing my fingers that he did. "How about you?"

"We're going to the opera," she said. "We have season tickets you know." Did I ever? She mentioned it often. "Tonight is the opening for La Traviata at the Bastille."

"How nice," I said.

"Have you been to the opera?" she asked.

"I've seen it from the outside," I replied. "It looks beautiful."

"You're thinking of the Palais Garnier in the ninth," she said. "That's the old opera house. It's popular, especially with tourists, but the performances are mediocre. They sell out no matter what they stage. If you want to see a decent opera, the Bastille is the one."

I knew that, but there was nothing to be gained by pointing it out. A few months back I would have told her what I thought and brought her down a notch. A lot had happened to make me think before I spoke and to hold my fury in check. Plus, meeting my parents had squelched some of the worst flames of my anger. They weren't who I thought they were, maybe I wasn't either. And, it was her intervention in the nick of time that helped save my father. I didn't know the right words to express how thankful I was to her. Besides, she appeared to be playing a role, at least in part. If it made her feel superior to boast about her knowledge of the city and the opera, I wasn't going to deny her the opportunity.

"I'll keep it in mind," I said.

"Anyway, as you can imagine I need to have my hair and make-up done so I'll leave early," she said. I had a hard time imagining she paid to look the way she did. I almost snickered, but I managed to cover my mouth and hold the impulse in check. "I'm sure you don't mind."

"Not at all," I said. "Leave as early as you need to."

If I hadn't been sitting down I might have fallen when she replied, in the tone she used only with Francois, "Great, boss, thank you."

When she said early she meant it. She didn't return to work after lunch. I didn't mind. I had filed all the paperwork and there were no active cases. There was little to do. I was restless, wishing for a workout. I might have sought out Rupert to get the excess energy out of my system, but he had called in sick that morning. At that moment, I received a call from Tadas.

"Danni, wives invite you to tea," he said as soon as I answered.

"Tea? Today?" I asked. "Since when do they drink tea?"

It must have been some traditional activity from Lithuania, their home country, and they didn't know the word for it in English or French.

"Me messenger. One hour," he said in his sometimes difficult to understand mix of languages. "Okay?"

"Sure," I agreed.

I liked to take toys and little treats for the children whenever I visited the families of our two Lithuanian workers, but I didn't have enough time to go shopping. I wrapped up the day at the office and walked across the complex to their apartment, wondering what Lithuanian "tea" was all about. They lived in two of the only apartments that had been modernized and were fit for habitation within our huge property.

Four children, his two and his friend's two, greeted me at Tadas's home. The eldest let me in, but after a few minutes, they told me to wait for their moms at the gym. I was confused, but after multiple attempts to understand what was going on I surrendered to the occasional chaos of their lives and went to the gym.

My annoyance evaporated when I walked into the gym to find it filled with my friends. Tadas and Giedrius along with their wives Ieva and Milda were there as well as Ernie, Marla, Michael, Sébastien, and Susanna. A banner in the back said "Congratulations, Danni. You Earned It."

"Surprise," they yelled in unison when they saw me.

My mouth remained open a bit too long. I must have looked a sight. Their smiles warmed my heart as they broke into laughter. A wall of hugs and kisses surrounded me.

"Wow," was all I managed in between so many greetings.

"Were you surprised?" Ernie asked me.

"Didn't it show?" I asked.

"I guess it did," he said, grinning from ear to ear.

"If your lips spread any further apart you might hurt yourself," I said, causing his grin to widen.

Sébastien who had been chatting with Susanna came to stand next to us. He wore an elegant business suit in dark gray, a starched white shirt and a beautiful pink tie with a pale green paisley pattern.

"What's with the banner?" I asked.

"It's about you finally being the permanent head of the

office," Sébastien said.

"Nothing has been announced," I said.

"It's coming," Ernie said.

"Do you know something I don't?" I asked him.

"I'm not saying I sneaked a peek at documents that may or may not have crossed my desk that may or may not have announced a certain promotion in Paris," he said, winking at me.

"Really?" I asked in a louder tone of voice than I meant.

"Yep," he said. "I wanted to wait until it was announced, but I have a big, hairy project that will suck all my waking hours starting Monday. This was the only weekend I could travel to Paris and organize a surprise get together for you. Also, Sébastien has a trip coming up too, and I thought you would want him here. I hope you don't mind that I jumped the gun a bit."

"The man has been driving us nuts," Sébastien said, patting Ernie on the shoulder. "He's been bossing everyone mercilessly, whipping us into shape, making us promise to show up on time on penalty of some horrible torture in his chamber of secrets."

"Yeah, right," I laughed. "Ernie couldn't harm a hair on anyone's head."

"I don't have a chamber of torture or whatever it was," he protested.

"The weapons master does," Sébastien said. "It might as well be yours."

"He's a sweetheart when you're around," Marla chimed in from behind me. "I'm with Sébastien. Ernie is a brutal taskmaster when he wants to be. While his weapon of choice may be his tongue don't let that fool you. He is relentless, like a dog with a bone." Surrounding me in a hug she asked, "How are you, my friend?"

"Good, I mean great," I said. "Today I'm doing great. You guys, that, this is amazing. Thank you so much."

"We just showed up, as ordered by Ernie," she said. "He did all the work. He called everyone, including Ieva and Milda."

"Everyone helped," Ernie said, studying the ground like a shy schoolboy. He also seemed to have grown an inch at the praise. "They found chairs and showed up when I was setting up the room. Giedrius hung the banner. Sébastien took care of the food and wine. I would have hired a caterer with waiters, but it's only a few of us and it gets complicated bringing outsiders into the complex. I thought you would rather something informal and private here with us than a big production at the Club."

As Marla stepped away to drop off an empty platter Susanna took her place.

"Mathis and I made you a gift," she said, giving me a hug and handing me a box wrapped in beautiful gold and silver paper and matching ribbon in both metallic shades. "Mathis couldn't make it to the party, but he sends his love." I was pretty sure the idea had been Susanna's. The last glimpse of him I had he had been a basket case. I imagined him sitting somewhere fretting about being kidnapped again. "It's a special blend that masks your scent. That means if you use your illusion to hide even a trained tracking hound couldn't find you. We, well he really, made it just for you. He's been working on it for weeks, and said to tell you he's still perfecting it. I hope you like it."

It was with difficulty that I rid myself of the tears that threatened, rubbing my eyes with the back of my hand while hoping she hadn't noticed. I didn't like anyone to see me crying. It always made me feel silly and out of control. Marshals don't cry, I told myself.

Susanna placed her hand on my shoulder and waited. After I swallowed, I felt more composed, realizing it wasn't her gift, or not only her gift, but the party and everyone gathering for me that was making an omelet of my emotions.

"Thanks," I croaked.

I wasn't known for my eloquence, but that was shorter than I intended. I was struggling to add something when Sébastien cleared his throat to catch everyone's attention. Once the room fell silent, he focused his eyes on me, drawing their eyes in turn. My cheeks felt hot.

"I don't have to tell you what a wonderful person Danni is," he began. "You know already. From gifting pastries to homeless people and their pets to helping new arrivals find a home here, she's selfless and tireless. As a boss?" He waited a moment like a showman before continuing. "She's equally selfless and tireless." I let out a breath I hadn't realized I was holding. "She's also unforgiving and tough." He laughed and they all laughed with him. His million-dollar smile lit up his face like a Greek god. "She always had my back, and my best interest at heart. In her company I learned more than I can say, especially about what really counts. I consider myself lucky to be among her friends."

He went on, but I missed the last part because I lost control of the waterworks and my attention wandered. At the end, I realized he had toasted to me or my promotion when I saw my friends zero in on me with their glasses in the air and a roar.

Less than an hour later, he returned to my side. Squeezing me he told me, "I meant what I said, you know. I'm glad to have you among my friends."

"There were days when I could've been more understanding, more patient, and certainly less crabby," I said.

He grinned before replying, "I didn't say you're perfect or miss sunshine. What you are is a true friend. I always know where I stand with you. That is hard to find." I opened my mouth to answer, but before I could speak he continued, "I have to go," and hugged me good-bye.

While I'm not much of a party butterfly, that night I had a wonderful time. Before I realized it, the evening ended and the guests were gone. Ernie and I were alone tidying up the room.

"They'll clear out the furniture and take care of the cleaning tomorrow," I said referring to our handymen. "The kids were tired and I told them to go home with their families. I just want to throw out any food, dishes, and cups. We finally got rid of the rats and roaches in this part of the complex, and I don't want them coming back."

"Got it," he said from across the room, where he was filling a garbage bag with dirty paper plates.

We worked in a comfortable quiet for a few minutes. It was the kind of companionable company I had missed since Sébastien had quit to become a big wig.

"Done," Ernie said as he dragged the last garbage back out.

"That was amazing," I said. "Thank you again."

"You bet," he said.

"You're welcome to stay the night," I reminded him.

"I wish I could," he said. His soulful look lingered on my face, making me wonder not for the first time what he was thinking. "But I have a big project to complete and all eyes are on me. I can't afford to make mistakes."

A sudden sadness came over me. It seemed anticlimactic to head home alone. It was more than that. I was going to miss him. I chucked the strong pull of emotions to the bubbly and wine I had.

"No problem," I said, unsure of what else to say.

"Do you mind using your portal?" he asked.

"Huh?" I asked, confused.

"Your badge still has the app for the portal, right?" he said.

"I guess," I said, pulling it out and looking at it. "Yes, it does. I figured it would shut down on its own or that it wasn't working anymore."

"As far as I know, your portal access is indefinite," he said. "That's a really big deal."

"It is?"

"Kinda," he said. "Most marshals and even Elders would give their right arm to have portal access. You sound rather matter of fact about it."

"Life is funny sometimes," I said. "I get that it could be a powerful tool, but I have no desire to use it."

He bent down his head a smidgen as he asked "You don't?"

"Every crossing has turned me into a vomit comet," I said. "Remember?"

His brows knit together as he asked, "Have you followed the arrows on your badge?"

I shook my head, asking "What arrows?"

"Hmm, I might know what the problem is," he said, his face opening with understanding. "If you enter the portal following the rotation of the planet it should be seamless. If you enter in the direction opposite the rotation, it can make you violently ill."

"Really? How do I know which is which?" I asked.

"Your app," he said.

"What about it?" I asked.

"The app usually points to the best direction," he said. "Make sure to check the app before going in and you should be fine."

"Now you tell me?" I asked.

"I thought you knew," he said.

"If you hadn't just thrown such a fantastic party for me I would be seriously annoyed at you," I said only half joking.

"Sorry," he said, lowering his eyes in a contrite expression. "I should have told you. I didn't put two and two together until now." After a moment, he lifted his eyes, holding mine. "On the good news front now that you know how it works, you can visit me anytime."

"I can?" I asked, surprised and delighted at once.

"Yes," he said, gifting me a meaningful look.

"Isn't it against the rules or something?" I asked.

"Not that I know of," he replied. "As long as you don't

mention the Daughters or the app, you should be fine. Keep it low-key."

"And, I can open the portal for you to cross?" I asked.

I was beginning to understand why he was excited about the app. Crossing from Paris to Portland whenever I felt like it would be fun, more than fun. It would be empowering to say the least. I was pleased about the possibilities it opened for us. Our budding romance had floundered when the marshals assigned me to Paris. The app could go a long way toward rekindling the flame.

"Pretty great, right?" he replied. I nodded. "Come visit me soon or if you rather I can come visit you when my project is over. Will you?"

"Maybe I will," I said. "Maybe I will."

Thank you for taking time to read
An American Weeia in Paris

If you enjoyed it, please consider telling your friends or posting a short review. Word of mouth is an author's best friend and much appreciated.

Sign up to receive updates and news of upcoming releases on Elle's website:

http://elleboca.poyeen.com/an-american-weeia-in-paris

About The Author

   Elle Boca is the author of the Weeia urban fantasy series about superhumans. The Unelmoija Series is set in Miami. In the Garden of Weeia, a novella, is set in Portland, Maine, and her newest Marshals Series is set in Paris, France. Elle makes her home with her king cat husband in South Florida. When not writing and creating fantastical beings she likes photographing nature and wildlife, pastries, movies, and dreaming of going on safari.

www.ingramcontent.com/pod-product-compliance
Lightning Source LLC
Chambersburg PA
CBHW020913200626
46814CB00001BA/319